AULT'S HEIR

C K CRIGGER

WOLFPACK
PUBLISHING
— EST 2013 —

Ault's Heir
Paperback Edition
© Copyright 2022 C.K. Crigger

Wolfpack Publishing
5130 S. Fort Apache Rd. 215-380
Las Vegas, NV 89148

wolfpackpublishing.com

Paperback ISBN 978-1-63977-265-0
eBook ISBN 978-1-63977-267-4
LCCN 2021952831

AULT'S HEIR

CHAPTER 1

"**T**hat dadgummed lunkheaded Dutchman."

RT Timmons's bellow rattled the low-hanging branches of a lone pine tree whose bark had been rubbed off by cattle scratching their butts. His beady dark eyes flashed fire amidst the wrinkles surrounding them, and his weathered face turned a girlish hot pink. "What's that old sauerkraut-eater up to now? Aside from letting them cows of his get fat on my grass."

RT asked a lot of questions and answered most of them himself. This time, as usual, he didn't wait to hear from the man riding next to him. Smiling a little, Knox Burdette clamped his mouth shut, wise enough not to mention his doubts the stray cattle were making a deliberate invasion.

"Burdette, there's a fence down somewhere between us and him," RT said. "You head on over his way and shove them critters back where they belong. While you're there, ride over and let Ault know. Tell him he needs to fix the fence on his side of the line, pronto. I'll get Warren to working on the Running T part of it."

1

"Yes, sir," Knox said, casting RT a glance as he gathered his reins.

Knox, the head wrangler at the Running T, sat his horse alongside his boss on a knoll a mile or so from a band of trees that marked the division between the Running T and William Ault's XYZ. Below them, in a wide, sub-irrigated draw, a group of maybe fifteen white-faced cattle bearing the XYZ brand had their heads down grazing. Unfortunately, they were devouring the rich grass RT planned on cutting for winter hay.

While Knox couldn't blame RT for getting hot under the collar regarding the hay crop, the downed fence was a yearly occurrence. William Ault owned the section of land on the other side of it and, for the most part, the German immigrant was as meticulous about maintaining his fences as RT. Maybe more so. Knox'd had to push XYZ cattle from the Running T onto their own graze more than once. Especially this time of year when winter snows and spring rains had done damage to the fences, what with runoff and washouts. But then, there'd been an equal number of times the push had gone the other way.

"And make sure you check on the old fart," RT growled. "Ask if he's all right. Last I heard he's been having trouble with his son-in-law. Folks are saying his daughter got sick and is about to die. She wanted to come home to do it, but her husband wouldn't't let her. Might've already. Died, that is. I figure it'll hit the old man hard."

"Who? Astrid?" Knox turned a startled look on RT. "About to die? What from?"

"Now *that* I didn't hear. Anyways, I don't know for sure. I heard a rumor is all when I was in town the other day. Clerk at the store was saying that son-of-a-seacook she married is keeping her prisoner, so she don't infect anybody. Some say he's probably killing her himself. Wouldn't put it past him."

"No. I wouldn't either." Knox had gone to school with Astrid back when she'd been young, and he'd been one of the "older" boys. She'd been a pretty little blonde girl but frail. Back when she'd been only seventeen, Anson Lowell had swept her off her feet and married her over Ault's protests. It'd been a kind of scandal back then, though Knox had lost track in the four or five years since. But he sure enough knew Lowell's reputation, about how he treated women rough. Knew the men Lowell ran with, too. Birds of a feather, as the saying went.

"Well," RT waved an arm, "get on with it before them cows eat everything down to the roots.."

Nudging his horse into motion, Knox rode off at a tangent from the cattle with the intention of checking the fence on the way down the hill. The most likely spot for breakage, he figured, was down by the creek where a hard winter and too much spring rain had made the ground extra soggy.

Water only ran there in the wet season, which made it prone to washing out a row of fence posts around this time of year. What his boss and Ault needed to do, as Knox'd mentioned to them both more than once, was to share the cost of mixing up some concrete and set the posts permanently. When the cattle came looking for water, it was too easy for the fence to be pushed over in muddy ground. A concrete base would stop that. But when did RT ever listen to advice, especially when it came from a man as young as Knox? But then, neither did Ault.

3

Leaving the boss to ride off toward home, Knox followed the fence line until he found the break. Exactly where he'd figured, and for the reason he'd figured. The cattle hadn't moved far from the downed part of the fence, he noted, sort of relieved, so they hadn't been there long. One less thing for RT to rail about.

"C'mon, Chick," Knox spoke to his horse and pointed him toward the cow that appeared to be the leader. Get her moving in the right direction and the rest would follow. Chick snorted in the cow's white face when she looked belligerent. It did the trick. Kicking up her heels, the cow ambled back the way she'd come, taking her time as the others fell in at her rear.

Chick pushed them across the creek to the fence, Knox whooping and hollering when they had a notion to stop. Once they were on the XYZ side, Knox followed them over, Chick stepping gingerly around the fence wire. Dismounting, Knox took the time to prop the fence with a downed tree limb for a brace and roll a rock over to keep it steady. It'd hold, he figured, until he could tell Ault so he could make a permanent fix. More permanent, anyway.

After finishing the chore, he, with the horse doing most of the work, urged the cattle over a couple hills to where a larger band grazed on grass every bit as good as what they'd found on the Running T side. Leaving them there, Knox continued on toward Ault's house. If the old man was away, he hoped to find Shorty Bonham, a roustabout who cooked, cleaned the barn, fed the chickens, and tended the patch of rose bushes Ault took inordinate pride in. He'd just pass the message along to Shorty.

He smiled as he rode, thinking of the way during every community spring roundup Ault complained about how much damage the cold winters did to his roses and how he had to replace a few bushes every spring. He figured the old man just liked to plant new varieties, like a man more interested in his roses than raising cattle.

Knox was still smiling and trying not to think about Astrid dying if she was even sick when he heard gunfire.

"Whoa." Drawing Chick to a halt, he cocked his head toward the sound and listened a few seconds more. "That ain't one man target practicing," he told the horse, clicking his tongue to get him moving again. "Sounds to me as if Ault is tied up in some kind of war. Get a move on, Chick. We'd better take a look-see."

The gunshots came from more than one gun. Knox figured at least three, or even more. There was a flurry of noise, then a yell, and another from a different voice. The words were unintelligible at a distance.

Swearing under his breath, he urged Chick to a gallop. A few minutes later, they burst from the woods at the side of Ault's house, rounding the corner to enter the yard.

A man lay sprawled between the house and the big, red-painted barn, his nose in the dirt and his arms flung wide. Blood pooled on the ground on either side of him in a shape like wings.

By this time, Knox had his carbine out of the saddle scabbard, holding it across his lap. "Oh, hell," he said, drawing Chick to a fast stop. At first, he thought the man, a dead body as he could plainly see, belonged to Ault. The gray hair led to the conclusion, but then he saw the body had faded red suspenders holding his britches over a sizable paunch and knew it was Shorty lying there. Ault, a thin, wiry man, belted his britches.

5

A bullet, close enough to whistle as it went past, came near to taking Knox's head with it.

"You on the horse," someone yelled. "Ride on while you got the chance."

The suggestion came from a tall man hunkered behind a galvanized metal watering trough, and his words drew gunfire from the house. Curtains moved in the window and Knox saw it was William Ault in there, pointing a rifle at the crouched man. Ault fired, causing the tall man to jerk back.

Knox rode, all right. He spurred Chick straight at the house.

"Don't shoot, Ault," he shouted. "Don't shoot. I'm here to help."

Well, at least he figured that's what he ought to do, seeing as how he recognized the tall man as Ault's son-in-law, Anson Lowell. And if the two were in some kind of a duel, he knew which side he was on.

To tell the truth, he was surprised Lowell hadn't gunned him down the minute he rode out of the trees.

Tried to gun him down, he meant. Like the feller that stuck a six-shooter out from behind a well-grown shade tree and popped off a shot at him. Without thinking twice, Knox returned fire.

The man screamed like a girl and dropped the six-shooter just as Chick slid on his haunches, going between a couple big thorny rose bushes before stopping right next to the porch. Knox tumbled from the saddle on the off side and slapped the horse on the rump to urge him to run, even as he flung himself at the door. Like magic, it opened before him. He fell inside, landing on his hands and knees with the carbine bumping on the red fir plank floor. Been nice if there'd been a rug to cushion the fall, he thought as the door slammed shut on his heels.

"Shorty's dead ain't he?" Ault squinted down at him, his face grim.

"Yes."

"Thought so. He weren't moving any." A string of German spewed out, and Knox didn't need to understand a single word to know the old man was cussing his son-in-law in the crudest form possible. "You say you're here to help? How'd you know I needed it?" While the old man cussed in German, he spoke English without an accent unless you considered Louisiana Bayou country something other than American. Knox had no idea how the old man had come to speak the outlandish patois.

Knox sat up and checked his carbine. "Well, I didn't until I heard the ruckus when I was still two hills over. I came to tell you the fence over by Polter Creek is down again. Found some of your cows on Running T grass."

Ault stared at him as if the words made no sense. "The fence?"

The fence didn't strike either of them as important at the moment.

Knox started to get to his feet, but the German laid a heavy hand on him and pushed him back down. "If you want to keep your head atop your shoulders, Burdette, you'll keep it below the windowsill. Looks like you showed up at just the wrong time. Wrong for you, I mean. Those boys don't plan to stop shooting until I'm dead, and the way they're pouring lead into this house, they'll kill anything in here with me. Probably even the mice, so that includes you. Just look what happened to Shorty." There was a catch in his voice at the mention of his roustabout. They'd been friends as well as employer and employee.

Knox nodded and scooted over to the doorway between the kitchen and the room facing the front yard. There was no lock on the back door, only a simple latch. He figured it wouldn't be long before one of those yahoos would think to go around the house and make a try to enter there.

"What *is* going on?" Knox thought to ask, settling in the doorway with his back to the jamb. He could see in both directions from there. "Beyond Lowell trying to kill you. What's he want?"

Taking his own advice about staying low, Ault knelt beside the front window a scant second before a bullet pinged through, another round of glass shards sprinkling the floor beneath. "Want?" The German scoffed and turned to stare at Knox. "Everything. He's after everything. He took my daughter and now he wants the rest."

"The rest?"

"The XYZ."

"The ranch? How's he figure?" Knox made a gesture. "It don't seem you two are real friendly. And excuse me, but I thought Astrid..." He didn't finish. It didn't seem right to bring up the old man's daughter.

"He says she ain't dead yet, and getting the ranch is the only thing he figures might make her well." Ault snapped off a shot through the broken window. A return bullet poked a hole in the wall next to him. "Yeah, so he says. I happen to know Astrid don't care two hoots for the ranch. Not for herself, anyhow. She never did, even as a girl. She'd live in a town if she could. Someplace like Spokane."

It looked to Knox like those outside were taking better aim or worse, depending on who was looking at it as he felt a splinter, blown from the molding by his head, scratch across his cheek.

"Anson showed up here first thing this morning." Ault continued as if he didn't notice the gunfire. His voice caught. "Said Astrid wanted me to sign the ranch over right now seeing as how she's my heir. Said it is the best way for everything to go smooth when I pass."

Knox shook his head as if his ears were hearing wrong. "When you pass? You aren't sick, are you?"

"Ain't sick yet but it's looking like I might soon be dead of lead poisoning. Lowell walked up to my door bold as brass and stated his claim. I told him to go to hell, so I expect he figures the only thing to do now is kill me. The thing is, last night Astrid"

Ault's face pinched up all of the sudden and it looked like he might weep. Knox sure in perdition hoped he wouldn't't.

The man gasped a little and went on. "The thing is, I think my daughter is dead and Lowell is trying to get hold of the deed before anybody knows."

"Why..." Knox started, but Ault talked right over him.

"See, he figures if the property is given over to Astrid before she dies, then he'll inherit it from her. And if both her and me are dead, that'll be sooner than later. Listen, Burdette, I was sound asleep last night. About two this morning, I felt a hand on my brow. And a voice spoke to me, a soft little voice. It sounded just like Astrid did when she was about eight years old."

"What did she say?" Knox scratched out. He wondered if the old man had lost his wits.

"She just said, 'Goodnight, Daddy. I'll see you in the morning.' Then I felt a big shudder and what seemed like wings whooshing all around and flying off." Ault sighed, tears forming in his eyes. "And I knew. Knew she was gone. But Anson wants those papers safe in his dirty hands. He figures nobody has to know for sure when it all went down or who went first Astrid or me. He's gonna say it was me." He sent Knox a sad look. "I'm sorry you came along when you did, Burdette. You're as good as dead yourself about now."

The funny part if you could call any of this funny was Knox discovered he believed every word Ault said. He'd overheard his granny say something similar about wings and hearing voices the night his gramps passed on. As for the rest, the part concerning him, well, he decided he had an opinion, and it didn't include Lowell's version.

"Well then," he said, "I guess we'd better make sure Lowell doesn't have his way." He started to his feet, intending to go on the offensive instead sitting like a duck on water when something or someone, heavy crashed against the back door. Shaking on its hinges, the latch slipped but held. Certain the next blow would find a way through; Knox sank back down and pointed his carbine.

At the same time, a bullet thunked through the wall where Ault was hunkering. He sort of sat up straight before his body sagged. "Hellfire," he said on a whoosh of air.

Knox had no chance to look at him, what with all his attention taken up by the man who, staggered by his own fresh onslaught on the door, charged in waving his revolver and firing aimlessly. Knox set himself, so when the feller spotted him sitting in the doorway and pointed the pistol at him, he was ready. Knox drilled him dead center in the chest, making the intruder into a dead man before he hit the floor.

Not, sad to say, before one of those random bullets

found a mark, scratching along Knox's side before plowing into the wall.

"Ow," Knox said. "Dadgummit." He stared at the body for a couple seconds before turning to Ault. Instantly, sour dread coursed through him. "You're shot."

Ignoring his own twinges of pain and the fact he was bleeding; he grabbed a towel he saw hanging on a knob and scrambled across the floor to the old man.

"Nothing is going to stop this bleeding," Ault spoke in his ordinary voice. "Do something for me, Burdette?"

"Whatever you say."

"Go in the room behind the kitchen. On the shelf behind the door. There's a key in a candy tin. Open the safe. It's where I keep my business papers. Top envelope. There's a paper I've got to sign. Bring a pen." The sentences were staccato. Breathless. "Quick now."

Knox wasted a few seconds staring at him. "A paper?" Seemed a strange time to worry about a paper.

"Yes, yes. Hurry. I ain't got much time."

Knox already knew as much since Ault was leaking blood like water spurting from a pump. He wasted no time in trying to crawl across the floor but jerked to his feet and ran. He hadn't even known Ault had an office. Pretty dang fancy, although since it was right off the kitchen he figured back when the old man'd had a wife and his daughter at home, it had been a pantry. Now the tiny room contained a small table in use as a desk, one chair, a single shelf with some ledger-like books on it, and the aforementioned safe. A little one, cheap, considering the simple key lock. In seconds, Knox had the top envelope in hand. Curiously, the envelope had been swaddled in a waterproof packet he'd wasted time unwrapping to make sure of what it was.

In the front room, Ault sagged lower, his face drained

of color. "This is it," he said. "Thanks." He wiped blood from his hands onto his britches and opened the package while Knox, seeing a couple men moving closer to the house, picked up his carbine and banged off a shot or two in their direction. It kept them ducked down even if it didn't stop them from shooting back. When the gunshots faded from his ears, he heard the scratch of pen on paper.

"All right," Ault said after a bit, his voice coming fainter now. Paper rattled.

Looking down, Knox saw the envelope closed and sealed. As he watched, the pen dropped from Ault's fingers and rolled across the floor. The man struggled over rewrapping the cover around the envelope.

The old man beckoned him closer and said, "If you get out of here, get this to the address on the front. Hand-deliver it, if you can. I surely would appreciate it."

He was fading fast. Knox would've promised anything to ease his mind, but he meant it when he said, "Yeah. Sure. Don't worry none. I'll get it wherever it has to go. I'm not going to let that peckerwood kill me."

"Good man." Ault's lips curled into a smile. "Astrid knew," he whispered. "Knew she'd see me this morning. I...I'm going."

And between one heartbeat and the next he went, although Knox didn't hear any bird wings or a celestial chorus or anything else except bullets thunking into the wall above his head. Yeah, and the reports of the weapons firing them.

For one thing, he was too busy. He grabbed up Ault's rifle and popped off a shot that took one man's legs out from under him. Spinning around, he used his carbine to shoot at the trough Lowell cowered behind. Knew he wouldn't hit him, but it made him feel good to keep

Lowell at bay. A minute later, the last of the men tried for a ricochet shot. Didn't do anything but make Knox mad.

Though barely aiming, he managed to pink the fellow. With all Lowell's men accounted for, he figured it was time to make his escape. More of his scant ammunition was wasted in firing at those outside, first with Ault's rifle, then his own carbine. Hoping the men would believe there were still the two of them putting up a fight, he stuffed Ault's packet of papers into his pocket and hightailed it out the back, stepping over the body on the floor without a second look.

From the back stoop, it wasn't far to the woods where last he'd seen of Chick, the horse had fled from the shooting. He, sure enough, hoped the gelding hadn't taken off for home. He'd as soon not be afoot with Lowell's men searching for him.

Knox dodged out of the house, slipped behind the woodpile when he judged nobody had him in sight and made a run for the woods. With a little luck, it would take Lowell a good long time to find out he had escaped.

CHAPTER 2

A few yards into the woods, Knox found Chick's hoof prints and followed them in the soft, damp soil beneath some big Douglas firs. After a while, the horse's stride shortened as he slowed from his startled run. Knox spotted where the tops of some young thistles had been chomped. He figured he'd soon find Chick when he came upon a rivulet cutting a new channel down a draw. Sure enough, when he rounded a clump of elderberry bushes, there was his horse, sucking up gulps of water from the ditch.

"Whoa, Chick, whoa. There's a good fella." He suspected the horse might be a trifle disgruntled over Knox slapping his rear back at the Ault house. Well, that and running him through some thorny rose bushes. In fact, Chick snorted his greeting, spraying snot. But the horse stood quietly while Knox tucked Ault's packet away in a spot safer than the hind pocket of his denims.

Gathering the loose reins, Knox mounted.

They hadn't gotten far when another fusillade of shots cracked the stillness, making Chick dance. Then came shouts, closer than he liked. A horse neighed and

Knox had to speak swiftly to keep Chick from answering. They must've gotten in the house and found Ault, Knox thought, along with the man he'd killed. Those shots were a puzzle though. What did they think they were shooting at? Or not what. Who?

What he did know was that Lowell wouldn't be any too pleased to find his, Knox's, body missing. They were bound to come after him. Just as soon, most probably, as Lowell figured out how to open the safe and discover the deed if that's what Ault had been reassigning, gone.

Could be Ault's new heir wouldn't be real happy when he collected his windfall. Appeared to Knox as though whoever it was, he'd have a fight on his hands if he meant to keep it.

Though curious, he figured he'd better get himself as far down the road as possible while he had the chance. He touched Chick with his spurs, a reminder they had business to tend and no time to waste.

Knox knew where he had to go. When he'd fetched the envelope for Ault, he'd seen the address on the front, and although he dreaded the promise he'd made the old man, he wasn't about to go back on his word to deliver it. Whatever Ault had written, he hoped it thwarted any of Lowell's plans.

They cut across the XYZ until they reached Perkin's land on the other side and followed the fencerow down to an old wagon trail, built before the county cleared a road elsewhere through the forest to town. At some point, they'd need to cross the river, but he had a notion once Lowell knew Knox's general direction, he'd send men to guard the bridge above the falls. Which meant he had to either outrun them or find a different way to the other side.

Knox cast a wary glance at the sky. Though only early

afternoon, it was already almost dark as night. Deep purple clouds blowing down from the north covered the sky, and as he watched, lightning streaked overhead, followed seconds later by a belly-shaking rumble.

Chick shook his head, his red mane whipping.

"Yeah," Knox muttered. "I see it. Looks like we're in for a soaking." He looked up at the sky again. "If we don't get lightning struck first.."

They loped then, stopping once to give Chick a breather and for Knox to stow his carbine in the scabbard. When he'd started out this morning the sun had been shining and he'd left his coat in the bunkhouse. A mistake, he realized in retrospect. Unseasonable cold stiffened Knox's fingers as he tied his neckerchief over his hat to hold it on his head. The wind was gusting something fierce as it ran before the storm. If he didn't find shelter soon, he'd not only be wet but half-froze before he got any place he could wait out the downpour already coming down in earnest.

And, he reminded himself, he still had to get across the river. Depending on how much rain those clouds carried, without the use of the bridge, it might be risky.

"C'mon, Chick, old son." He thumped Chick alongside the neck. "Get a move on."

Giant raindrops as hard as ice pellets struck his face as they ran from the wind and rain. Chick didn't much care for the weather either, shaking his head under the onslaught. Lightning blazed across the sky and struck somewhere up ahead, lighting the way for a doe and her fawn running for the safety of the forest. The air smelled of ozone. Thunder cracked and bellowed. Somewhere off to the side, he heard the snap of breaking branches as a tree fell across its mates.

Knox spurred Chick to greater effort until after what seemed an unconscionably long time, they emerged from the woods just where the road divided, and the river came into view. Water spilled over the banks, cutting into the road.

Up ahead, in full spate, the falls roared. Spray rose in a heavy mist above the treetops.

Knox cursed softly. Any potential ford was several miles away. No harm, he decided, in taking a quick look at the bridge. Could be Lowell hadn't gotten there yet. Chick had made good time through the woods, even though the road was shorter and better going.

Keeping far enough within the timber to remain hidden from anyone on the road, Knox got to where an old bridge, wide gaps separating the boards, spanned the river. Clearance between wood and water, he noted, was less than a foot. Should the river rise much more the whole shebang was likely to be swept downstream. From where he stopped, he could hear the bridge creaking a protest. But whether the bridge held wasn't his problem. Not at the moment, anyhow. No, his problem lay with two of the hombres he'd last seen at Ault's place where they'd been shooting at anything with moving parts. By which he meant at him. They were standing under some trees with their horses tied nearby. The men looked miserable; their hats pulled low, so rain ran off the brim. Knox figured they probably weren't as miserable as he was. At least they had coats.

Lowell had sent them to watch the road, no doubt with the intention of shooting him dead. In fact, they should've been watching the road, but just then one of them turned away and began to unbutton his britches. At the sudden move, one of the horses threw up his head, jerking his reins loose from where he'd been tied. This caused the other man to whip around, and as he did, lightning struck not twenty feet from where Knox and Chick stood.

Not only did this illuminate the two of them clearly, but the following almighty crash of thunder startled Chick into hopping forward.

No possible way for the men to miss the movement. And they didn't.

"It's him," one yelled. "That Burdette yahoo. I see his horse."

"Git'em," the other said, leaving his half-undone britches loose and hauling out his six-shooter.

Knox didn't figure this was any time for finesse. He urged Chick onto the road and touched him with spurs. The horse leaped forward, racing for all he was worth toward the bend just up ahead. They were going in the wrong direction, but Knox figured anywhere *away* suited their purpose best just now. With a little luck, they could head into the woods and circle back around to the bridge, all while those two were chasing them down this road.

But nothing quite worked according to plan.

Chick galloped down the road, his feet sticking in the gluey mud. The two men had mounted their horses and were following, shouting at each other. Every once in a while, Knox'd hear a shot from one of them, they were shooting any old which-way as they charged forward. A shot buzzed past him, close enough to burn a divot in the bark of a nearby tree. He was actually looking over his shoulder when *it*, meaning the next catastrophe, happened.

Chick dug in his hind legs, sliding forward on his haunches, his head thrown back as he tried to stop.

Knox had just enough time to see a tree laying across the trail, its broken branches poking out like sharpened spears blocking the way. Chick took the only route open to him, laying himself and his rider down. His momentum kept him going until they slid all the way off the road to the river's edge. A river risen above its banks, the edges softened so soil and rocks and tree roots dissolved under the weight of horse and rider.

Chick couldn't right himself. He went into the water on his side, feet thrashing, head tossing, a frantic neigh cut off as he went under.

As for Knox, he went under too, trapped for too many seconds beneath the horse. He struggled to fight free, one foot still caught in the stirrup, pushing, and twisting to no avail. Then Chick managed to get his head above water, pulling Knox along behind him, both of them churning and bobbing in the rushing torrent before they went under again. Water flooded over Knox's head, blurring his eyes, filling his nose, his mouth, washing away his hat, tugging at his boots.

Cold. So cold.

Frantic to avoid Chick's thrashing hooves, Knox kicked out with his free foot, pushing against the horse's side. Chick rolled and came up. Knox didn't. Still under-water, something, some bit of debris caught in the current, rushed along underneath him. Whatever it was, lifted him far enough to yank his foot free. Beating at the water, he rose to the surface, gasping as air rushed into his lungs. He blinked muddy water from his eyes and saw Chick had gotten ahead of him. Once freed of his rider, the horse swamstrongly for shore, headed for the opposite side of the river. As for Knox, he went where the current took him. He beat at the water, trying to stay afloat and avoid the debris swept down by flooding upriver. Most of the debris, anyway, until a lightweight canoe bobbed up in front of him and floated on by before he could grab on to it.

Half a tree went past, close enough to put the fear of God into him. Then a drowned cow, bobbing wrong side up, all four of its legs pointing into the air. A sudden surge knocked the cow into him and pushed his head underwater yet again. When he came up, he was coughing, puking, growing weaker with each passing second.

But then, enough to rouse Knox to greater effort, a white cat appeared, riding a piece of wood until it tipped when it struck his shoulder. The cat spilled into the water.

Hardly aware of what he was doing, Knox grabbed its tail, whereupon the cat curled around his arm, climbed onto his back, and dug in its claws.

He swam then, sort of, the cat riding above his head and agile enough to shift whenever he twisted. It all seemed to go on forever, until he was breathless, exhausted, too weak to stroke against the water but simply moving enough to keep his nose in the air when the cat didn't push it down.

Chick had gotten far ahead and out of sight while Knox drifted that's if the horse hadn't gone the way of the cow.

At some point Knox slammed into a downed tree, one with its roots still partially connected, dipping, and driving like a many-armed skeletal prehistoric beast. Clinging to the bark with hands too cold to feel, he pushed himself and the cat into a fork formed between the tree trunk and a branch. Sometime later, the tree lurched and ran ashore, its rootball wedged between boulders. That's when he discovered he'd somehow gotten trapped, wedged in so tightly he couldn't get loose.

Cold. He was so cold.

One thought lingered until his last moment of consciousness. *Looked like he wouldn't be fulfilling his promise to William Ault after all.*

CHAPTER 3

Trying to beat the storm as it rolled in from the north, Tinker O'Keefe donned her workaday britches before going out to 'batten down the hatches' as her late 'uncle' Patrick O'Keefe used to say. Who wanted a skirt whipping around when the wind came up? Not her, that's for sure. Her dog, a mixture of several big breeds with curly brown hair, was already hiding under her bed in the room just off the rooming house's lobby. Had been since the first distant rumble of thunder.

He'd somehow managed to squeeze himself almost flat in order to slide under the overhanging quilt, the sight of which made her laugh every time she thought about it.

From the blasts of wind and the lowering dark sky, this promised to be a big storm. A whole lot of rain looked to be stored up in those black clouds, plus the treetops had begun swaying in the gusts of wind. She didn't want anything blowing into the next county. She'd already brought in wood for the fires since the woodpile often caught the brunt of any bad weather, wind, or wet stuff but especially when it came out of the north. Trying to burn rain-soaked wood caused the chimneys to smoke and spread through the rooms even with no more than a stiff breeze.

She'd had to bring in sheets from the clothesline, too, yanking them from the wooden pins with the damp fabric slapping her face like an angry lover. If she'd ever had a lover, which she hadn't, but goodness knows she'd heard enough about them from a couple of the house "clients."

Well, back before, anyhow, when she'd been a kid and her mother was still here running the house. The so-called rooming house. That was after her 'Uncle Pat O'Keefe' took up with Maisie, and Tinker herself got saddled with his last name. Legality had nothing to do with it. Besides, who knew what her name should really be? If Maisie knew, she wasn't saying.

As to why Tinker had the first name of Tinker, well, there was a story to that, too.

Maisie told her it came from an old poem. One that started off: *A Soldier and a Sailor, a Tinker and a Tailor, Had once a doubtful strife...*

That might've sounded romantic, except Maisie said since she didn't know who her child's father was, he could have been in any one of those named professions, she chose Tinker. After all, whoever heard of a girl named Sailor or Tailor?

Tinker always wondered who ever heard of one called Tinker? And yet, when all was said and done, *she'd* turned around and named her dog Soldier. Why not? Even if he wasn't very brave and cowered at the sound of thunder.

She sighed and let the wind carry her into the house where she flopped the sheets onto the kitchen table just as the sky opened up and dumped down rain. Dashing about, she slammed shut windows on both floors of the house, stopping to mop water blown in on the windward side. The chairs on the front porch had to be brought in next, and she'd best get that done before the wind knocked them over and paint that was hardly dry, the chairs being Tinker's latest project, scratched and chipped.

She had the first chair inside the house and gone back for another when she heard a horse neigh. Frowning, she set the chair back down and listened. Fancy, her pinto mare? No. The sound had come from the other side of the house. The river side.

"You're hearing things," she muttered to herself and scooted the chair inside. One more to go. But this time the wind died for a moment as she picked it up and the horse's cry came through clear, more a squeal than a whinny. It sounded... "Distressed. No, scared. That's a scared horse. Or hurt. Maybe it's hurt."

It seemed odd to her the animal was down by the river, not up on the road. How had it gotten there? There was no road fronting the stream. Not really even a trail, although it was possible to pick your way along the riverbank as long as you didn't get too close or in too much of a hurry.

But she couldn't leave an animal in trouble. She'd have to go see what had happened. The worst thing was, she'd only once before heard a horse cry like that, and it'd had to be put down. Heart heavy, she stowed the chair, got out the big old revolver Pat had left behind the night he disappeared, loaded it, and carried it with her into the gale. Just in case.

Even in the last few minutes, the wind had picked up, pushing the rain ahead of it. Tinker heard the river roaring and crashing while she stood on the porch. That meant before the storm got here, it had hit upriver first, adding to the already high water.

To tell the truth, she felt nervous even walking, well, she actually planned to run across the field and down to where the river cut through the valley. Lightning was flashing all around and if she'd had her druthers, she would've locked herself in the house with Soldier, though not under the bed, and waited until the storm passed. But even as she made a half-turn to go back, the horse squealed again.

Tinker swore, a word ladies weren't supposed to know, or at least not use. But who was there to hear whether she did or didn't? Besides, she wasn't noted for being a lady. Far from it.

Bowing her neck, she pushed on through a headwind, rain washing hard against her face, until she finally reached the dubious shelter of the tree belt along the river. She'd stay well back from the bank, she assured herself, in case the soil went soft.

And then the horse called again, and she rushed toward the sound until finally, she spotted the animal.

"Oh, no!" Her mouth gaped open. "Shite fire and save matches." She said it just like O'Keefe had always done, Irish accent and all.

The horse, a pretty sorrel with its coat dark with mud and the wet, stood shivering, front hooves striving for purchase on the bank, with his rear submerged in the rushing water. He had a saddle on his back, turned half off to the side, with most of it covered by the water. *Pulled* off to the side, Tinker amended, seeing a stirrup had caught on something sunk in a drop-off. Not only that, but a rein had caught on the same obstacle and the horse, with his neck twisted, could go neither forward nor back. No matter how hard he tried, and from the look of things he'd tried very hard indeed. He'd managed to paw the bank into a slurry in his struggle.

Tinker's heart sank.

"Whoa, boy." She did her best to keep her voice soft and calm. Not that she felt calm. Far from it. "Easy now. Let me help you."

Leery of getting close to him considering a panicked horse, especially a *strange*, panicked horse, was nothing to fool with, she approached carefully, making sure she had his attention.

"Whoa there, mister. You are in a pickle, aren't you? If you'd be so kind as to not trample me to death, I might be able to get you out of it." At least her chatter didn't anger or frighten the horse any worse.

Still, she used all due caution. Two things to contend with, she reminded herself. The river washing ever higher, and a horse already twisted into a knot, bent on tying himself tighter with every flash of lightning and crack of thunder.

"Whoa," she said again, drawing a sharp, thin hunting knife from the sheath buckled around her waist. A knife she was never without. "Whoa, whoa."

Lightning crackled and the sorrel horse tried his escape again, straining at the rein and pulling it taut. Quick as could be, Tinker slashed down, cutting the leather through, and jumped back. His head released, although the stirrup still held him in place, the horse whinnied again.

"Stand," Tinker told him. "Hold still. Let me see what's going on." Her heart sank. She'd have to get closer, maybe even into the water.

Oh, Lord. She really didn't want to do that. A river that could wash a horse downstream, for obviously, the animal had come from *somewhere*, could take a girl like her and kill her dead in about ten seconds flat. Maybe twenty if she fought hard to live.

Like the man who'd been riding this horse, most probably. A fairly long-legged man, judging by the length of the saddle's fenders. Who was he?

She cast the question aside as something to worry about later. If she got the chance.

Returning the knife to its sheath, she unbuckled the heavy Merwin & Hulbert .44 and set it under a sheltering boulder well away from the water. Then she approached the horse again.

At least he didn't seem to be a biter. He nuzzled her head as she stepped up alongside him. Barely avoiding getting a foot crushed, she shuffled forward into the loblolly of mud he'd churned up. Tinker grabbed hold of one of the dangling thongs, the rope it had once held no doubt long gone into the river. Inching out as far as she could, she bent forward to peer into the muddy water.

"Hold still," she told the horse. "I can't see a blamed thing."

Something, she never knew what although she thought antlers were involved, bobbed out of the water just then and bumped into him. He squealed and renewed his struggle. This time, with his head free, he had more range of motion.

Good for him, maybe. Not so good for Tinker. If she hadn't had the presence of mind to wrap the thong around her wrist, she would've been tossed into the water like a paper thrown into the wind. As it was, she hung by one trapped hand, swept completely off her feet.

Her squeal joined the horses.

He settled before she did.

No time left to salvage the saddle whole. Whipping out the knife again, she sawed frantically at the latigo, terrified she'd miss her aim and slash the sorrel's belly. Easy to do, seeing she was shaking worse than Soldier ever did. But she managed. Just about the time she thought her grip on the knife would give out before the leather did, it sliced through, and the horse lunged forward, the saddle dropping into the water behind him. Tinker just managed to grab onto his tail as he went past, hanging on as he pulled her onto solid ground.

Exhausted then, he stood spraddle-legged, his head down. So did she, although, having landed on her hands and knees in the mud, she didn't actually stand.

It took them both several minutes to regain their breath.

"Well," she said, at last, still panting. "That was an adventure, wasn't it?"

If the horse answered, she didn't hear him. When she felt able to move again, she re-armed herself and headed back to the house, the horse following her like a well-trained puppy dog.

Tinker led him to the barn where her little white and black pinto mare was already snugged away in a stall. Not that she was locked in or anything. Fancy liked to wander in and out at will and was smart enough to stay out of the rain and wind. She nickered a greeting to her visitor. He snuffled a reply, shivering as Tinker wiped the worst of the rain and river from him with a rag. He seemed more interested in the grain Tinker gave him than the creature sharing the stable.

He must've been starved after fighting the river for survival. He gobbled the oats and indicated he'd like more. After complying, Tinker hobbled to the house, leaving the horses to associate. Soaked through and freezing to boot, a hot bath sounded just the thing provided she could summon enough energy to heat water on the stove.

Alas. Energy or no, a hot bath wasn't in the cards. She had visitors before she got to that point and in retrospect, was darn glad she wasn't in the tub when they showed up.

As it happened, those particular visitors sent a squiggle of fear writhing through her stomach like a nest full of snakes. They were the kind of visitors that explained why she always carried a knife and kept the .44 handy.

CHAPTER 4

The water in the biggest pot she had in the house had almost come to a boil when Tinker heard men shouting in the yard.

Call her some kind of visionary but coming on the heels of 1) the storm, and 2) the horse she'd rescued, the noise struck her as more than a coincidence. She hadn't seen a soul lately except for the once-a-week mail carrier who dropped off mail for her to deliver to folks in the outlying areas, those who didn't come to collect it themselves from the boxes located in her enclosed side porch. He, the carrier, was a sour old man who seemed to think she'd contaminate him if he stayed to chat.

Oh, and there'd been another fellow who hadn't previously been in the area since before Maisie left. It had come as a shock to him to discover the house was no longer a "house."

"Especially," he'd said, "since you is a real pretty girl and got a mighty fine ass."

Tinker had been wearing her britches at the time then, too, being busy mucking out the barn. Personally,

30

she didn't think the smear of manure on her cheek did her any favors.

She'd threatened him with the pitchfork until it had finally sunk into his pea-sized brain that she wasn't for sale. Vocally disgruntled, he left in a hurry.

The shout she heard now had her pick up the Merwin & Hulbert and check the loaded chambers. Not that she really needed to. O'Keefe had been adamant about teaching her an unloaded gun was worse than no gun at all.

Maybe she could pretend to be away? But no. Smoke coming from the chimney put that premise to the lie.

Her nerves were on edge as she went through what had been the lobby to the door. It opened from the outside in and slammed against the wall before she got there. A tall man stood in the opening, dripping water on her clean floor and tromping mud on the mat.

"Get out of my house." Tinker's voice was firm and cold. "It is no longer open to the public, as you can see from the sign outside. No one enters my home without an invitation."

"Yeah?"

"Yes. And you," she added pointedly, "have not been invited in."

She knew the man, even if she wasn't going to say so. Worse, she didn't like what she saw. Not one bit.

"Well, little Miss Tinky, you ain't very friendly. How do you make any money with an attitude like you got? Sour as an old maid."

That wasn't all he said but Tinker acted like she didn't hear the last part.

"Get out," she repeated. "Not only are you uninvited, you aren't welcome." Though hidden at her side, the roll of the chamber as she cocked the .44 was clearly audible.

Anson Lowell's eyes narrowed as he looked down on her. "The day I've had, Tinker O'Keefe or whatever last name you're using nowadays, you don't want to mess with me. I got one question. Depending on the answer, I'll leave."

"Then ask it."

"You seen a man ride past here an hour or so ago on a sorrel horse?"

Sorrel horse, eh?

"No." Well, she hadn't.

"You sure? Just after the rain started? Think carefully, gal. Like I said, I've had a day."

Tinker had no desire to ask him about his day. She didn't want to know. From the time her mother ran the house, the slight acquaintance she had with him raised only fear and disgust.

"You're the only man I've seen for a week," she said, "and I'm done with looking at you. Now get out."

He studied her for a moment. "I got a feeling you're lying. Why do you suppose that is?"

Her stomach quivered. "I have no idea. Probably because you'd like it if I were. Which I'm not."

His eyebrows drew together, and she saw his hands clench into a fist. "Watch your mouth, girl. You'd best not depend on that peashooter you got behind your back, either. I can take it from you any old time I like. Then you'll see what I can do. Maybe you won't have as pretty a face when I'm finished with you."

Tinker did her best to remain inscrutable, although judging by the slow grin that broke over Lowell's face, she didn't quite succeed. But then she leveled the.44 about where his belly button should be, and his grin disappeared.

"Can't anybody miss a shot like this, Anson Lowell,"

she said. "Gut shot sound good to you? Would a hole in your belly button improve your day?"

Could be they both were saved when one of Lowell's hired toughs yelled to him from outside. "Nobody hiding in the barn, boss. Just a fancy little pinto and a broke-down red horse."

Tinker's muscles went tight. Would Lowell realize she'd only ever had one horse?

Evidently not, because he winked at her and started backing out. "Saved. Oh, sorry about the mess." He looked down at the bedraggled mat and carefully wiped his boots on it until it stuck together with mud from the yard. "Might want to shake this out."

He went as far as the porch edge, stopped, and looked back at her. "I find out you lied to me, missy, I'll be back. And you'll be sorry."

There were three of them, Tinker saw. Anson Lowell himself and two more. One of them carried his arm across his chest in a blood-spotted sling. The other limped when he went to get on his horse.

She didn't close the door until they were truly gone, disappearing over the hill into the rain. Soldier had worked his way out from under the bed by this time. He padded over to stand beside her and watch them go.

Tinker looked down at him. "The thing I want to know is, who are they looking for? And why? It's for sure they don't mean him well, whoever he may be."

Pressing against her leg, Soldier whuffled.

"Yes, they have that attitude, don't they?" She gave his ear a scratch. "By the way, Soldier boy, you weren't a whole lot of help just now. What do you say to trying to do better?"

Soldier's tail wagged.

Doing better meant getting out into the weather

again. On the upside, although it meant Tinker had to forego the bath for the present, at least she wouldn't be caught buck-naked if those yahoos came back.

But she did wash off most of the mud and put on dry clothes. Strange Anson Lowell hadn't asked how she'd gotten so wet and dirty. Wouldn't have been too hard to come up with an answer, but she was glad it hadn't been necessary.

She also made a packet of gear for what she had in mind to do next. A rope, her knife, her revolver, some bandages, matches, a canteen of clean water. Soldier stood by with questions in his eyes, so she put a collar on him and added a leather lead. Tinker knew what Soldier was silently asking. He wanted to know what she was doing. Why were they going out in the rain? Huh! Chances were good she should be asking herself that same question.

Because that red horse had come from somewhere, that's why. It seemed clear he was some man's prized cow pony, and since he'd been saddled up and ready to ride, it also seemed obvious whoever the man was he'd fallen on perilous times out there afoot. Or adrift. The horse had been washed up in the flood. Had his rider washed ashore somewhere also? The question struck her as especially serious since Anson Lowell was looking for a man on a sorrel horse. And because Lowell's hired guns had fresh wounds.

Was this man they were looking for alive or dead? Tinker intended to find out.

One thing for sure. Lowell bore him no good intentions. And since Lowell was after him, Tinker figured that put her on his side, whoever he might be.

For the first time in a year, she found the house key where it hung from an inconspicuous hook on the wall and locked the house doors, front and back when she left. With Soldier leading the way, Tinker climbed aboard Fancy and rode out, leaving the exhausted sorrel to eat and doze.

THE VIOLENT PART OF THE STORM HAD PASSED ON TOWARD the south as Tinker guided the pinto onto the main road and headed east. A few sunbreaks split through the overcast although they did nothing to warm the afternoon. She shivered even in her heaviest coat, still chilled from the dunking at the river. Only a couple hours remained before dusk. If she hadn't found the sorrel's rider by then he was apt to be in a sad state of circumstances.

Or if she did find him, he was apt to be a corpse. She had to prepare herself for that, but Lordy, she hoped not. The small experience she had with corpses gave her no joy.

The sorrel had to have come from somewhere upstream and once in the water been swept down by the raging current. He'd been lucky to land where he did, as there weren't many places along here he could've gotten as far out of the water as he'd managed to do. He'd have saved himself if the stirrup and rein hadn't gotten caught.

She intended to take the road a couple miles before cutting back down to the river and starting her search. Just below the bridge, in point of fact. She worried that it might have been washed out, causing the horse and his rider to be swept away.

Setting Fancy to a fast walk, it didn't take long to reach the bridge. She stopped as soon as she came in sight of it, saw it shaking, but still whole and spanning the water. There were men guarding it, one on each side, both carrying rifles. Anson Lowell's men? She thought she recognized the short one as having ridden with Lowell earlier. *Dang!* One thing for sure, she didn't want them spotting her. Every one of the men he hired were as bad, almost, as Lowell himself. She often wondered how the ladylike Astrid Ault, who'd been several years ahead of her in school, Tinker's schooling having been intermittent had become tangled up with him.

She backed Fancy off. At the first opening in the thick underbrush, leafed out and dripping with rain, she guided Fancy down to a narrow trail more suited to fishermen on foot than to a horse and rider. She didn't find any tracks, a disappointment.

"Soldier," she said.

At his name, the dog stopped and looked up at her.

Tinker swung her arm wide. "Seek," she said. Immediately, he put his nose to the ground and dashed on ahead. She smiled, watching him. The dog, admittedly a scaredy-cat, had nothing wrong with either his nose or his brains. If a man was out there, Soldier would find him.

As long as he hadn't landed on the other side of the river, always a possibility. The horse had been on this side, so most probably his rider would be too. Tinker had no desire to contend with those men at the bridge.

Fancy found it slow going through the wet underbrush, Soldier not so much. Tinker had a difficult time keeping him in sight, with his speed and the way his brown fur melded into the background. In fact, she'd lost sight of him when she and the horse came to one spot where the ground had been torn up, bushes broken, rocks rolled out of position. From the looks of things, a tree had fallen and slid into the river, roots, and all.

The ground slanted steeply here, especially dangerous to the four-footed. She dismounted, thinking it wise to lead Fancy through the area. Soldier had been here, and he'd left his paw prints in the mud. Lots of tracks, so he must've discovered something and paused to examine the area closely. Then finally, he'd gone on. She did too but progressed only a few yards before spotting where he'd dug under one of the rocks half-hidden by a tree limb. She knelt for a closer look at what had caught his interest.

Tracks of a horse. One whose scent he'd smelled before?

Looking at the traces with fresh eyes, Tinker studied the ground. To her best judgment, it showed where the horse had come part way out of the water, then, unable to gain purchase, had fallen back in. And, even more telling, a couple long red hairs. From the sorrel's tail, she'd be bound. Apparently, the horse had been here at some point. At the beginning of his ordeal? Or perhaps tried for land and been swept away again? And what about his rider?

"Soldier," she called, not loud. In case Lowell had set his men to patrolling the riverbank, she didn't want her voice to carry far. Mostly, she relied on the sound of rushing water to cover anything short of a full-out scream. After a couple minutes, when the dog didn't appear, she went on. His paw prints were clear. Hoping he knew something she didn't, Tinker followed.

They rounded a sharp curve in the river, upon which the path widened enough for her to remount Fancy. Tinker kept a wary eye not only on the embankment but on the river itself in case of a surge. God knows the rush and tumble as it sped over boulders was fearsome enough to warn off any thinking person.

Every once in a while, she called out to the dog but

heard nothing in return. Long enough, in truth, that she'd begun to wonder if he'd found his way home. Then, in answer to her last call, she heard a responding bark. Close enough to surprise her, actually, and she hurried Fancy to catch up.

She found the dog standing on a boulder overlooking the river, his eyes intent on something below him.

"Soldier? What have you found?"

He turned his head and barked. A demanding bark, as though he were saying, "Look for yourself."

So she did. Feeling more than a little uneasy, she crawled on hands and knees onto the boulder beside him. The rock was wet and slippery with slimy debris washed up from the river. Cowering close to Soldier, she blinked spray from her eyes until she spotted what the dog had found.

"Hah," she said, one part glad to find her effort justified, one part not so much.

Or not at all.

Not four feet below them, a man was caught in the fork of a tree, which in turn was stuck between more rocks poking out of the stream. The tree may even have been the very one washed from its spot upstream. Wedged in the juncture, while his body was submerged, the man's head rose above the current. Somehow, he'd managed to twist, or maybe the tree had, so a branch kept his face afloat and pointed his nose up.

Tinker's eyes narrowed. Was that movement? Movement on his own, she meant, not caused by the boisterous stream. And indeed, as she watched, his eyes opened, then closed again.

"I never heard of dead people's eyes doing that, did you?" she asked Soldier. He responded with a half-bark.

But now she had a dilemma. She'd saved the horse.

Could she do less than save the man, as well? Whether alive or dead, the question remained, how was she to get him out of his predicament? Should she go back and ask the men at the bridge for help? No. She put that idea out of her mind right away. Lowell and his men were looking for him with if she was any sort of judge, murder in their eyes. So, if Lowell was after him, it meant if she did that, she'd just put him in more danger.

Tinker made her way off the boulder and back to Fancy and the rope. There was a tree far enough off the bank she thought the rope, even tied around the man, would reach. From there, she hoped to pull him out by herself. If not, she'd have to risk Fancy and she didn't want to do that. Look at what had happened to the sorrel, and Fancy was a smaller horse. Easier for her to be pulled off balance and swept away.

Once back on the boulder with the rope, she lay on her belly and leaned over. "Hey, you," she called down. "Mister. Can you hear me?"

His eyelids fluttered again. She was sure of it. Almost.

"Hey, mister, are you alive?"

This time, she knew he was, as his eyes opened to maybe half and followed her movement as she scooted over the rock to the narrow piece of land separating the dirt and water.

Now she'd have to save him for sure. Quickly, before the river finished him off. She wondered why it hadn't already, the way it boiled and bubbled around the tree and the man trapped there.

The question of how she planned to pull off the rescue remained.

CHAPTER 5

I f, Tinker told herself, *he isn't dead by now, and he's not, it must mean he's plenty tough. Maybe he's still got enough grit to help.*

"Mister," she shouted to him, "can you hear me?"

His jaw shook as his mouth moved. No sound came out, though he seemed to try hard. But anybody could tell what he wanted to say. *Yes.*

"If I throw the end of this rope down to you, can you catch it?"

She read his reply this time, too. *No.* Dang. That meant she was probably going to get wet again. Why couldn't he at least make a try?

But just then a swirl in the river gave the tree a strong push. In the surge, she saw one of his arms wedged tighter than a peg in a hole into the fork, and the other hooked around a branch helping hold his head above water. So, no. She guessed he really couldn't do much to help, which left it all in her hands. For a moment she despaired, then caught herself up. She'd try anything as long as it meant thwarting Anson Lowell. And if pulling this man out of the flood alive went against Anson's preference, so much the better.

Aware of the scowl on her face, Tinker inched closer to the edge of the riverbank. Water gushed over her; a shock as cold as winter. She couldn't imagine why the man hadn't died from the cold by now and for sure, his lips were blue.

"I'm going to fit this rope over your head and try to get it under your arm. Your free arm." Free being a bit of a misconception as its job included holding him where he could get air. The river lapped at her as she stretched as far as her body could go. Her stomach muscles ached with the strain, but at last, she got the rope beyond his neck working fast at this point and over one shoulder to fit under his arm. If she had to pull hard, she figured he'd have a righteous rope burn, or maybe a broken neck, but it was the best she could think to do. As she inched backward, a splash over her entire face warned her of the tree loosening in its moorage. That's all she'd need, she thought in disgust, to go to all this risk only to have tree and man float off down the river. And most likely take her along with them.

Tinker didn't know if the panic she felt showed, but she did notice the man's eyes were glued to her, his pupils flaring in their hazel depths. He looked if she spared a thought for it, which really she was too busy to do, as if he didn't believe what he was seeing.

Her knees digging into the softened bank, she squirmed them in deeper. If she managed to get the rope's loop to fit over the shoulder above where the man's arm was trapped, it would give a more balanced load. Then she could move back, hitch the rope around the tree with sturdy roots, and start pulling. All without strangling him. She hoped.

41

It all worked pretty much as she planned until a surge flooded over the man. A mighty frothing ripple drenched her too, even though by this time she'd wrapped the rope once around the anchor tree she'd selected. But then the log with the trapped man began to move. First bobbing up and down, then from side to side as the rocks holding it loosened.

The man bobbed too. His head rose above the water as the log shifted. He cried out once, before his mouth filled with water.

Tinker felt a hard yank as the tree floated free. Still attached, the man jerked as the rope snapped taut. Caught in-between, the skin on Tinker's hands burned and shredded as the rope slid through them. Determined to hang on, she dug in her boot heels.

He was heavy and the river kept trying to snatch him along with the tree.

"Soldier!"

Her cry brought the dog to her side. She skated a little farther as the rope tightened and pulled. All she could do is point with one finger at its dangling end. Give her another hitch around the tree and she could keep the man from being washed away.

Dead or alive.

"Get it," she said. "Get the rope."

Soldier, after a moment, took the rope in his mouth and eyed her.

Though smart, he might not be smart enough for what she wanted him to do next.

"Good boy." Pointing her one finger at the tree, she said, "Around." This was the thing. Normally the surround instruction would be accompanied by a wide sweep of her arm, indicating he should circle something, whether to herd the chickens in the yard or to forbid him from splashing through a mud puddle. Right now, she dare not let go of the rope. Would he understand?

Ear cocked, he didn't move.

She waggled the finger and pointed at the tree. Soldier's head followed the motion. "Around," she said again.

Slowly, too slowly for her liking, he started in the right direction even as the man's weight dragged her another foot closer to the stream's edge.

A lull in the river's roar as the tree swung sideways of the current carried the man's voice to her. "Let go," he said.

At least, that's what she thought he said.

Let go? After getting this far? The tarnation she would.

A small "woof" made her look at Soldier, returned to her side. Her other side, with the rope, wrapped a second time around the tree and the end still in his mouth.

"Good boy. Steak for you tonight." If she'd ever had a single doubt about Soldier being the smartest dog in the world, it disappeared in a flash.

A giant tug just then would've ripped the rope from her hands if it hadn't been for the second turn. The bobbing tree only gave up its grip on the man with difficulty, but at last, it floated free and went on its way leaving him behind. Tinker pulled him toward shore like a fish on a line.

Soldier helped her then, too, taking hold of his shirt collar while Tinker pulled him by his hands. He cried out at the first jerk, then went underwater yet again. When he surfaced a second time, he stayed quiet. Too quiet.

Frantic now, Tinker gave a final yank, throwing herself backward and dragging him onto the riverbank.

He didn't move.

"C'mon, mister. Breathe." Not knowing what else to do, she pumped his arms a dozen or so cranks until he coughed and spewed water, panting and gasping for several minutes afterward. All very well, but his lips were still blue as he shivered.

But shivering is good. Isn't it? She seemed to remember hearing something of the sort.

As for Tinker, sweat ran down her face to mix with river water. She'd never worked so hard in her life and still had more to do. Now she had the man out of the river, she had the care of him. And that meant getting him on her horse and taking him home with her.

Like a stray kitten.

She'd have laughed, except for him being in such a bad way. That, and she'd best not forget Lowell already had her in his sights. Helping this man, should Lowell find out, put her in an awkward position. No, not awkward. Dangerous. Well, she'd just have to watch out for him, that's all. Watch out for both men, come to think of it. Avoid one, while keeping the other safe.

How do I get myself into these predicaments?

There was no more time to dwell on the question.

Dusk had begun to draw down, making it fairly dark under the trees. Which was to her advantage. If Fancy were able to safely make her way along the river's side path, they'd be out of sight most of the way to where the sorrel had come ashore. And by then, if they hurried to the house in the full dark without making light, Anson, or any of his men who might be keeping watch, wouldn't be able to spot her bringing the man inside.

She gave him a little shake. "Mister, are you awake? Can you talk?"

His eyes opened. He didn't say anything.

Tinker gave it another try. "Can you sit up? I'll help."

He still didn't speak but shifted around and held out a shaking hand as if he wanted her to pull him up.

He wasn't a big man, not like Anson Lowell. But he wasn't real small either. She'd discovered that much when she pulled him to shore. Doubly glad of it now, she took the offered hand and tugged until she had him sitting with his back braced against the basalt boulder. It served a second purpose of getting him out of the wind.

Since he was still shivering and she still sweating, Tinker took off her coat and put it over his shoulders. The coat stopped short of going around him and was wet besides, but even so, it beat nothing.

"Are you hurt?" she asked. "Aside from being knocked around in the river and nearly freezing to death. Oh, and drowning."

She noticed his quick look toward his left arm and spotted the gouge through a rip in his shirt. His blood-stained shirt.

"I lost my horse," he whispered.

"A sorrel gelding? Had on a saddle with KB incised in the fender?"

If possible, he appeared more mournful than ever. He answered with a nod.

Tinker opened her mouth to let him know she had his horse safe in her barn when Soldier emitted a loud *whuff*. Alarmed and unable to see him anywhere, she stood up. "Soldier?"

A hiss, a squeal, and a massive rattle of bushes answered.

"Soldier?"

The dog pushed through the bushes at her call. Blood dripped from his nose.

"What..."

Hard on his heels, a white cat slouched into sight behind him. The fur on the cat's back, mussed and full of dog spit and river water, raised up in stiff peaks like porcupine quills as it stalked toward them.

"You found a cat? Soldier!"

The cat gazed at them all like a king surveying his peasants. Zeroing in on the man, the cat approached fearlessly, jumped up, and secured a place on his lap.

Dumfounded, Tinker stared at the pair of them. "You have a cat?"

The man shook his head.

Stray kitten indeed!

Somehow, she thought he would've smiled if he could've crinkled his face.

———

KNOX BURDETTE HADN'T GOTTEN MUCH BEYOND climbing onto the girl's pretty little pinto. Once there, he concentrated hard on not falling right back off. If he'd been able to think halfway straight, he might've wondered how this girl, woman, came to find him. Especially in time to save him from drowning, trapped as he'd been in the fork of that tree. Miraculous is what it amounted to. Plain miraculous.

But for now, he didn't even care where she was taking him, as long as it was someplace warm and dry and away from the river.

His head swimming and his eyes half-closed, he figured if he hadn't spent most of his waking hours on a horse for the last twenty years of his life, he most probably would've landed on the ground at the first step. And never made it back up. It had taken everything he had, and all her strength as well, to get him aboard the pinto in the first place.

She didn't try to talk, either, which suited him fine.

So he just held onto the saddle horn and let her lead the horse where she willed. All he knew was that it seemed to take an awful long time to get where they were going. Long enough for full dark to come on, and he so cold his teeth clacked together like some of those Spanish castanets.

Also, he was aware of the cat following them as good as any stray dog, while the woman's curly-haired mutt pointedly ignored it.

He'd have laughed out loud if he weren't having so much trouble just staying awake and on the horse.

But something occurred to him later when he'd warmed up some. It had been when they climbed the bank to the edge of a meadow separating a house from the river. Fine. Then, instead of taking the shortest route straight across the meadow, she led the horse all around the clearing. Took longer, but the thought struck him they'd be harder to spot if anybody chanced to be looking. He couldn't help but wonder how she'd known to do that, then lost the thought as another round of shivers about shook him right off the horse.

A big old house loomed out of the darkness as they approached from the back. Kind of cagey for a woman with nothing on her mind but helping someone. Did she have gunmen after her, too?

They came to a stop where she positioned the horse until it stood right up against the porch.

"Whoa, Fancy." She gave the horse a pat and came around to stand at his side. "Can you get off?" She looked up at him, doubt on her face.

He guessed he'd have to. Sure couldn't expect her to pick him up and carry him.

"Yes'm," he muttered, trying to round up the strength. Maybe if he just tipped himself over and fell. But that meant he'd have two choices. Either get back up or crawl on his hands and knees into the house. Both options insulted him just to think about, so he'd keep his feet, if possible.

And it was, just, which mostly he owed to her shoulder being tucked under his armpit to hold him steady as he reeled through the door. A door she'd had to unlock to let them in. In these parts, nobody locked their door. What if someone, even a stranger, needed shelter?

Something else for him to wonder about later.

She ushered him into a small room enclosed from part of the back porch. A couch stood along one wall. Opposite the couch, which seemed a sort of afterthought in the room, a cabinet containing a double row of pigeonholes had been bolted onto the wall above a counter. A stool had been pushed under the counter. The pigeonholes were all fronted with little glass doors.

Knox, breathing hard by then, didn't stop to wonder about the room, as he and the girl both staggered under his weight. She turned him around and pushed his legs against the couch until he sat.

"Get those wet clothes off and lie down. There's a blanket folded on the end of the couch. I'll stir up the stove and make some coffee. Warm you from the inside out."

He stared at her. *Take off my clothes?* He knew why, saw the sense in it, he just didn't know how. His hands were frozen, his fingers as fat and stiff as the plate lifters on a kitchen stove lid. Besides, it wasn't his habit to disrobe in front of strangers. Especially strange women.

She hurried out of the room, giving him privacy. Not that she needed to bother. He hadn't moved, still sitting on the edge of the couch with his head hanging when she came back bearing a cup of coffee and a basin of warm water, a washrag, and a towel.

It took effort to lift his head far enough to see her.

Her mouth compressed, forming dimples in both cheeks. Knox thought he most probably would've been charmed by them if he'd felt a tad perkier.

"How long were you in the water, anyway?" She set the basin on the counter and approached with the coffee which she held to his lips. To his surprise, when he sipped, he tasted whiskey and felt the burn in his innards. A good burn.

"Too long," he croaked, although he wasn't sure the question called for an actual answer. That he spoke seemed to surprise her as she stood back and stared at him. What? Was she astonished he knew how to form words? "Don't know," he added after a while.

She motioned toward the untouched buttons on his shirt. "Can't do it, can you?"

Though not sure what she meant, he shook his head.

Emitting a sigh, she started undoing the buttons. "Should've known." She eased him out of the shirt, upon which she wrapped the blanket around him. "I think I can find a shirt for you. This one is due for the rag bag. Meanwhile, put your hands in this water. It'll help thaw you out. Then skin out of those britches so they can dry."

Knox knew he blushed or would've if his blood hadn't been frozen solid. "My britches?"

"Yes," she said, as though impatient with his lack of understanding. "Britches, trousers, pants."

"Yes, ma'am." He paused. "Boots?"

She did one of those dimple things again. "I'll get them."

Water flew across the room when she yanked them off and he heard something that sounded remarkably like a cuss word as she left, taking boots and shirt with her. It's what got him to wondering who she was and why she was helping him.

Huddled into the blanket, he thawed slowly. As the minutes went on, he came to understand why she'd put him in this room and provided the basin of water, and the hot coffee. The room evidently backed onto the kitchen where a fire in the stove passed the heat through almost too well. And the water did indeed thaw his hands so that after a bit, he removed his soggy britches. Not his drawers though, he wasn't about to get bare and take a chance of full exposure.

Knox, when the pain in his chilled hands finally abated enough for him to flex his fingers, lay back on the couch and pulled the blanket over him. Aware of drifting in and out, he slept for some time, jerking awake every so often thinking he was back in the river drowning. Once he heard her, the girl, talking to someone, and the door opening and closing. Next thing he knew she was there in front of him, shaking his bare shoulder. He jerked.

"Mister," she was saying, quietly, so that he opened his eyes slowly, his alarm falling away. "Mister, sit up and have some food. You can sleep after you eat."

The white cat had followed her in. It sat staring at him out of bright green eyes as he dropped his bare feet to the floor and sat up.

Knox couldn't help staring back.

The girl noticed. "I fed your cat," she said. "And gave

him a good brushing. He looked pretty awful after being doused in the river."

Knox shifted under the blanket. "It ain't my cat."

"No?" She smiled. "He seems to think he is. Or at least that you're his human."

And to prove it, the doggone feline jumped onto the couch beside him and commenced purring.

CHAPTER 6

With the man settled, Tinker led Fancy to the barn, removed the saddle, and got out the brush. Running it in slow strokes over the pinto's coat, still in its final stages of shedding winter hair, soothed her as much as it seemed to please the horse.

All right. So now she had the man that belonged to the horse she'd rescued. The problem was, what should she do with him?

Tinker didn't mean the horse. She glanced at the sorrel. He still seemed worn out from his struggles in the river. Well, she didn't blame him. What had the man said? *I lost my horse.* Yeah, that was it. His first concern had been his horse. This sorrel horse.

Her opinion of the man rose a notch. If it had been Anson Lowell whose horse got swept away in a flood, she could imagine what he'd say. "Don't matter. There's plenty of horses in the corral."

The man lying on the couch in the post office hadn't reacted to her description of the saddle, only the horse. Yet another point in his favor. It had been a good saddle, too.

Making sure both animals had water in a bucket and hay in the manger, Tinker made her way along the well-worn path to the house in the dark, pleased to see no light showed around the curtains she'd drawn over the windows. One advantage, she guessed, to living in a former whorehouse. It had funny little touches like that. Heavy drapes, hidden rooms, well, not really whole rooms hidden. The only real one was no larger than a small closet. Still, it almost disappeared in the wall, the door into it having been disguised so cleverly as to become invisible. At least to anyone who didn't know it existed. And what about the extra outer door, which formed the back wall of the hidden room? It opened onto the north side right into a group of bushes deliberately planted thickly enough to provide cover even in the middle of winter. O'Keefe, in his job as whoremaster, had added it so a customer could escape if somebody came looking for him. Like the sheriff or maybe an abandoned wife.

She'd put a padlock on the door when her mother left and hadn't opened it since, but still, it was there if the need ever arose for a quick escape. If she hadn't lost the key.

Tinker slipped into the house, entering the kitchen. She'd left a light on, a single lamp that barely broke the gloom. Enough to remind her of the bloody shirt she'd set aside in the sink and, after a short examination, thrown in the trash bucket. She made a simple supper then, enough for two. Or three. Soldier needed his share, and so did the cat.

Although she hadn't heard a sound from her guest, she picked up the plate she'd fixed him and bore it into the room. There were questions she wanted, needed, answers to. Before Anson Lowell came back. And he would, she felt certain. Just as soon as that mention of a sorrel horse sunk in.

"Mister," she said, quietly, so as not to startle him. Setting the plate down, she lit a lamp, although even that didn't disturb him. The even rise and fall of his breath told her he slept.

Deeply, to all appearances. She reached out, touched his shoulder, and felt him jump.

After a moment, he sat up. His nose flared and his head turned to follow the aroma of food.

Probably the bacon.

"You're hungry, aren't you?" she asked. It would be a bad sign if he were not, and she, sure enough, didn't need a dead man on her hands. Not after she'd gone to so much trouble to save him.

"Yes," he said but when she drew up the stool for him to use as a table, he studied the plate before looking up at her. "Is it morning? Did I sleep all night?"

"No. Only a couple hours." She pushed the plate forward an inch. "Eat. Then I think we'd best have a talk."

Gripping the edges of the blanket to hold it around him, he picked up the fork. His fingers were swollen and clumsy. "You're sure it's not morning?"

"I'm sure." Her chin jerked up and her eyes narrowed. "What's the matter? You don't like eggs? Never had'em for supper before?" Tinker thought she'd finally figured out why he kept nattering on about it being morning.

"Nope never did." He took a bite anyway.

She was proud of those eggs, fresh from the nest and whipped up with some salt, pepper, cream, and a bit of the cheese she'd bought in town. Tinker liked cheese. She especially liked it in eggs. There was toast, too, heavy with butter and a blob of wild strawberry jam, along with a half-dozen rashers of thick bacon. Nothing to complain of there, and by jiggerdy, he'd just better not.

The food disappeared down his throat almost before she had a chance to think this part through. Somewhat mollified by the speed with which he polished it off, she cleared the plate and sat herself down on the stool opposite him.

"There's a bullet hole in your shirt," she said abruptly.

His free hand crept to a spot under his arm. "Yes. I expect there is. Got one in me, too. Or might just be a graze."

"Do I need to sew that one up?"

"Don't think so. I hope not. Seeing as I ain't dead it must not be too bad."

Tinker matched his hope and doubled it. She had no experience plying a needle in living flesh and had no desire to learn.

Shifting on the stool, she met his eyes, hazel eyes, as she'd noticed before, verging on brown. She cleared her throat. "I suppose you have a name."

It wasn't a question, but he nodded in agreement. "I do. My pa gave it to me. My mama says she'd have called me something else." He paused. "Do you want to know what it is?"

"Just the name you use." Tinker took in a breath. "If it's not too much trouble." Was he teasing her? Because this was a strange conversation. Unless the fellow was simply a raving idiot who talked in circles. Lordy be, that might make him as dangerous as Anson Lowell, if in a different way.

Thoughts of Lowell erased the brief moment of levity.

"No trouble. I'm Knox Burdette. I work over on the Running T. You know RT Timmons?"

"Know of him. I don't believe he was ever a regular customer." Tinker had a moment of relief until she saw the big, puzzled frown come over Knox Burdette's face. Now, why'd she have to go and say that, anyway? It only served to paint her with the same brush as Maisie, which she had never been. *Never.* And here she'd been working so hard to get beyond those times.

Which is why she hurried with another question before he had time to form his own. Maybe he wouldn't even take note of what she'd said. Maybe he couldn't tell how her hot face mirrored her mortification. "How'd you come to get shot, fall in the river, and lose your horse?"

"Well, I..." he started, then stopped and sent her an inquiring or no, make that a worried look. "Did you say something earlier about a saddle with KB, my initials, carved in the fenders? Did you find my horse? Is he dead?"

Tinker's eyes widened. She hadn't thought he'd remember. "I did find your horse. Or he found me. He washed up on the riverbank below the house and I heard him squealing."

"Washed up," Knox repeated. His shoulders drooped.

"Yes. Turns out when he tried to climb onto the bank he got caught on a downed tree. Hey, just about like you did! I had to cut him loose." The similarity of their circumstances caught at her enough to stop the story. Until she noticed Knox's woebegone expression. "Oh. He isn't dead. Far from it. He's in my barn right now eating his head off. A near-drowning seemed to do wonders for his appetite."

Knox sat straighter, his face alight. "Chick's alive?"

"Yes. Sure." Then, after a moment, "Your horse's name is Chick? Like for a baby chicken?"

"Yeah." He avoided her eyes. "As a foal, he had fuzzy hair. Like a baby chicken. You know."

Tinker almost laughed. "So you raised him from a foal."

"I did. He's a good horse."

"Oh, I can see that." She wasn't about to argue. He was strong, too. He'd had to be to survive the flood.

"But my saddle." Knox glowered as a thought seemed to strike and he started to stand up. Making a grab at the slipping blanket, he leaned toward her looking more anxious than ever. "What about my saddle? Have you got that in your barn too?"

"No." Alarmed by his reaction, Tinker scooted the stool backward. "I told you, I had to cut the horse loose. Had to free him from the saddle, I mean. It was caught in the tree, holding him so he couldn't move. Reins, too. He could barely breathe."

Speaking of breathing, Knox was snorting through his nose as if he were the one having trouble drawing in air and muttering something that sounded crude. His mutters made her stand up and prepare to flee.

"I had to do it to save the horse," she said in her own defense. "It was just a saddle. Anyway, as things turned out, I'm glad I didn't save it. You should be glad, too."

"I should? Why?" Knox looked confused. "That was a dandy saddle. But the saddle's not what concerns me."

She waved the business about his saddle aside. "You should be glad because Anson Lowell showed up a while later asking about you. He didn't say your name, but he described your horse."

"You know Anson Lowell?" Knox's jaw clamped. "What did you tell him?"

"Everybody in this part of the country knows Lowell. Or of him, most often with a warning to stay out of his way. Good advice, as it happens." Tinker heard the dread in her voice and cleared her throat. "I told him I hadn't seen you, of course. His men looked in my barn. They saw your horse but didn't recognize him. He looked pretty rough just then, his tail dragging, and he hadn't dried off yet. I'm guessing that's not his usual state."

"No. It's not."

"If your saddle had been anywhere on the premises, they would've spotted the link. Before it sank in the river, I saw the KB carved in the fenders. Anyway, I...," She hesitated. "I didn't want anything to connect me. He, Lowell came busting in as if the place was open for business. Which it's not and hasn't been for more than three years. Ever since Ma Maisie left. I didn't, I don't want him coming here again."

He blinked at her. "Open for business?" He looked around the room. A thought seemed to strike him, and his eyes opened wide. "Maisie? Is this the old Red Light Pleasure Palace?"

Tinker couldn't help the way her voice rose louder and her face glowed bright enough to be the aforementioned red light. "Not anymore, I assure you." Though she didn't mean for it to happen, her voice carried loudly enough for Soldier to chuff a question from his rug in the kitchen. The cat leaped off the bed. "This is the Middle Fork Post Office and Rooming House."

"Oh. Sorry, sorry, Miss. I, uh, I didn't mean to offend you. It's just, uh..." Knox fumbled with his blanket again.

Tinker shot erect. She was so embarrassed she grabbed the empty plate and turned to leave, the cutlery rattling against the crockery.

"Wait." He was talking to her back. "Please. I'm sorry.

The name. I'd heard it before, is all, and Maisie is an unusual name. A pretty name. I want to thank you. Thank you for saving my life, for saving my horse's life, for taking us both in. And the cat," he added a little desperately. "Even if he isn't mine."

Tinker heard him speak, though not with any real idea of what he said. She didn't stop mid-flight. Once in the kitchen, she dumped the plate and fork in the dishpan with such force water splashed not only the wall but onto the floor. Which meant she had to mop it up before she slipped and broke her neck and, well, shoot. A broken neck didn't sound like such a bad idea. Put her out of her misery.

Rag in hand, on hands and knees she sopped soap-suds before crawling over to where Soldier watched her with sad brown eyes. She hugged the dog.

"I'm so stupid, Soldier. Why didn't I just pass it off, about this formerly being the Red Light Pleasure Palace and skip any mention of my 'famous' mother? It's not like everybody doesn't know already. All I have to do is say it's changed hands and is now the post office. And a legitimate rooming house. No soiled doves. I don't have to say anything regarding the rest of it."

Soldier gave her cheek a swipe with his tongue.

"He's heard of my mother, though." Her chin wobbled and she firmed it up. "I don't want to tell him my name. My stupid name. He probably knows that, too. He'll think I worked here. Worked here as a dove. I expect everybody does." She stroked the dog. "Well, who wouldn't. But I swear I never did."

Anyway, why did she think it important he, this Knox Burdette, know the facts and believe them? It didn't matter what he thought. The sooner he got on his horse and rode out of here, the better off she'd be. She didn't want to think of what would happen if Anson Lowell came back and found him in her house. To Burdette or to her.

Although that might take care of the broken neck problem. Lowell had already warned her.

———

KNOX'S STOMACH GROWLED, TELLING HIM HE COULD'VE used another plateful of those eggs. He should've told her they were good and thanked her before she ran off, but whoever would've thought she'd be so touchy?

He leaned back on the couch and propped his feet on the armrest. The girl had said the old Red Light Pleasure Palace had been turned into a rooming house. Considering it no doubt still had several rooms with real beds, it would've been fine if she'd put him in one of them so he could stretch out. The too-short couch didn't quite do the trick. Exhaustion gripped him and he knew, after what he'd learned about Lowell, that he ought to pull on his britches and boots, find his shirt no matter how ragged, and ride Chick on out of here. Yeah, bareback, seeing as he lacked a saddle. Because if, as the girl feared, Lowell did come back, he didn't want her to suffer on his account.

As for his saddle, well, he'd ridden bareback before, plenty of times as a kid. He didn't suppose it would hurt him none to do it now. And it wasn't the saddle's monetary loss worrying him, either. Or not much, though Lord knows he'd spent plenty of money on a good one that fit Chick well. RT would find a saddle for him to use, once he got back to the Running T. They'd send for the sheriff first thing and let him know what had happened to Ault. Maybe find out for sure if Astrid were dead or alive.

No. It was the letter. Ault's letter, that he'd slipped into a hidden pocket beneath the saddle's rear housing and the skirt.

A thought struck. Might it be possible to find his saddle washed up somewhere with Ault's letter still intact? It had been in that oiled packet. He remembered the slippery feel of it beneath his fingers. Ault had sent him on a mission he still wanted to complete. More than ever, truth be told. If the document hadn't been destroyed. If it wasn't gone for good, taking Ault's final wishes along with it. Guilt filled him. He should've been smarter in avoiding Lowell's men. He should've been faster. He should've shot first when he still had a gun.

And now this girl was apt to be in big trouble due to him. She'd be better off if he left right now.

But his eyes closed before he found the necessary stamina to get up. It isn't every day, after all, that a man gets caught in a flood and survives.

The next thing he knew, the girl had a hand on his shoulder shaking him out of a bad dream. Again. Only this time she wasn't carrying a plate of food.

CHAPTER 7

"**K**nox. Knox Burdette. Wake up. Wake up, drat your hide!" The whisper in his ear was forceful, the shaking more so. He smelled gun oil and felt the unmistakable shape of a revolver when he reached out. *A gun.*

He couldn't think where he was. Why he hurt in every part of his body.

At least the gun moved away when she did. *She* being the girl in possession of the agitated whisper. *And the gun.*

Knox blinked his eyes open. Not that it did him a particle of good. The room was dark to the point he thought maybe he'd gone blind. "I'm awake." His mumble put his words to the lie.

"Shh. Be quiet. You've got to move, mister. Right now."

"Huh?"

She tugged on his hands, urging him to his feet. "Hurry. Get up. *And be quiet.*"

"I..." he started, but she hushed him again.

"They're here. Damn him, he's come back. Come on! You've got to move."

"What...who?" But then his brain clicked into action, and he remembered. Both the who and the what. The river and the shooting. And the girl. Most decidedly the girl. "Anson Lowell is here?"

"Yes."

He swung his legs onto the floor and stood. The room felt as if it were whirling around him. He staggered, hardly aware when she thrust boots and britches into his hands and grabbed his arm.

"I'll guide you. It's only a few steps." She tugged, leading him forward.

From outside, he heard voices. Men shouting, laughing. Drunk, or halfway there, he'd be bound. Somebody began pounding on the front door and, startled, he heard a voice yelling from right outside the porch wall, only a few steps away. They were surrounded.

"Where are we going?" Knox shuffled behind her, nearly running over her when she abruptly turned to face him. The most he could see, and that not well, was the white of her face, shining out in a ghostly fashion considering the cloud of her nearly black hair that surrounded it.

"Right here," she said.

"Here? Give me that gun."

She acted like she didn't hear. As close as he could tell, they'd stopped right in front of a blank wall. Blank, as best he recalled, except for a hole a couple feet down from the ceiling where a stovepipe entered. Also, as he remembered, the wall was papered with a brightly-colored random pattern of birds in trees. It had made his eyesight swirl.

But then, though he had no idea what kind of trick

she pulled, to his surprise a portion of the wall swung out and she pushed him through the opening into a cavity barely big enough for him to turn around.

"What the...?" he started, but she ignored him except to say, "Hush."

"I'm going to close the door," she told him, still whispering. "Don't you dare say a word until I let you out. Don't move around. Don't even breathe too loud, you understand?"

She shut him inside before he could answer.

Knox didn't care for it at all, the total darkness, the closeness of walls barely big enough for his shoulders to fit. Nope, he didn't like it one bit. What's more, her actions riled him. He should've been looking out for her, not the other way around.

Even though it all at once occurred to him, he had yet to discover her name. Had a growing suspicion he might've heard of her, though.

The fall of her soft footsteps moved away. A few long seconds later he heard the pounding at the front stop. A couple minutes went by. Voices rose again, a man's, the girl's, the brown dog adding his vocal protest. More minutes passed. Then a gunshot that made him thrust against his confines. If he'd known how to open the door, he would've done it no matter what she said, but he found, when he ran his hands down the wall, there was no handle and pushing did no good.

Then he heard her voice, strong, angry, and clear. At least nobody had shot her. Yet.

He stopped his ineffectual fumbling when someone entered the room and walked around. Not the girl. He would've recognized her quick, light stride. Whoever this was tripped over what Knox assumed was the stool. Cursing, a man complained of the dark and slammed the door as he left. A moment later footsteps thudded from right overhead. Lowell and his men, Knox surmised, searching the place.

As he found out later, he had only one thing wrong. Lowell was occupying himself elsewhere.

———

TINKER HAD EXPECTED LOWELL TO SHOW UP SOONER OR later. Known he'd come at night, too, no doubt thinking he'd catch her sleeping, all unaware. It was how men like Anson Lowell thought, always looking for an advantage, especially over women. Especially over a lone woman of certain reputation without a strong man to take her part.

Which is why Tinker hadn't bothered to go to bed but dozed on the couch in the front parlor where Maisie, posing proud as a queen, used to greet the special customers. The ones with influence. No doves were ever allowed here, and Tinker only on special occasions, until she got older. But now it was only her and Soldier and even the white cat, waiting for the midnight hour. That's when people like Lowell did his dirty deeds, wasn't it? In the dark at midnight?

It's also why she was fully dressed, her revolver tucked at her side, and a rifle nearby but out of sight.

Lowell and his gang were plenty stupid. Especially considering Lowell seemed to think of himself as the smartest man in the county, or maybe the whole world. They made no attempt at quiet, so she knew when they came off the road, whooping and yelling, and down the trail to the post office. Just as she'd predicted.

Yes. The *post office*, not the Pleasure Palace, exactly as she'd told Knox Burdette.

No matter how you figured it, their drunken racket

gave her a few minutes' leeway in which to stow Burdette in the secret cubbyhole. He'd be safe as long as he kept his mouth shut and stayed where she put him.

Taking her time as Lowell beat on her front door and called out her name, Tinker lit a lamp with shaking hands.

This won't do. She took a steadying breath. A supposedly steadying breath. It didn't do much since she nearly shook the match out before she got the lamp lit. But finally, she succeeded and went to open the door.

"Who is it?" she demanded through a crack only a couple inches ajar. She clutched the robe she'd put on over her clothes as though she'd been abruptly awakened. "Go away. This—" She broke off. "Oh, it's you. What do you want now?"

She hoped her acting ability proved convincing. If not, well, she'd best not let the thought creep into her mind. Surreptitiously, she touched the revolver secured in the waist of the britches she wore beneath the robe.

Anson Lowell leered and pushed her aside as he entered the room. "You know who I'm looking for. Where is he?"

"No, I don't actually know who you're looking for. Where's who?"

"Knox Burdette is his name. A no-account hand of some no-account rancher. Where is he?" He stopped, glaring at her. "We had this talk earlier, Tinker O'Keefe. Don't try to play all innocent and bewildered with me. I ain't falling for it."

"I told you then and I'm telling you now, I haven't seen anybody ride past here today, except you and your rowdies. I don't know this Burdette person." Her gesture took in a short, bearded, stocky man trailing behind his boss who gawked around as if at a zoo, and a taller, darker fellow who hung back. "What do you want with him, anyway? It must be important for you to come here at this time of night."

"He's got something that belongs to me. Not that it's any of your business." He smirked. "But I intend on having it. One way or another."

She huffed. "None of my business *and* nothing to do with me. Leave me alone. In fact, just leave. You and your yahoos. If any of you damage anything, there'll be a bill to pay."

For instance, someone seemed intent on kicking in her locked back door. In the kitchen, Soldier stood and made nervous little yips. "In case you haven't noticed, the weather hasn't been fit for traveling. And tell your man to stop trying to pulverize my door. It's against the law to destroy post office property. Federal law."

She had no idea whether it was not, but felt sure Lowell, not nearly the brilliant thinker he thought himself, wouldn't either. Aside from the fact she owned the property, not the postal service.

"The hell you say." His gaze smoldering, he studied her. "How about taking off that robe. I'm curious what you got on underneath. You've grown up to be quite a looker, Tinker. Tinky. Little Tinky O'Keefe."

He made her name into an insult.

"How about not. I'm sure you'd be disappointed." She loathed the way he was eyeing her, like a subject to be conquered. A frisson of fear traveled her nerves. Her hand inched toward the opening in her robe, closer to the revolver. In the kitchen, the lock between that and the post office porch gave way and the door slammed open.

Tinker glanced over her shoulder. The man who'd

been pounding and kicking it fell inside. Literally fell, sprawling face down.

Soldier whimpered and cowered under the table.

Lowell, with a disgusted snort, pushed past her and stomped through the front room into the kitchen. He nudged the man in the ribs with the toe of his boot. "Get up, Ed, before I kick your worthless ass."

Although Tinker thought, from the way the man groaned, it might already have been more of a kick than a nudge. Just not in the behind.

But then Soldier, upset by the noise and violence, took up a protective stance and, something evidently clicking in his brain, decided to take action. He snarled with a show of teeth and, in an unwise decision, lunged at Lowell.

Quick as a striking rattler, Lowell had his six-shooter out and fired a shot. Too fast, as it happened. The bullet, meant for poor Soldier, thudded into the floor.

Tinker moved pretty fast herself. She grabbed Soldier by the scruff and yanked him out of the way, tucking him in behind her before Lowell could pull the trigger again.

"You put that gun away, Anson Lowell, right this minute." Her yell most likely scared poor Soldier even worse. Her ears rang from the gunshot, while the man on the floor poked fingers in his ears to block the sound. A little late, but what could you expect? And maybe her actual words carried a more descriptive designation of the gun than just 'that' gun. She hardly knew.

Lowell waggled his gun in the air. "Make me."

"Oh, for..." She took a firmer hold on Soldier, not the easiest thing to do when he wanted to struggle, and she had to hold the robe closed at the same time. "Go ahead."

She made a careless shrug. "Look around. See for yourself. And hurry up about it. You're boring me."

She knew the insult bothered Lowell. He just wasn't sure what to make of it.

Certain he'd won some kind of advantage over her, he told his men to spread out and get to searching, holstering the pistol as an afterthought. "Take a good look around. Every room. Don't miss anything. I'll wait here with little Miss O'Keefe." He laughed down at her, he being a tall man and she barely of average size. "Bet you wish you had that bouncer here, don't you? What was his name? The big Indian, remember? I always figured I could take him in a fight."

Tinker didn't look at him.

Lowell sidled closer.

So did Soldier, fidgeting and showing off his teeth. Not, Tinker couldn't help thinking, the best time for him to find his courage. "You be quiet," she told him. Her fingers clutched into his thick fur.

Boots thudded on the stairs as one of the men went up to check the empty second-floor rooms. So far, the only roomers who'd stopped here had stayed for only short durations and had all moved on, which didn't do much for her bottom line. Some had no doubt been disappointed by the lack of female companionship.

She heard doors slamming at the side of the house, too, in the area away from the kitchen, in the unused dining room and a parlor. They were being thorough.

His men's absence must've been what Lowell was waiting for. Before Tinker could guess his intention, he reached out and with both hands, yanked on the edges of her robe. Mouth open, he stared at the result. "What the...you've got clothes on."

"You bet I do. Now get away from me." Tinker

reared back, nearly falling over Soldier. The stumble helped hide the motion as she drew her pistol. She didn't shoot though. Not yet. She slapped at him with the pistol barrel, rapping his fingers smartly. "Hands off."

"Ow. You sneaky little bitch." Glaring at her, he shook his hand. "That hurt. You made me bleed! See, the deal with you sluts is always the part about paying some money and then getting to slap 'em around if you feel like it." He reached in a pocket and flipped out a silver dollar. It twirled in mid-air before dropping to the floor. "They don't get to slap back. Got it? Looks like somebody needs to teach you the rules of the game. Looks like that somebody is me."

She backed away, pushing Soldier with her knee, managing to shrug out of the robe and kicking it aside. *Should've shot him when you had the chance, Tinker.* Her little brain voice had finally decided to speak up and give advice, about a half minute too late.

Lowell used his height then, diving straight at her before she had a chance to get out of the way. She crumpled all the way to the floor under his weight. He dropped on top of her, crushing her lungs and pinning an arm and the hand holding the gun beneath her body. Her shoulder wrenched and she cried out.

He laughed and ripped at her shirt. A button popped, flying across the room. Lowell's face came close to hers as though to kiss her, liquor-laden breath a smothering miasma.

"Ugh." It was a sound of revulsion.

Lowell knew it, too. He slapped her. Slapped her hard.

Jaw aching from the blow, Tinker somehow got a knee raised beneath him and jerked upward with all her strength. He yelped, then screamed, and as though tussling with a bear, fell off her onto his side.

Astonished with the success, Tinker stared.

Soldier, scaredy-cat Soldier, had transformed himself into a guard dog at last. The dog's teeth had a grip on Lowell's ear, and he was wrestling the man as if fighting a wolf.

Blood streamed. Soldier growled. Lowell screamed.

One of Lowell's men yelled out from whatever part of the house he'd invaded. "Boss? What is that?"

Tinker skidded backward on her butt until she had room to get her pistol pointing the right way. The *right way* meant dead center of Anson Lowell's belt buckle.

"Soldier." She called to the dog, her tone firm. "Drop it."

He didn't want to. That much was clear. She understood the attitude all too well. "Drop it," she said again, and this time the dog gave Lowell's ear a final shake and let go. Back to his normal self, he sidled under the table.

She made it to her feet before Lowell's men arrived, their feet pounding the floors. They crowded into the room. "Boss?" Seeing his boss writhing in circles on the floor, the bearded one's eyes bugged out like they were on stems. "What've you done to him?" he said to Tinker.

Meanwhile, Lowell's eyes watered as if he'd had pepper blown in his face. He clapped a hand over his damaged ear. Three of his fingers had already swollen to sausage size where Tinker had smacked them with the pistol barrel. Blood poured down the side of his head from his wounded ear.

"When I say hands off, I mean hands off," she told him.

"You can't..." the dark man began, but Lowell interrupted.

"Get her. Hold her. I'm gonna beat the holy living..." Fury emanated from him like a forest fire. "And somebody kill that damn dog."

One of the men started forward, drawing his gun from a holster. He didn't move nearly fast enough.

Tinker pinked the one threatening Soldier in the leg, not quite an accident as at the last second she changed her aim to something less than lethal, upon which he fell down and forgot all about shooting her dog. She took more care with her second shot. This one, aimed at Anson Lowell, nicked him neatly under the arm. Not quite as deeply as she'd intended but good enough. The position bore a remarkable similarity to where Knox Burdette had received his wound.

"You two, get over here." Glaring, Tinker waved her pistol at the unmarked men, the bearded one and the dark one. "Haul these pieces of trash out of my house. I can't stand their stink. Nor yours."

They seemed frozen. The short one looked toward his boss.

"Right now." Tinker had to shout to finally get them moving.

But if she expected them to waft away on currents of air, she found herself mistaken. First of all, the man she'd shot in the leg whimpered and moaned and since she didn't, after all, want him bleeding to death in her house, she found a clean rag and tossed it at him to bind his wound. Although, come to think of it, why not let him bleed? After all, he was no invited guest, but rather an invader of her home. She had the right to defend her property.

The same went for Lowell, although she didn't bother to hide her lack of concern over either of his wounds. He couldn't make up his mind which to complain most about, dog bite, gun shot, or smashed fingers. Tinker wished she felt like laughing.

"Enough!" Standing back and watching his men obey her commands, she snickered, which most certainly didn't endear her to him. "I suppose you'll want an earring to put in your ear next. You know, like a pirate." Soldier had gnashed a tooth right through the lobe.

"Although," she added, "you know what they do with pirates." And in case she wasn't clear, finished off with, "They hang them."

But at last, they all got squared around and shuffled outside to mount their horses. The raiders left, riding up the hill to the main road, the two wounded men carrying on like children. She and Soldier watched them until she was certain they wouldn't be back. Not tonight, anyway. But later? She shivered. Oh, yes. Later.

"You're a good boy, Soldier, you know it?" Reaching down, Tinker stroked the dog's furry head. "But you almost got yourself shot. Bet you wouldn't have moaned and cried nearly as badly as they did." She finally managed the wished-for laugh, until a more serious thought occurred to her. "No. You'd probably be dead."

Then, a moment later, "He didn't act like that."

Soldier gazed up at her as if asking a question, his eyes soulful.

"Knox. Mr. Burdette, I mean. He didn't say a word about being shot. Didn't complain a single time, not even when I yanked him out of the river with a rope. And that must've hurt like blazes."

Speaking of which, she'd better rescue him again, this time from the cubby. She knew for herself it wasn't the most comfortable space in the world. Maisie had hidden her there more than once when some man thought the young girl more alluring than an experienced woman. It was hot, dark, and more than a little scary considering as a little girl she'd needed someone to let her out. Kind of like being trapped in an upright coffin if you let yourself think along those lines.

Unless you knew the trick on how to release the door's catch, which the man stuck in there didn't.

Tinker figured Knox would be grateful when she opened the door, but she had it all wrong.

He was furious.

CHAPTER 8

Knox lunged from the closet as soon as it opened, his face white, air wheezing in his lungs. Almost falling, he caught himself on the jamb. Apparently, he'd been leaning against what he thought was a wall. Close, as it happened, but still a miss. His eyes squinted against the lamplight and his expression, had he only known it, was enough to scare the ears off a donkey.

The girl's eyes opened wide. Blue eyes, although they looked almost black at this moment.

"I heard shooting," he bit out, thinking he wouldn't mind shooting somebody himself about now if only he could decide who deserved the first bullet. And if he had a gun handy, it would help.

"You did indeed."

"Who was it? Lowell?"

"Yes, of course." She slanted him a look as though wondering what else he had to say. "Things did get somewhat out of control for a while. As I'm sure you can guess, Anson Lowell is on the prod because he can't find you." Her brows pulled into a frown. "Do you mind telling me *why* he's looking for you, Mr. Burdette? Because he's going after you hard. Real hard."

He staggered away from the closet and drew a deep breath. A deep calming breath. He shook his head. "Better if you don't know. But just now, since he didn't shoot me and he didn't shoot you, who did he shoot?"

"No one, though not for lack of trying. He took a dislike to my dog, and his attitude needed settling. Turns out I fired a couple of those shots myself." She studied him. "You don't look well, Mr. Burdette. You should sit down. Or lie down. They won't be back tonight." Her lips compressed, bringing the dimple into being. "I don't think. I doubt he can get a gang together before daylight."

"Thought he already had a gang." He mumbled that much, then spoke more clearly. "You haven't told me your name." His voice rasped like a saw blade on nails. "If somebody is gonna pen me up in a coffin for half the night I ought to at least know who to thank."

She blinked. "Pen you up in a coffin? Mister, it's very possible I just saved you from being killed."

He hesitated. No more than the truth. She most probably had. He couldn't have fought a two-year-old baby and won. Shucks, he hadn't even been able to fend off a white cat.

"I don't much care for shut-in places, is all." He closed his mouth on the weak admission, vowing not to say anything else before he made a fool out of himself. More of a fool, he meant.

Her mouth twitched. "Well, no. I'm sure you don't. I'm sorry it took so long to let you out. Believe me, I came as soon as I was sure they were gone. All of them."

"All of them?" he repeated. "How many men does Lowell have with him?" He realized she'd most likely been plenty scared although she wasn't admitting to it. At least she hadn't been shut up in a hole in the wall. But a girl alone in this big house with Anson Lowell on a tear? Could be they were about even on some kind of scale.

"Four," she said. "There were four, including him."

"Four?" Astonishment registered before a grin twitched at his mouth. But then he turned serious. "How many did you kill with your two shots?"

She huffed. "I didn't kill anybody. They all rode away, each man upright on his own horse. A couple may've been a little worse for wear, is all." She started edging her way out of the room. "And since you asked, my name is Tinker. Tinker O'Keefe. You'd better be ready to ride out come daylight, Mr. Burdette. Before he comes back. For now, you should sleep."

She ducked out of the room before Knox could say anything else, leaving him to stew even as he followed her advice and settled on the couch again. He couldn't guess why Lowell thought the girl was hiding him. Unless he knew she had Chick in the barn and had lied to him about it. That's all he could figure.

That, or...there was another thing. Tinker was a pretty girl. Black hair, and dark blue eyes, and dimples. She'd, sure enough, caught his eye. Could be she'd caught Lowell's eye, too, and he was using the hunt for Knox as an excuse to make a move on her. A wife dead within the last twenty-four hours would hardly matter to a man like him. But there was something else making Tinker shy off.

Then he knew and he kind of choked.

As he recalled, the woman who'd owned this place had called herself Maisie, even though it was generally acknowledged Maisie wasn't her real name. A few years back all the young men had been talking about her, though none had got up the nerve, or the funds to buy time with her. She'd been the Madame who ran the Red Light Pleasure Palace right up until she took off with someone new and the feller who owned the place closed it down. Then he left too. Simply abandoned it.

Knox had heard Maisie had a daughter, one she kept close and away from other people, especially the men who frequented the place. Since he hadn't been one of them, he couldn't say for sure.

Sure as the world, Tinker was that daughter, left behind in an empty whorehouse to try to salvage some kind of life.

Knox had an idea it was no easy task. Kind of like putting a fence between the Running T and the XYZ. Some of the cattle were apt to spread beyond their bounds, no matter what. Just like rumors about the exclusive madame who'd been unavailable except to a select few. Who'd taken off and left her young daughter to contend with decent folks' contempt?

And now Lowell had Tinker in his sights.

Knox's fault, most likely, for drawing him in her direction.

————

THE AROMA OF FRESHLY GROUND COFFEE AWAKENED Knox in the morning. The blinds over the window were still pulled down, but sunshine crept in at the sides. It felt late to him, but then he was accustomed to rising before daylight. He sat up and stared around. Even though he knew where the door to the cubbyhole should be, he saw no sign of it. Somebody, he thought, had done a real fine job of making joins so precise, then using paper to cover them further.

He found his britches folded, along with a worn, but clean shirt, atop the stool. His boots stood side-by-side on the floor below. Both had dried overnight. Deciding he felt fine, aside from being as hungry as a starved dog, he got dressed and followed his nose to the kitchen. Tinker was there, pouring coffee into two cups.

"Mornin', Miss O'Keefe."

"Good morning, Mr. Burdette. Feel better?" Avoiding his eyes, she kept her back to him, busying herself turning some bacon strips frying in a skillet.

"Fine as hair on a chicken." He didn't figure to mention the sting from where the bullet had grazed him, every time he moved his arm. Plus, the purple bruises that practically covered his body.

Her cheek bore a matching bruise, he saw as she turned toward him.

"Glad to hear it." She spread a few dollops of flapjack batter on a griddle that'd been heating next to the frying pan. "Because I've got an idea."

"Idea?" He swallowed down anger. Her bruise was something more to put on Lowell's account.

"Yes. Sit down. Breakfast will be ready in a minute. Want milk or sugar for your coffee?"

"No, ma'am!" No self-respecting ranch hand he knew would consider drinking his coffee any way other than black. And the stronger the better.

He saw the smile that touched her lips when she set the cup in front of him and figured she'd known that. He took a scalding swallow and judged this example as pretty fair. "What's the idea?" he asked.

"First thing this morning I walked down to the river to where your horse got tangled up. You see, the only way I could save him was by cutting the saddle loose. I remembered seeing it sink to the bottom when the horse scrambled up the bank. The tree the stirrup caught on was wedged tightly between some boulders and some rooted trees, so I went to see if it's still there. It is."

Knox caught what she was getting at. "And the saddle?"

"Also there. The water is quite murky, but clear enough I saw the stirrup is still attached to the tree limb."

His heartbeat sped up. "You think I can save it? Or at least bring it high enough to look at?"

"I think *we* may be able to. If I'm not mistaken, it'll take us both."

———

KNOX BURDETTE'S PHRASING CONCERNING HIS SADDLE struck Tinker as off kilter. Oh, not the saving part. That made sense although she had a notion waterlogged leather might not stand up so well to the treatment it'd had. But no. The bringing it high enough out of the water to look at part is what had her wondering.

Nevertheless, if raising the saddle was apt to somehow put the brakes to Anson Lowell's wheels, she wanted in on the action.

"We'll need some tools." Tinker set a loaded plate in front of Knox and a less loaded one in her own place at the table. "A rope, a very sharp knife, maybe a saw in case we have to remove a limb."

Knox, already busy eating, simply nodded.

"We need to get this done as quickly as possible," she added. "He's going to be back, you know, just as soon as he can get here, and he'll be looking to make war."

"I hope you got someplace safe to go for a while."

Looking up from his plate, Knox cast her a concerned glance. "Lowell doesn't have a good reputation around women."

She snorted. "He doesn't have a good reputation around anybody." She touched her cheek. Thus reminded of her dog's heroics in defending her the night before, she slipped Soldier, waiting patiently at her side, a bite of bacon.

Knox put down his fork and, reaching for his coffee, breathed in the steam. He frowned. "Yeah, but I doubt you know the half of it."

"Why don't you tell me?"

Tinker noticed he still moved slowly this morning. No doubt he'd been rigorously banged about on his trip down the river while hung up in a tree. A purple bruise, much larger than the one she bore, colored his left cheek. She figured he was lucky his jaw wasn't broken. Then he'd been shot besides. How much would he be able to do, raising the saddle and making good an escape? Maybe he was thinking slowly, as well, because it took him a bit to reply.

"Lowell is married. Did you know that?" he said at last.

She paused, her fork in the air. "Don't know as the subject ever came up. What does that have to do with why he's after you? Did you and his wife decide to run off together?"

To her surprise, he blushed like a schoolboy and for a moment she thought she might be on the right track.

But then, sounding a bit testy, he said, "No! Why would you think... Aw, forget it. Here's the thing. He is or maybe was, married to William Ault's daughter. Astrid is her name."

She nodded. "She was ahead of me in school. But you said, 'is or maybe was.' Don't you know?"

"No. See, it depends on whether Astrid is alive or dead. And that's what I don't know. Neither did her dad, although he was sure she's dead."

Tinker opened her mouth, then shut it again. Finally, after seeming to think over his words, she said. "Neither *did* her dad? As in the past? As in maybe, he's in no condition to know?"

"Yeah. Like that."

Pushing away from the table, Tinker stood up. "I think you'd better explain, Mr. Burdette. All of it, this time."

Knox's lips twisted. "I suppose you've been wondering how I got shot."

Tinker couldn't help herself. "I imagined it was with a gun."

Blinking, Knox paused with his mouth open before saying, "Funny, ain't you? Guess I should've said, you're wondering *why* I got shot."

"You'd be right." She poured them both more coffee and sat again, Soldier's head on her knee.

"It's like this," he said and, despite being a man of few words, spent a whole minute filling her in on how he came to be on the scene of Lowell's attack on Ault, Ault's death, and Knox's own escape with the packet of papers.

"Does Lowell know you have the papers?" she asked when he finished.

Knox shrugged. "Dunno. But if he got Ault's safe open, and I suspect he did, he won't have found what he's looking for. What he needs. And he'll be wondering if I have them."

"What are these important papers?"

"Ault said something about the deed to the ranch."

Tinker pondered, wondering what she'd do if she were walking in this William Ault's boots. "What did Ault want you to do with the deed?"

"Take it to a lawyer in Spokane. Hell, woman!" The words burst from him. "I have to try. Can't go back on my word to a dying man."

"What do you think the letter he wrote says?"

He swallowed the last of his coffee and thumped the cup down on the table. "Don't know. Don't want to know. That's between Ault and the lawyer. All I do know is Ault was sure his daughter died during the night, which is why Lowell is in such a hurry to get the deed and get it signed over to her."

Tinker shook her head, her brow furrowed. "I'm not following."

"Easy. From what Ault told me, if Astrid outlived him, even by a minute, she'd inherit. Then, when she passed on, Lowell would inherit from her. But if she died before her pa, Ault could assign anybody as his heir and Lowell couldn't contest it. I'd've figured maybe old Shorty Bonham who worked for him as the heir, but Lowell's gang killed him first off. Far as I know he's still laying out in the dooryard." He paused before adding, "Lowell will say Astrid died after she heard her pa was dead. A few hours might not make that much difference, see when folks look into the time of her death, but any longer and folks will know."

With an exclamation of disgust, Tinker rose again and gathered their plates, taking them to the sink and dumping them in a pan of hot soapy water. She turned around to face Knox. "Mister, I think you're in deep..." she hesitated over the next word, "...trouble."

"Yep. You'd be right. I'm a witness to the murder of William Ault and I've got something they want. If I don't get to that lawyer before they get to me, I'm a dead man."

She stared at him. "There's another thing, Mr. Burdette. Do you know what it is?"

"Know what, what is?"

"The part where he plans on blaming you. You won't come across as a witness. He'll say you killed Mr. Ault and his hired man. He'll say you stole the deed and he had to fight you, kill you to get it back. And then it was too late because his wife died."

He eyed her. "He can't get away with that."

"He might if you're dead and can't defend yourself."

Knox shot to his feet. "Then I guess I'd better not let him kill me. Let's go fetch my saddle."

In the barn, while Knox made a fuss over Chick, Tinker dusted off an old saddle O'Keefe had taken in trade from some down and out drifter, pronouncing it better than nothing.

Knox eyed it doubtfully.

"You won't be able to use your saddle until it dries out, if then," she said. At least there was a decent saddle blanket to ease the transition between the strange saddle and Chick's back.

She saddled her pinto and, calling to Soldier, they all, horses, people, and dog, trooped across the meadow to the river. The white cat, who'd followed them out, was left sleeping in Fancy's manger in the barn, curled up on a bed of hay.

They found the river still running high from yesterday's storm, though not so thunderous as before.

Tinker pointed down at a spot where the tree, a big old jack pine, lay wedged between boulders and riverbank, its top bobbing in the swirling current. "See it?"

Barely visible in water rife with churned up weeds

and mud, among less savory things, the stirrup's shape drew them forward. With the water down from the day before, a ten-foot-wide mudflat awaited them.

Knox scowled. "Looks like I'm going to get wet again. This ain't quicksand, is it?"

"No." Tinker eyed the set-up. "How's your balance, Mr. Burdette?"

"My balance?"

"If you walk the log, I think you can get to the saddle without getting wet. Attach a rope, loosen the stirrup from where it's caught, and I'll pull the saddle to shore."

Able to tell by his expression he didn't much relish the task before him, Tinker could commiserate. After his hours in the river yesterday, only a fool would risk a second dunking. A fool or a desperate man.

"Once you get a rope on the saddle, throw the end to me." Tinker watched Knox remove his boots and start out onto the tree trunk. "I'll hold on while you cut the saddle loose from the tree."

Knox nodded and began to crawl on his hands and knees, bracing himself on side limbs as he traversed the trunk. But at last, he found a position where by stretching full length he could reach the saddle.

Easing out of the rope he'd crossed over his shoulder bandolier style, he used it to tie off the saddle. After three failed throws, he got the rope to her as she waited on shore. Finally, he detached the stirrup. Immediately, the saddle sank farther into the water, nearly pulling him off the log and dragging Tinker into the mud.

Tinker dug in, fighting the tug of the river, and watching Knox's only partially successful struggle to stay dry and not fall as he made his way back.

He grinned at her when he stood beside her again, although she noticed his face had turned a shade or two paler under its dark stubble. He slid his feet back into his boots and dug the heels into the mud. "Now to reel it in," he said as if the saddle was a huge lunker fish.

Hand over hand, not easy with the saddle a dead weight fighting the river's pull, they finally drew it onto the rocks, water sheeting off it.

Knox surveyed the sodden mass, his expression rueful. "Got knocked around pretty good. Look here. The tree is broke, the skirt is pulled away, the horn is knocked off."

"Beyond saving, I'm afraid," Tinker added as her opinion. "Looks like Chick probably kicked it around. It was turned almost underneath him."

Knox nodded. "Just let me look'er over. Then I'll throw it back. Let the river have it."

Soldier, who'd been nosing the saddle, looked up then, his head turning toward the road, out of sight once they'd dropped down to the river. The dog whuffed a small sound. An alert.

Taking heed, Tinker put her hand on the dog's back where a ridge of hair stood on end. "What is it, Soldier?" She turned to look toward her house.

Carrying across the meadow, they heard a yell, which soon was joined by more voices. A howl like a pack of coyotes rose to break the morning stillness. Tinker cocked her head.

"Who is that?" Knox asked, but not as if he really wanted to know. More like he already had the answer but didn't want to believe his ears.

"Lowell and his men," Tinker said the name as if spitting out nails. "They're here, and they're looking for us. Both of us."

CHAPTER 9

"**B**e quiet," Tinker whispered to Soldier when the dog showed signs of fussing and breaking into howls. Although come to think of it, there was no need. Lowell's gang of ruffians made enough noise to cover ordinary talking. To Knox, she said, "Hurry."

Knox didn't need Tinker urging him to speed. He pushed Soldier out of the way, yanked the waterlogged saddle onto its left side, and pawed in the vicinity of the back housing and the skirt. An extra flap of leather was attached between the two pieces, one Knox had added when he still carried around his military discharge papers and a few other important documents. All now safely stowed in RT's safe, by fortunate chance.

But Ault's papers? What about them?

His fingers were clumsy with cold, but even so, he felt the edges of the packet he'd stowed there the day before. It was a tight fit for the available space, especially with the leather swollen from its dousing in the river.

"Hurry," Tinker said again, her urgency clear.

He yanked the packet out and held it up. "It's here. Don't know if it's ruined."

"Doesn't matter. We have to go. Now." Already mounted, she had Chick in hand and thrust the reins at him. "I heard one yell something about tracks and the river. They'll come looking."

The news didn't exactly cheer Knox. With a swift heave-ho, he cast the saddle back into the river and swung aboard his horse. "What's the best way out of here?"

It struck him that she might be a little unsure herself, but she nodded toward the right. "Lawyer in Spokane?"

"Yes." He didn't have to look. He wouldn't be forgetting the address on Ault's packet anytime soon. "Go," he said. "I'll follow."

Tinker urged her pinto into a pace that to Knox felt faster than the way supported but Chick, unfazed, kept up with her. The racket of Lowell's men soon faded behind them.

They stopped once to talk; their voices low even knowing the outlaws were long out of earshot.

"You got someplace you can hide out the next few days?" Knox asked. "Until I can get this delivered and set the law looking for Lowell?"

Her blue eyes darted toward him, wide and dark. She shrugged.

"You'd best not go back to the Plea…to your house. Not for a while. It's too dangerous."

"Worry about yourself." Her words snapped. "It's fifty miles to Spokane and Lowell will be after you every inch of the way."

"Yeah." They were at a wide spot, and he drew Chick up beside the pinto. "What I can't figure out is why he keeps coming back to your place. He searched the house and barn. Why doesn't he move on?"

Tinker pulled Fancy to a halt. "A couple of reasons.

One, he knows there's a river landing right below the house. It's one of the few places people could beach their boats and the first place he'd look for anyone coming ashore, including dead bodies. It wouldn't be the first time high water has washed up a victim."

"That where Chick and the saddle came out of the water?"

"Just below there. So they'll look until they find it, and our tracks." She clicked her tongue to put the pinto back into motion.

"You said a couple of reasons. That's one. What's the second?"

"One of his men found your shirt last night. He asked me about it and the bloodstains. I told him it was just a rag. That I'd killed a chicken and mopped up spilled blood. He acted like he believed me, but he may have mentioned it to Lowell. It's a good thing nobody asked to see the chicken's carcass." She sighed. The dimple appeared as her mouth compressed. "So actually there's a third reason. Me."

"You?"

"Yes. Remember I told you I fired a couple of those shots you heard? It was because Lowell seemed to think I'm for sale. Or there for the taking, which would suit him better. To show him any different, I had to shoot him a little bit. He's a man who carries a grudge. He won't forget or forgive me for besting him."

"Shoot him a 'little bit'?" Knox didn't try to stop his spurt of laughter although he couldn't quite decide if he was amused, astonished, or appalled.

"I'm afraid so. Right in front of his men. As you can imagine, it didn't set well with him." She shook Fancy's reins and clicked her tongue at the horse. "Enough talking. Let's go."

Miss Tinker O'Keefe, Knox thought, was turning out to be a dangerous woman to know, even if she had saved his life. He had an idea she was every bit as likely to get him killed. But one thing he knew. She had to come to Spokane with him. He couldn't leave her to face down Lowell another time on her own, and that was a lead-pipe cinch.

They argued.

"No," she said. "I'll be fine."

"No, you won't," he insisted. "So I can't go if you don't come with me."

"But you have to," she said. "You promised."

"I know, but Ault is dead and you're alive. I mean to see you stay that way."

She heaved a big breathy sigh like a wearied warrior and gave in. "Well then, come on. Let's get a move on."

Tinker, having lived here most of her short life as it turned out, was well acquainted with the local byways, shortcuts, and potential traps. She led them through draws used only by deer and the occasional elk, across land where fences were non-existent, and around a rocky bit of ground where the footing for horses meant a pace slow and careful, but which left no traces. And that was in the first five miles.

All those side trails she led them onto, Knox found, were meant to make it harder for Anson Lowell and his crew to track them. Sometimes she even led in the direction opposite of their destination. At the time, it seemed a needless waste of an hour. Turned out Miss Tinker was plenty smart.

Not only aching and as stiff as a poker from his rough and tumble trip down the river yesterday, not to mention unaccustomed to the worn old saddle Tinker had dedicated to his use, Knox called for a break. "Need to lengthen these stirrups," he said, hoping the girl wouldn't hear the pain in his excuse.

She had just announced they were only a couple hundred yards from the main road, and that after this they'd have to take special care. "If you hear anything, horses, people talking, wagon wheels, *anything*, say so and we'll get off the road. Even if it's not Lowell or his men, it might be someone who'd rush off and let him know he'd seen us."

Knox snorted. "It'll take two days or more to reach Spokane at this rate." He fell silent, then after a moment, said, "I can hear people talking right now."

"You can?" Face cocked to the side, Tinker looked up from where she'd been holding a small tin bowl of water from which Soldier eagerly, and noisily, lapped. "Ah, yes. You do."

Setting aside the bowl, she attached a rope to Soldier's collar. "Stay here and hold him, will you? Don't let him follow me. I'll take a look." She swung aboard Fancy and before he could do more than blink twice and begin a protest, she rode off weaving a path through the woods toward the road.

Minutes ticked past. Once several voices lifted in shouts, though none belonging to a female. Long minutes stretched into half an hour. Knox paced, dragging a resisting Soldier along with him. He had just prepared to mount Chick and head out looking for her when he heard a sound. Spinning, he saw the pinto limping through the woods toward him. It took a moment to spot the girl walking beside the horse. Turns out they were both limping. Added to that, Tinker's blouse had a rip in the sleeve, her boy's britches had the knee torn out, and a scratch left bloody trails down her cheek.

His heart thumped in alarm. "What happened to you? You're all bunged up. What took so long?"

"First of all, those voices you heard; it was them. Lowell and his men. They're patrolling the main road."

———

A SPLIT-SECOND DECISION HAD SENT TINKER FROM GIVING water to her dog to hurtling through the trees, once narrowly missing being knocked off her horse by the low-hanging branch of a dead spruce. Aggravated, she slowed Fancy to a walk. Which, in a strange twist of fate, turned out to be a good thing. If not for those few seconds of delay it cost, she probably would've emerged onto the road at the precise moment two of Lowell's men passed in front of her. She'd have had no chance to avoid them.

As it happened, she caught only a quick glance at their faces before they were all the way past. Plenty long enough to recognize them, because even if she hadn't seen them, she would've known their horses. They were the same ones who'd been at her home the previous night.

The two appeared oblivious to any noise she and Fancy made rattling through the bushes. They were too busy talking among themselves. She even heard one of them say, "Look. There's a deer. Wish I had time to do a little hunting."

"Not on Anson's time," the other man said. "He'd have your hide."

"Yeah, I know. Only hunting he approves is going after this Burdette feller. Did I ever tell you about...?" His voice faded as they passed beyond her hearing.

But just because Tinker and Fancy had come to a

quick and complete stop, even when the men vanished around a bend in the trail it didn't mean the brush stopped moving. Or the noise. The commotion continued; sounds consisting of a peculiar, pig-like grunting, and some babyish sounding squeals. Then the appearance of some dark shapes, one quite large and two quite small, moving deceptively fast. Right toward Fancy and Tinker.

Fancy caught one whiff, took one look, and stampeded into motion so fast Tinker's head whipped backward and she almost fell off. They broke onto the road where Fancy spun in the direction headed away from the bear and her cubs. The horse ran flat out until Tinker finally regained both her senses and her balance and pulled her mare to a halt. She figured they'd outrun the bear and her cubs by this time and couldn't help worrying about Knox waiting in the woods for so long.

What she hadn't counted on was a second set of voices coming from around the bend. They were headed in her direction and probably no more than fifty feet distant. Worse, she didn't have to see the speaker to know who it was.

"Lord love a duck," she muttered and willy nilly turned Fancy into the timber. This time to hide. Maybe, just maybe, she thought, Anson Lowell and the man with him would meet up with the bear.

Poor mother bear.

The need to get off the road gave Tinker no time to judge the terrain. She forced Fancy through a narrow opening between a couple of small cedars, and then into the center of some bushes. Their flight ended there as the rain-soaked ground gave away beneath Fancy's feet. Not dumping them into a rushing river, like had happened to Burdette, for which Tinker had reason to be grateful, but into a morass of slippery mud. Fancy fell to her knees. Tinker went right down with her, barely stifling a scream.

"What was that?" Lowell's companion asked, no doubt hearing the ruckus.

"Don't..." Lowell began an answer, only to change whatever he meant to say to, "Holy Hell. Look out, Jeff, it's a bear. Run."

And run they did, the bear, according to all the shouting, following. Tinker had thought they'd simply shoot the animal.

Fancy struggled to her feet, finding purchase in the slippery mud. Her threshing freed Tinker, whose leg had been pinned between the horse and a fallen tree. Whimpering, Tinker slipped sideways from the saddle. Fancy, she noted, was bleeding from a gash in her leg, which made them a matched pair. Bait for the mama bear if the critter, satisfied with chasing away the humans, returned this way and scented horse blood. Or woman blood. They needed to get back to Knox. And to Soldier, who might at least discourage the bear from attacking.

The dog was a fine guardian as long as other humans weren't concerned. Or thunder.

Although Knox and Tinker were probably no more than a quarter mile apart, it seemed hours before she met with them again.

Chick was grazing peacefully on a patch of new grass. Soldier faced toward them, tail wagging. And Knox. Knox paced, the scowl on his face a definite indication of his mood. Or would've been if he hadn't had the kind of face most folks liked to look at. Tinker had to admit she didn't mind.

"As to what happened to me and Fancy..." She finally

got around to answering his hail of questions, beginning with a choked laugh. "A bear happened."

"A bear?" Knox's mouth dropped open. "No. Those were voices I heard. Human voices."

She sank down onto the decaying stump of a fallen tree as if her legs would no longer hold her. "Oh, yes. That too. I've never heard such talkative men before. Yap, yap, yap. But in this case, I'm glad they were."

Knox followed Soldier, the dog pulling his leash taut as he strained to reach Tinker. She welcomed him with soothing words and caresses. The dog's waving tail nearly felled Knox as he knelt beside her and poked anxiously at the hole in her britches, the fabric wet with blood.

"Did the bear get you? You and the horse? We've got to get you both cleaned up. Bears are dirty critters. You'll be infected."

She slapped at his hand, which unaccountably turned and gripped hers. "The bear didn't get me or Fancy. We took a fall getting away, is all."

Knox sat back and surveyed her and the horse before he let go. "A bad fall, from the look of things."

Tinker had to agree. "Bad enough. Listen, Knox, Fancy isn't fit to be ridden. We aren't going to make it to Spokane with you. We'll have to make our way back home."

His hazel eyes bored into hers, intense, concerned. He shook his head. She felt downright faint under his regard, then caught herself up. What was she thinking, anyway? So much concern for her? Pure silliness.

"You can't go home," he protested. "More than likely Lowell's set a watch on the place. He's probably read enough sign by now to know I was there."

"I don't know. He doesn't strike me as being any too smart."

"Yeah, but one of his men might be. You said it yourself, about a man seeing my shirt and putting two and two together. Sort of."

"I'll be careful." Tinker shrugged, but Knox still shook his head.

"You'd best ride double with me, at least until we get some place you can hide out. Chick can handle it. You're not very big and I ain't gonna leave you to Lowell or his men. Your pony can follow us if we go slow."

Though incensed over Fancy being called a pony, Tinker had a little, well, no, a substantial thrill at hearing this. At least Knox thought enough of her to keep her out of Lowell's clutches. And as for walking herself and Fancy the five rough miles back to the Pleasure Palace, Post Office, she meant, she didn't care much for the idea. It had taken about all she had just to get from where they'd fallen back to this clearing.

"All right, if you insist." She forced herself onto her feet, wincing with the effort to straighten her leg. "Just until we find somewhere safe. If there is any such place."

Truthfully? She couldn't think of a one.

Once they reached the road, Knox dismounted for a closer look at the tracks marking the day's traffic. He took care not to bump her leg as he slid past her and studied the ground. "Don't think the signs add up to more than Lowell's group," he said, adding, "as far as I can tell. Except for the bear and her cubs."

The critters' paw prints stood out clearly, which proved of great interest to Soldier. Tinker insisted he be kitted up in collar and leash again when he showed signs of preferring to follow the bear instead of them.

And Knox, being a pretty fair tracker, was able to see

where Lowell and his pal had split and each run around the bear before racing to follow the first members of his search team. Which meant all of Lowell's men were ahead of Knox and Tinker.

"I don't think much of the situation." Knox, his expression grim, stood in the road and ran his fingers through his thick brown hair as if searching for his missing hat. "They could be setting an ambush just around the next bend."

Tinker started to nod, then stopped. "You're right. You should take the train to Spokane," she said, apparently out of the blue.

"The train?"

"Yes. There's a water stop about a mile over that way." She pointed at a tangent from where they were. "It's out of your way, but you can catch up the time once on the train. They pick the mail up there, too. The crew often lets folks ride, and as long as there's room in a stock car, you can load your horse."

Knox's mouth gaped. He closed it with a snap. "Could've mentioned it before."

His voice remained cool, but Tinker heard a trace of underlying doubt.

"Could've if I'd remembered it," she said. "Excuse me if I'm not accustomed to planning escapes from a bunch of bloodthirsty hooligans."

CHAPTER 10

K nox didn't exactly appreciate Tinker's sass. Except two seconds later he was ashamed of himself. He busied himself in checking the worn cinch, trying to hide the flush he felt climb into his face. He suspected the prospect of catching a train was something he should've known himself. Although seeing the Running T was not only upriver from here, but also on the other side and several miles away from the tracks, he may have had some excuse.

Probably looked to Tinker as if about drowning in the river yesterday had washed all his smarts out of him. If he'd ever had any.

"What'll I do about Chick if there isn't room?" he asked, already figuring what she'd say.

"Then I'll take him and Fancy somewhere Lowell won't find me. I'm not without resources, you know."

Knox eyed her. Resources?

His mouth clamped, but a second later, he had an idea. A good one, he thought. "If it comes to that, you'd best make your way over to the Running T. Tell Timmons what's happened. I expect he's heard something by now. Don't know if it'll be the truth. Anyway, he'll look out for you 'til I get this situation straightened out."

Quick as water gushing into a bucket, her pretty blue eyes filled up and she blinked six or eight times.

Alarmed, he said, "What's the matter? I say something wrong?"

His question went unanswered because just then, a whisper of sound, a wail as soft as a crying dove, reached them.

Tinker jerked, sniffed, and scrubbed at her eyes. "That's it. That's the noon train. The whistle means it's about halfway up the grade over Baldy. We've got about thirty-five minutes until it gets to the water tower."

He wondered how she knew until he remembered she'd said the room where she'd put him up last night served as a post office. She'd be fully aware of the train's schedule.

"A mile, you said?" He got back in the saddle in front of her and felt her nod rub across his back.

"Plenty of time," she said. "Even with Fancy limping along."

Her 'plenty of time' turned into scant minutes to spare. The train had already arrived and was filling the boiler when they broke out of the woods. The fellow up top watching the water shut-off valve gave her a wave as they approached. Chick pranced some seeing as how he didn't appreciate being so close to the monstrous puffing locomotive.

The engineer poked his head out the window. "What happened to you and Fancy, Miss Tinker? You all right?"

"We will be, Mr. Binwell. We took a fall on the way over, is all. Slipped in some mud."

"You sure?"

Tinker nodded.

The engineer shook his head in a commiserating fashion. "That's too bad, Miss Tinker. Jediah already picked up the mail. Looks like you wasted a trip."

Yeah, but anybody could see the curiosity on his face as he eyed Tinker perched behind an unknown and possibly no-account ranch hand. Knox most certainly could.

"I'm not actually here for the mail," Tinker said. "This is Mr. Knox Burdette. He was in a shootout yesterday with Anson Lowell and his pack of coyotes over across the river at the..." She looked at Knox as if asking for help.

"Ault's ranch," he said. "William Ault of the XYZ."

"Mr. Burdette tried to help, but Lowell murdered Mr. Ault."

"Shorty Bonham, too," Knox muttered.

"And murdered Mr. Ault's roustabout, Shorty Bonham, too," she repeated. "Now Mr. Burdette, who barely escaped with his life, is trying to follow Mr. Ault's last wishes. He needs to get to Spokane as quick as he can."

The engineer's eyes narrowed. "You sure about this, Miss Tinker?"

Right away, Knox figured rumors were already going around the countryside. Tinker had spoken right on the money when she said Lowell would try to put Ault's murder onto him. If anybody believed him.

"I'm sure, Mr. Binwell." Nodding in a decisive manner, she took a breath. "Anyway, Mr. Burdette needs transport for himself and his horse. The sooner he can fulfill his promise, the sooner this can all be cleared up and the law can get after Lowell."

She was a durned fine advocate, in Knox's opinion.

He also thought maybe he needed one, going by the doubt still showing on the engineer's face.

He spoke up. "Need the transport for Tinker and her horse and her dog, as well. Lowell's taken after her and she ain't safe."

This last did much to convince the engineer. "I can believe that, knowing that hell-hound. Well, the stock car is pretty full, but I reckon you all can squeeze in." He shook his head. "I'd druther this didn't get noized around. The minute we hit the yard in Spokane, you folks get off. No dilly dallying. Got it?"

"Got it."

Tinker smiled, pretty as a picture for all her scratches, bruised cheek, and hair gone wild from riding through the woods. "We'll be quiet as mice and quick as lice, Mr. Binwell. Thank you very much."

So that was the way of it. They led the horses up a ramp into the stock car, crowding several other horses, one mule, and two fine looking Jersey milk cows to make space. A little room had been left at the door to the car, fortunate as they found a spot to seat themselves on the floor where they could avoid being trampled. At least they could breathe fresher air there, as the animals all seemed called upon to void themselves several times. Soldier, his big body trembling, pushed against Tinker, not liking his ride on a train one little bit. Knox actually smiled to see him.

The clack of wheels on the track and the rush of wind through the slats of the car made it impossible to talk as the train wound its way over hill and through dale. Probably just as well.

Afternoon was wearing thin by the time they hit the rail yards along the Spokane River. The moment the locomotive rumbled to a halt Knox pushed the door wide open and got the ramp in place. In a matter of minutes, he'd led Chick and Fancy onto solid ground. Soldier followed warily behind with Tinker limping after them, squinting into the sun.

Once out and the car closed up again ready for authorized personnel, he tightened cinches and lifted Tinker onto Chick. He hated to say it, but the shabby old saddle on his good horse's back sort of embarrassed him.

"Nice," the girl said. "Nobody will ever know we bummed a ride."

"Bums," A dirty word in Knox's book. "What the engineer was getting at, isn't it?"

"I'm afraid so."

"Huh," he said.

"Do you know where to go?" Tinker asked when they'd found their way out of the stockyards, not an easy task for folks accustomed to wide open country. The convoluted series of tracks and slow-moving trains disturbed the penned animals and confused the people. Trains tooted, cattle bawled, and the myriad stock pens seemed to have been set in place by a dizzy madman.

Knox, sweating over that very question, spotted an opening and got them all through it. "I've got the address," he said, gaping as a motorcar driven by a dude in a long gray duster, a flat, clamped down hat and bug-like goggles over his eyes zoomed past them. The driver apparently guided the vehicle with a stick poking up through the floorboards.

Chick shied at the *chug-chug* racket of its engine and Fancy pulled on her lead. Soldier stood and snarled as if confronting an opponent much worse than a bear.

Tinker buried her face in Knox's back and giggled. "Oh, dear," she said.

It was late afternoon by the time they found the

street, then the address on the envelope Ault had asked Knox to deliver. Outside an imposing red-brick edifice four stories high, they dismounted, tied the horses to a rail, bade Soldier to stay, and entered a small lobby. The space was as deserted and somber as a funeral home with no guests.

Knox peered down a hall, then up a wide staircase that emptied into darkness. Was he going to have to knock on every door?

Meanwhile, a glass-fronted directory had caught Tinker's attention. She jiggled his arm and pointed to it.

"Who are you looking for?" she asked him.

"A lawyer by the name of Eastman."

"There he is," she said after a moment. "Third floor, number 6."

"Do you suppose the higher the floor, the more important they are?" Knox pondered the question as they began climbing the wide staircase up. "Or the opposite?"

Tinker, using the smooth and polished stair rail to help her climb, shrugged and said she didn't know. "But I've read stories where something called penthouses are the most prestigious places to live and they're always at the top."

When they found the door with Eastman, Ritter, and Tombeck, Attorneys at Law written in gold on an interior window, they also came upon a skinny little man in the act of locking the door as he prepared to depart.

"Are you Eastman?" Knox asked the man.

The man tittered as if Knox had said something funny, or silly. "Oh, my no. I'm Mr. Adkins. I'm clerk, secretary, and general assistant to Mr. Eastman and Mr. Ritter."

"What about Mr. Tombeck?" Tinker peeked around Knox to ask.

Adkins gave her dirty britches and torn shirt a disparaging glance and brushed at his own immaculate suit jacket lapel. Did he think it might have gotten dusty while standing there talking to a pair as disreputable as they? "Mr. Tombeck died a couple years ago."

Knox eyed the key in the man's hand. "I don't suppose Mr. Eastman is here."

"Of course not," Adkins said. "It's 5:30 in the afternoon. The office is closed for the day. Call tomorrow and make an appointment. I warn you. It may take a week to fit you into the schedule should Mr. Eastman decide to see you."

Behind him, Knox heard Tinker give a little gasp. "A week?" she said.

"Decide?" he said.

"Yes, yes." Adkins started down the hall, walking fast. "Mr. Eastman and Mr. Ritter are very busy men, I assure you."

"Oh, but this is a matter of..." Tinker started.

Knox knew what she meant to say. A matter of life or death. Which is exactly why he shook his head sharply at her, cutting off the words. He'd met people like Adkins before. Self-important fellows who liked to intimidate anyone they considered less consequential than they were themselves. He might be only a ranch hand, but he knew appealing to the secretary would get them nowhere. And might make things worse.

"Well then," he said as if it didn't matter, "I reckon we'll just have to bide our time."

"Indeed," Adkins said and outpaced them down the stairs. A few seconds later, they heard the outer door swing closed and a muffled "woof" from Soldier.

Tinker tugged Knox's sleeve. "What are we going to do now? This business can't wait a week."

"No, it can't."

"By tomorrow, the story Lowell's telling is sure to be spreading far and wide. Do you think we should go to the sheriff?"

Gruff, he said, "I'd rather talk to the lawyer first."

"I know. But you heard that man. You need an appointment, and it takes a week. If he'll even see you." Her worry came through real strong.

"He'll see me all right." This time he sounded even gruffer. "You must think I'm as paltry as that feller. That I'm satisfied to wait around. Well, I ain't. I don't figure a *secretary*"— emphasis came down on the secretary part, "has the uh...gumption to keep me from seeing this Eastman. First thing in the morning. See, there's no damn way Lowell isn't aware Ault did his business with this outfit. He probably knew before him and Astrid even got married. He'll remember and be nosing around right away. I've got to get Ault's papers into Eastman's hands first."

"Oh." Tinker's voice was small. "Good. That's good."

They reached the bottom of the staircase before she spoke again. "I'm hungry."

Knox had to smile. "Me too." But then his smile faded. She was hungry, he was hungry. He had no doubt Chick, Fancy, and Soldier were every bit as hungry and more, even if they couldn't exactly say so. And worn out. After all, it was only yesterday he, and Chick had been caught up in a murder, a flood, shot at, and dang near drowned. And she, this little girl had singlehandedly saved his hide. And his horse.

Thing is, they had a big problem. His brow furrowed.

105

"I'm a shaney." The force of his words brought her to a stop.

"A shaney?"

"A blamed fool. Somebody who isn't too bright." His jaw clamped down hard. He thrust his hand in his britches pocket and felt around. Came up with the two thin dimes he knew were there and held them under her dismayed gaze. "This. This is what I have for money." Another problem he didn't know how to solve.

———

TINKER, SINCE SHE'D BEEN THE ONE TO DRY KNOX'S clothing the night before, very well knew that if he'd ever had any money, the river had washed it right out of his pants pocket. Under different circumstances, she might've been amused at the way realization of his poverty dawned on him. But not now. The timing wasn't right.

"Well then," she said, sitting herself down on the next to last step of the impressive stairway, "you're in luck."

"I am? How do you figure? Looks to me like we're all gonna be plenty durn hungry by morning."

"Oh, hush."

Maisie had taught her daughter one thing that would serve her in good stead. Always, *always*, have a few dollars secreted upon your person, no matter if you were only going to the outhouse. Although Tinker drew the line at wearing a money belt to bed, she often wondered how her mother had come by this knowledge. She suspected it had been hard-won.

Under Knox's disgruntled, but interested, gaze, she loosed the tangled strings of her left boot and drew it off. A hard twist of the heel released a ten-dollar gold piece from a hollow space. The coin fell out and rolled onto the bottom step.

"This should keep us all going for one night." She smiled up at him.

Knox bent and picked up the coin. He whistled. "Aren't you the clever one? That's a good trick."

"Good planning," she corrected. "And a clever bootmaker."

The heel back in place and the boot reinstalled on her foot, Knox helped her to rise. Once out of the building, they stood a minute on the boardwalk. Tinker noticed it ran the whole length of the block, which she surmised meant they were in the better part of town.

A city, she discovered, was a busy place. Lots of people, both men and women, children and...dogs. She found a length of twine curled around her saddle horn and used it to tether Soldier close to her leg. It kept him from getting too close to the shiny steel rails upon which a trolley car traveled up and down the middle of the street. Horses and carriages added to the confusion by dodging around the front and in back of it. And what a racket. People shouting, horses neighing, the dogs barking, bells pealing, sirens blowing, plus the hoot of trains over in the rail yard. Add in the scream of saws from the sawmills on the river and the noise seemed endless.

"Have you been in Spokane before?" she asked Knox, sort of wishing she could grab hold of his hand to keep him near. Just like Soldier.

Slowly, he nodded. "A few times. You?"

"I was once, a long time ago." She'd been eleven or twelve when she and Maisie rode in on a stagecoach from somewhere south of here. She wasn't sure just where, as a series of towns had all turned into a blur. Anyway, it had been night and Maisie had bundled her up fast. She hadn't wanted anybody noticing the young girl mixed in with the four doves come to populate the newly erected Red Light Pleasure Palace fifty or so miles north of the city. O'Keefe had been their escort and he'd hurried everyone out of town before the police caught sight of them. The Spokane Police would demand a fee just for letting them pass through, and Patrick O'Keefe held his expenses close.

Nowadays, Tinker was smart and quick and fairly well up to date, but she had no experience with cities. Nevertheless, she knew what order of business they needed to follow at this moment.

"Do you know of a livery for the horses? Then a cafe? And a hotel?" She said the last a little shyly. What would he think?

"No." Knox stepped back into the shadows cast by the tall buildings and shook his head. "Been almost a year since my last trip. Then it was only as far as the stockyards." He cleared his throat. "You saw what it's like around there. The hotels are nothing more than flop houses. Okay for ranch hands but not for a lady. I never did get into the city proper where the fine folks gather."

"Oh." Tinker's voice came out small. Did Knox really think of her as a lady? She knew all too well what cowboys did when they got away from the ranch and came to town. The same thing they used to do at the Pleasure Palace, if only on a larger scale. "Well." She spoke louder. "Then I suppose we'll both find out."

They started out walking, although Tinker's knee, still aching from Fancy falling on it earlier, gave out after a while. Knox soon noticed and sat her up on Chick.

The odor guided them to a big livery stable down by the river. At least the wranglers, a bevy of them, maybe four, were friendly enough to give advice on hotels and eateries. Tinker had an idea they had wandered out of the finer part of town again by now. Nary a boardwalk to be seen. Probably just as well, she thought. Finest always meant most expensive, not necessarily best value. She might be inexperienced, but she'd at least heard about how they lived here. Theaters, music, schools, activities. A myriad of stores where every want got satisfied immediately and folks didn't have to order out of catalogs. Yeah, right along with the grifters, drifters, gamblers, and, dare she say it, whoremasters.

Wistful, she rued that their job here wouldn't include the opportunity to visit a place like the grand Auditorium Theater. Or the Rockaway Cafe, famous for its steaks. Or the Crescent Dry Goods Company store where you could buy most anything your heart desired.

Although, since she had handed her emergency money to Knox, she had nothing to spend anyway.

CHAPTER 11

"**I** am not leaving Soldier in a strange place with strange men. He might run away." Tinker, arms akimbo adamantly refused to leave her dog at the livery with the horses. "Who knows what they might do to him. I've heard rumors about the dog fights held in this town with gamblers betting on who lives and who dies. And while Soldier might be big and look like a fighter, he isn't."

Soldier, as if to magnify the situation, sat at her side and stared up at her out of trusting brown eyes.

Knox tried not to look at the dog. It was like kicking a kid out of the way. He already knew the dog was gentle as a purring kitten. A vision of the white cat rose in his head. Gentler, he amended, rubbing at a scratch on his shoulder where the cat had clamped on during their trip down the river.

"We'll tie him up so he can't run away," he said. "The wranglers here know he's no stray. They'll take good care of him." Knox hoped the reasonable argument would get through to her, eventually.

Her snort made her thoughts very clear. "He can

chew through any rope in about a minute. Besides, I don't trust these men."

He gave her a look. "Yet they're keeping our horses."

"Horses are their business. Dogs aren't. I won't risk it."

With the argument, conducted in whispers, settled, they pushed out of the stable into the early evening with Soldier at Tinker's heels. Businesses had mostly closed for the night. There were fewer people out now, and fewer people meant less noise unless you counted the shriek of saws cutting through logs down at the Sawmill Phoenix on the river. A flour mill's giant grindstones made an addition to the din. The higgledy jiggledy pacing of the day faded away, calming Knox and, he hoped, Tinker, if only a little.

"What is your preference?" he asked, a bit diffident since it was her money they were spending. "Hotel first or restaurant?"

"Hotel. I need to make myself presentable, best I can." Tinker's lips pressed together until she looked almost stern as she eyed him. "Wouldn't hurt you to have a wash, either, even if you did go for a swim yesterday."

Knox smothered a grin, figuring she had a point.

He did well, not saying a word when at the first hotel the wranglers had recommended wouldn't allow the dog. The second one, a step down, wanted to charge extra, an idea Tinker soon pulled the plug on.

"You've probably peed on a rug since he has," she told the officious clerk. Broken veins on his nose and cheeks led one to believe he might be a heavy drinker, and his flush said she was probably right about the peeing part.

The clerk ignored Soldier into non-existence after this exchange. Pushing a guest book forward, he handed

Knox a key. "Sign in, mister. I'll fetch a couple towels. Do not wipe your boots with them."

"Wait," Knox said, stuttering a little. "We need two rooms."

Pretending not to hear, the clerk stalked over to the front window and hung a sign before retreating into a storeroom off the lobby and closing the door behind him. Knox and Tinker stared openmouthed at the sign.

So there they were with another dilemma. Already.

"Does that sign say what I think it does?" she said.

Knox tilted his head. "I expect so."

"No Rooms To Let?" Tinker whispered, staring at him with worried blue eyes. "Does he think...that is...does he expect...us to...uh?"

Knox had a buzzing in his ears.

"Oh, dear," she said, then sighed. Her mouth tightened and her voice dropped lower. "Well, you don't have to sign your real name. Nor mine. We can be...we can be somebody else for tonight."

But some perverse notion made Knox sign the book the way he wanted to.

Their room turned out to be on the shoddy side. Not exactly a surprise. Plain, a little dirty, the blanket thin, the mattress sagging. Later, after a surprisingly good meal in the hotel dining room, exhaustion let Knox fall asleep as soon as they got to their room. He spent only a couple minutes arguing about sharing the room, if not the bed, which she insisted he take.

"You're the one who almost drowned yesterday with a bullet hole in him," she said, and Knox had been so close to sleeping on his feet, he let her push him down. "And today hasn't been real relaxing. I can sleep in the chair."

An untruth because he woke once during the night

and found her lying close beside him. He kept his hands, and other parts, to himself, in a slightly regretful, but true gentlemanly manner.

When morning lit the room, he roused to find her sitting in the chair reading a newspaper and acting as if she'd been there all night. Soldier lay at her side, his nose cushioned on his paws.

Holding back a grin, he raised himself on an elbow. "Where'd you get the newspaper?"

"Found it outside in the hall."

That sounded innocent enough. At least she hadn't stolen it. Or had she? Because when he eyed her more closely, he thought she looked guilty of something. Or if not guilty, disturbed, and thoughtful. He didn't think it was because she'd spent the night lying beside him. He wasn't supposed to know about that.

Yawning, he swung his feet off the bed, stood, and stretched his stiffened muscles, cartilage popping. Sitting again, he pulled on his boots.

Tinker didn't look up.

Her preoccupied silence bothered him. "Something the matter?"

She rattled the paper in an agitated sort of way. "There's an article here you'd better read."

That's as long as it took for a sick feeling to travel all the way from his dry mouth to his stomach. "Ault?"

"About Ault. And Astrid. And about the shooting. There is one piece of luck. Your name isn't mentioned. Yet."

His curse, though softly spoken, made no pretense of sheltering her delicate feelings. Clomping over, he snatched the newspaper from her.

To his relief, the business hadn't made front page news. The article, buried on the second page, required only a couple inches of one column. First, it announced the death of Mrs. Anson Lowell, nee Astrid Ault, age 22. Then, aside from the usual hysterical outrage over the current lawlessness giving the area a bad name, the main message was that two men had been found lying dead at a remote ranch house. Both men had been shot. Murdered. One of the men was Mrs. Lowell's father. A suspect, name not released, was at large.

"So Astrid is dead. Ault thought so. Said he felt her go." His comment won him a questioning look as he read on.

"Two men?" he said, not quite to himself.

The comment earned him Tinker's sharp stare. "How many dead men should there be?"

"Three, by my count." He ought to know having accounted for one of them himself. "One of Lowell's men bought himself a one-way ticket on the train to hell."

Her eyes narrowed. "Well, I don't suppose Lowell could leave one of his hired men there for someone to find. Too easy to figure out he must be involved." She thought a moment. "Too bad the dead outlaw wasn't the one who intended to shoot Soldier."

The dog, hearing his name, flicked his ears.

Knox shrugged as he refolded the newspaper into a neat rectangle and handed it to her. "They're all pretty much alike. One is as bad as the other. Better put this back where you found it. Then we'll eat breakfast and get over to Eastman's office. I want to catch him before that secretary throws a fence up around him. If possible."

According to plan, they got to Eastman's dark and silent office building before the officious secretary. The lobby, to their great good luck, was open, and, walking on tiptoe, they went silently up the stairs and settled in to wait in the hall outside the lawyer's office. Knox leaned against a wall and Tinker, ignoring her sore knee, paced around the landing like a squirrel hiding nuts. Soldier, with nothing better to do, followed her every step.

"What are we going to do if he, Mr. Adkins, I mean, won't let us in to see the attorney?" Tinker paused outside the dark office and tried the door for a third time as if expecting it to open.

"We'll get in. I'll see to it."

"But what if he calls for the police and has us arrested?"

"Arrested for what? Last I heard it's not against the law to see an attorney. Or even enter a public office." He paused. "Appointment or no appointment."

"Yes, but?"

Her limp grew worse with each turn around the hall, her grimaces giving Knox a new worry to gnaw on. He couldn't help being conscious of his ribs where the bullet had grazed, as well. What with one thing and another, he was stiffer and sorer than he had been yesterday. A damaged pair is what they were.

"Settle down, Tinker. We will meet with Eastman today." He interrupted one of her rounds, trying to reassure her. "This morning. I guarantee. I guess you know I didn't come here to be tossed out on my ear."

"Yes, but?"

A cheery male voice interrupted whatever she meant to say. It came, like a disembodied specter, from the stairwell at the end of the hall. "Who is going to toss you out? Eastman? Why would he do that? Mr. Adkins? Don't make me laugh."

Whoever he was, he wasn't actually laughing.

Knox spun to face the stairwell. He hadn't heard the

man approach, which concerned him. How long had he been listening anyway?

A head poked around the corner and a youngish fellow wearing a new looking, gray-colored bowler hat stared at them through the little round spectacles perched on his nose. Brown eyes magnified by the glasses, his inspection traveled from man, to woman, to dog, and back again before choosing Knox as the spokesperson of the group.

"I'm Eastman," he announced, at last, his expression pleasant as he bounded over the last step toward them with his hand extended. "What seems to be your problem? I'm correct, am I not? You have a problem? Well, sure." He answered his own question. "You wouldn't be here if you didn't. People only visit an attorney when they're in trouble."

The men shook hands, Knox nodding while Tinker heaved a relieved sigh. "Oh, thank goodness," she said. "Why, I don't believe you're an ogre after all."

"Who said I was?" Eastman grinned.

Figuring he'd better get ahead of their business before the whole morning got away from them, Knox finally got a word in. "I see you have the morning paper under your arm, sir. Maybe you'd best read a certain article before we settle in for a serious talk."

Eastman's expression hardened. "All right. Just a minute."

He fished in his pocket and drew out a key, unlocking a door made of a heavy dark wood with a fanlight above it. He pushed open the door with a flourish. Turning on lights as he went, he ushered them into a good-sized office.

A working office, Knox observed. A big desk with baskets of paperwork awaiting attention. A tall file cabinet. A swivel chair for the attorney and a couple others for his clients that were upright but bore pads on the seat and back. Shelves of books covered one wall and a single window with an uninspiring view looked out onto an alley and the brick wall of a neighboring office building.

The electric overhead light glared as they all took good looks at each other.

"Second page, far-right column," Tinker said when Eastman had seated first them, then himself. He opened the paper.

Tinker, to Knox's amusement, sat primly, feet crossed at the ankles, back straight and barely touching the chair, hands folded in her lap. Just like a real lady. Except she gawked around the room as if memorizing every detail. As for himself, he leaned back and tried to act like a man who visited a lawyer's office every day.

Eastman was quick. Knox had to give him credit as the attorney glanced briefly and said, "The shooting up north?"

"Yeah."

Eastman read fast, his indrawn breath indicating growing agitation. He looked up, only to be interrupted by the sound of the outer door opening and a rush of quick footsteps.

"Sir," a voice announced. "Sir, you're in early. Good. I came to warn of a couple disreputable appearing characters who..." Adkins, bursting into the office, shut his mouth with a snap. For a moment only. "You," he said to Knox. Then to Eastman, "Should I send for the police?"

"Not necessary," the lawyer said. Then, with another glance at Knox, "Is it?"

"Nope. Not on my account."

"Sir." The word sounded like a protest. "These people

117

were here after you left yesterday. They don't have an appointment."

Eastman's gaze dropped to the newspaper in front of him before lifting and steadying on Knox. He briefly eyed the big brown dog who'd risen to his feet, attention fixed on the secretary.

"Soldier," Tinker said, a soft warning.

"We are in a meeting, Mr. Adkins. We're fine here."

For a moment it appeared the dismissal wouldn't work, but the secretary finally gave in. The door closed behind him with a decisive click.

"Mr. Adkins gets a little excited," Eastman said, his smile both apologetic and wry. "He's very strict when it comes to protocol. As he thinks I should be."

"Full of..." Knox muttered.

Tinker's elbow, unfortunately for his sore rib, stopped the flow of words.

Clearing his throat, Eastman leaned forward in his chair. "Formal introductions are in order, I believe. As I said, I'm Thaddeus Eastman." He held out a hand to Tinker. "You are?"

"I'm Tinker O'Keefe. I'm just along for the ride. It's Mr. Burdette who needs to talk to you." Blue eyes wide and a little spooked, she spoke in a rush.

The lawyer touched her hand and transferred his attention to Knox.

Knox stated his name and said, "I work for RT Timmons north of here. His spread butts up to Ault's XYZ."

"All right." Eastman settled back in his chair and placed his forefinger on the newspaper article. "You're here, so I assume you know Ault is...was...my client. Tell me, how do you figure in this tragedy?"

"It's like this," Knox blew out a breath and gave the

lawyer a succinct explanation of fence-crossing cows and hearing shots. "I came on Shorty Bonham's body first, shot dead and laying in the yard. Ault was in the house, fighting off Lowell's men."

"You're positive they were his son-in-law's men?" Eastman's sharp gaze fixed on him.

"I'm sure, all right. Lowell was there shooting right alongside his boys. They blew enough holes in the house to sink Noah's ark." Knox reached in the back pocket of his britches and drew out the oiled packet and stared down at it a moment. "Ault gave me this as he lay dying. Asked me to bring the papers to you. So here I am." Almost plaintively, he added, "I couldn't turn him down, could I?"

Eastman's face pinched. "Don't know how. Not if you're a decent man, which I see you are."

Knox reddened. "Whole situation is a bucket of maggots. It almost got me killed right alongside Ault, and now this lady is in danger because of it." *Lady* meaning Tinker. He handed over the packet with notable signs of relief and started to get up.

Frowning, the lawyer motioned him back into the chair. Taking the packet, Eastman examined it, then undid the flap holding it closed. A second layer revealed, he said, "I see the ink has run some. Fortunately, the writing is still legible. How did it get wet?"

"Went for a swim in the river. My horse, me, and that dadgummed packet."

Eastman opened his mouth, murmured, "Tell me," and listened closely to the ordeal from first Knox's, then Tinker's perspective. Finally, he opened the envelope and extracted the paper within. The document looked damp, but not wet. It did already smell a little musty. The attorney read, interrupted himself to look up and stare at

Knox through his spectacles, then reread the whole document.

Without speaking, he got up and went to the file cabinet, unlocking the topmost drawer and withdrawing a folder. Minutes were spent with his back to them before he returned the folder to its place and closed and relocked the drawer.

Tinker fidgeted; her eyebrows arched as though asking a question as they waited. Knox shook his head.

Sitting again, the attorney put the papers on the desk. "Do you know what this document says?" he asked Knox.

"Nope," Knox said. "None of my business. I'm just the messenger."

Eastman bellowed a sudden, loud laugh. "Oh, I think you're more than that, Mr. Burdette."

Startled, Knox glanced over at Tinker as if wondering if she knew what was so goldurned funny. So far, he hadn't found any part of the situation amusing.

Blue eyes wide, she shrugged.

CHAPTER 12

T haddeus Eastman's laughter brought his assistant on the run. The secretary opened the door and peered through the crack. "Sir? You called?"

Eastman waved him in. "I did not. But as long as you're here, you can do something for me."

"Sir?"

"Call the sheriff on the telephone. Ask him to come to this office right away. I have some news he needs to hear immediately."

Adkins gazed triumphantly at Knox and then, harder, at Tinker. "The police. Most certainly, sir."

Tinker heard approval in his voice until Eastman said, "Not the city police. The sheriff. And only Sheriff Dempsey himself, not one of his deputies. Hear me?"

Adkins cast a sideways glance at Knox. "Sheriff Dempsey himself. Of course, sir, as you say." He darted away.

The attorney grinned at Knox. "I think he's convinced you're a crook. He's going to be mighty disappointed when he finds you're a client. Disappointed and surprised."

As Knox stood, Tinker got up as well.

"Me? I'm not a client." Knox reached a hand toward Tinker. "Reckon we'd better be going now. I wish you luck with this, Mr. Eastman. Lowell is apt to be unhappy and you might want to watch your back. He came after me and he came after Tinker, Miss O'Keefe when she got crosswise of him. Best thing you could've done is call the sheriff and sic him onto Lowell."

"Thank the Lord. He'll forget all about us when the sheriff gets after him." Tinker, much relieved, couldn't see why Anson Lowell would have any reason to continue his persecution. He'd have more important matters on his mind—like going to jail. That's if they didn't hang him.

It was the troubled look both the attorney and even Knox, gave her that caused her stomach to tighten up again. "What?"

"I don't figure you can rely on Lowell giving in easy," Knox said. "He'll try to fight his way out of trouble. With his gun, if that's what it takes. Look at what he did to Ault and Shorty. And I'm a witness."

Eastman twiddled with his pen and looked worried. "I'm afraid Mr. Burdette is right, Miss O'Keefe. William Ault told me a bit about his son-in-law when he was making out his will and from what he said, Lowell is a violent, vengeful man. A dangerous man."

Knox nodded gravely. "He's all of that and born mean besides. You oughta know that, Tinker O'Keefe. Look how he treated you. How he came after you when all you did was run him off the other night. Before he even knew you'd fished me out of the river."

Eastman's eyebrows rose. "You ran him off, Miss O'Keefe? Somehow you left that part out of the report."

"Yes. Oh, it wasn't anything I said. I'm afraid I had to

use a gun to persuade him." Tinker sighed, then smiled and reached down to run her fingers through Soldier's thick fur. "And with my dog's help."

"I sense an interesting story waiting to be told. Sit down, Mr. Burdette. Miss O'Keefe. We've got time. Let's hear it." The lawyer got up. Going to the door he shouted at his secretary to bring coffee for three, then settled into his chair again.

Knox tried to protest. So did Tinker, not that it did them a particle of good as Eastman proved himself not only stubborn but persuasive. One who seemed ready to bar their escape with his body, if necessary.

"You're not leaving until you meet with the sheriff. I insist. Believe me, it will be to your advantage. Sit down." Eastman spoke his final command in such a strong voice, they gawked and did as they were told.

Because hiding someone in the old Red Light Pleasure Palace, in a hidden room, no less was a little hard to explain, Tinker was relieved to skip over certain parts of the tale when a knock on the door announced Sheriff Dempsey's arrival. Almost relieved, anyway. At first. She came to think the whole explanation would've been easier than meeting him.

Mr. Adkins ushered Dempsey into the office, upon which the room grew overcrowded with the sheriff's presence. He was that kind of man, at least as far as Tinker was concerned, with his portly figure and thick, dark mustache. His hard stare didn't seem to bother Knox, but it made her very nervous indeed. She blamed Patrick O'Keefe and Maisie, both of whom always had an eye out for the law.

"Ma'am," he said to her, eyeing her torn and stained garb and raising a thick eyebrow. Made her wish she'd been able to do more than finger-comb her hair that morning. His gaze lingered a moment on her bruised cheek where Lowell had hit her before moving on.

Certain of his disdain, Tinker's face grew hot. Apparently, she didn't adhere to his opinion of what a lady should look like.

"Don't get on your high horse, Christopher," Eastman said, reading the sheriff's expression as easily as Tinker. "These folks have had a rough time making it to town."

"Yeah?" Sheriff Dempsey didn't seem terribly impressed by their troubles. Not until Eastman began introductions, anyway. At the words *Knox Burdette* he stiffened. His gaze sharpened. "Who did you say?"

"Knox Burdette," Knox said for himself, his mouth in a grim line. He'd heard the menace in the sheriff's tone, just as Tinker had.

Dempsey, quick as a trout hitting the line, snatched out the pistol he carried in a shoulder holster under his suit coat and drew down on Knox. "Hold it there, Burdette. You're under arrest."

Knox, looking into the bore of Dempsey's .45, froze. His mouth opened, shut, opened.

The sheriff, when Knox didn't move, swiveled his head between Eastman and Knox. "Well, Thaddeus, thanks to you it looks like we got our man."

"Got your man?" Knox choked out the words.

Dempsey fumbled one-handed with a pair of steel cuffs. "I've been hearing about you, Burdette. There's a warrant for your arrest been issued. I've got to say I'm surprised you've gotten yourself an attorney already. Thadd, I'm surprised to see you sitting here calm as an etherized frog. You don't usually do criminal cases." His gun, trained on Knox, didn't waver. "Here, help me get these cuffs on him and I'll take him in."

Leaping up to stand beside him, Tinker felt Knox tense up like a strung wire. She grabbed onto his arm.

"Arrest?" he gritted. "Me? What for?"

Eastman ignored the cuffs the sheriff dangled in front of him. He made a throat-clearing kind of sound and spoke to Knox. "Well, Mr. Burdette, I imagine you can make a pretty accurate guess. Looks like Anson Lowell's already spreading his poison around. Wish you'd gotten to me sooner. We could've stopped it before it got started."

"Did my best to get here right after it happened. Had a cartload of trouble getting it done. But it isn't against the law to defend yourself if somebody is trying to shoot you, is it?" Knox spoke through clenched teeth.

"That's true, Mr. Eastman," Tinker said. "We tried. If we hadn't had to dodge Lowell and his men so many times, we'd have caught a faster train to the city."

His attention seized by her excuse; the sheriff turned to stare at her. "Dodge Lowell and his men? What are you talking about?"

"Just that. They were intent on killing us and we were determined not to let them." She reached down and gave Soldier a pat on his head. "That scum even tried to kill my dog." When she looked up to meet his eyes, her gaze was hot and angry. "You see, Lowell and some of his men burst into my house night before last, and I had to defend my honor when Lowell attacked me." She touched her cheek. "The dog helped. He bit a hole right through Lowell's ear. So when I picked myself up off the floor after Lowell knocked me down, I shot him. Lowell, I mean, and one of his men, too. Just grazed them both. Looks like I should've aimed a little deeper."

"Grazed them?" Dempsey's mouth, almost hidden beneath his mustache, had rounded. "That dog is what put the hole in Lowell's ear? *You* shot Anson Lowell?" His voice rose with each question, then dropped as he said, "He told the local deputy, fellow by the name of Caldwell, that Burdette shot him, then stabbed him with an ice pick when he was down."

"An ice pick? Why on earth would Mr. Burdette have an ice pick?" Tinker allowed every bit of her scorn to show. "Who'd ever believe such a silly thing?"

Eastman choked as the sheriff's face turned red.

Tinker continued her story. "He lied. Like I said, I shot one of his men, as well. I don't know which one. Didn't hurt him much. I'm not apologizing for it, either." Tinker didn't bother to keep her satisfaction from showing. "But it was enough to put them out of the harassing mood and the whole kit and caboodle of them left. Trouble is, they came back the next morning, yelling for Mr. Burdette and making threats. Threats to both of us. There were more of them, this time. Mr. Burdette and I, we had to run."

She made no mention of the packet they'd rescued from the river. That was for Eastman to talk about. And Knox.

Tinker thought the expression that tweaked the sheriff's mustache had more to do with disbelief than admiration for her abilities. He turned to Knox.

"I don't understand. How'd you end up at this woman's house, Burdette? What's your connection with her? Is she in on this?"

From the way Knox frowned, he didn't much care for the sheriff's insinuation. He slid a wary glance toward Eastman before he spoke. "In on this what? Not sure what you mean by that, Sheriff."

Dempsey started to say something, but Tinker answered. Even to herself, her voice sounded high and

126

thin. "He ended up at my house because I brought him there. After I fished him, half-dead, out of the river."

"Fished him out? How?"

"With a rope and the help of my horse and this dog." Her fingers sought Soldier's fur again. "I didn't say it was easy. As I'm sure Mr. Burdette will agree. Thought I might strangle him to death myself before he fetched up on shore."

Dempsey blinked and looked at Knox again. "Well. I guess that was downright lucky she spotted you, wasn't it, Burdette?"

Tinker answered again. "Luck had nothing to do with it. I went looking for him, or someone. It could've been most anyone although I thought at the time it might be a dead body." She held up a finger as the sheriff started to speak. "The reason I went looking is because I'd just rescued a horse that had washed up on a portion of my river frontage. Poor critter had gotten caught there and could neither go forward nor back. That's when I figured for sure there'd be a body. But then Lowell rode in and pushed his way uninvited into my house. He had two of his men search around." She gave a delicate shiver. "Rude sons of...guns. That was the first time they showed up. Anyway, when they left, I rode out along the river and, thanks to Soldier, I found Mr. Burdette stuck in a tree bobbing along in the water."

"What soldier?" Dempsey's gun was pointing more at the floor now, his attention clearly diverted.

She pointed her finger at the dog. "Him. His name."

"Thought you said you shot Lowell."

"Not the first time he hassled me. The second time, when I shot him, was around midnight."

Dempsey's mouth silently formed the word *hassled*. "Hmm. I don't suppose it occurred to you Burdette

127

might be a dangerous outlaw and Lowell might be helping out?"

Tinker gaped. "No. Why should it?"

"Well," the sheriff said, "seems to me most women would be pretty leery of a man after Lowell came looking for him."

Tinker huffed out something like a short laugh. "The one main thing that convinced me to back Mr. Burdette is when Lowell showed up and shoved his way into my house like he had some right. You see, Sheriff, I know all about Anson Lowell. He's a bad man, a liar, and a bully and now he's turned into a murderer."

As a conversation stopper, her blunt words worked a treat. But only temporarily.

Dempsey blustered. Eastman sat back and smiled. Knox looked anxious, though he tried to hide it.

"How can you know that?" Dempsey stared at her, his eyes like polished agates.

It was Eastman who stopped her from answering. "Enough. You can put your shooter away, Christopher," he said. "And she's telling you the truth. I've got the word of a dead man to prove it."

"What?" The sheriff snorted.

"A letter in William Ault's own hand and stained with his blood." He tapped the letter still sitting on his desk with his forefinger.

Dempsey, remembering at the last minute to point his pistol elsewhere, made a grab for the letter. "Give it here. I want to read this letter."

"Have a care," Eastman said, complying. "It's been wet and is a bit fragile. I imagine it'll be exhibit one when we bring Lowell to trial."

Dempsey read, frowned, looked up first at Knox, then at Eastman, and read again. Tinker, spared the ire of that glance, wasn't about to bewail the fact. She leaned forward, hoping to catch a glimpse of the writing.

"You, I suppose you know what all this says?" The sheriff glowered at Knox.

"Nope. Don't want to. Whatever it says is between Ault and Mr. Eastman."

Dempsey cocked a brow at the attorney. "Any part of that true?"

Eastman was back to fiddling with his pen. "Asked and answered, I believe, Christopher."

"Well." Dempsey made a breathy sound of disgust as he pressed forward. "Well. Are you sure this is the real thing?"

A grin twisted Eastman's mouth. "I'm sure. I checked the handwriting and the signature with some documents Ault signed previously. Remember, I'm considered something of an expert when it comes to matching handwriting."

While the sheriff and the attorney settled into some convoluted argumentation and expoundation, as Tinker recalled O'Keefe saying as he described a cursing match he'd gotten into with one of Maisie's customers, she reached over and poked Knox' arm. When she had his attention, she whispered, "What do you suppose is in that letter?"

Knox shrugged. "Dunno. But it must be important. Sounds like maybe Ault wrote down about who shot him."

"Bless his heart." Tinker's eyes opened wide. How nice for Knox to be the recipient of such generous fore-thought. She'd never been. Most folks, the local women came to mind, had always been more of a notion to condemn her because of her mother than to support her efforts to get past her upbringing. "Does this mean we can leave now?"

"Seems as if."

She got up, wincing as she put weight on her sore knee. Another thing she could blame Anson Lowell for. But there was the attorney, waving her down yet again.

"Sit, Miss O'Keefe. We're not quite finished."

Dempsey shook his head. "Don't need her here, do we?"

"Depends," Eastman said. "Mr. Burdette? Would you prefer to have the lady wait for you in the outer room while we discuss business?"

"Business? What business?"

"The business of getting your name off the wanted list, among other things," Dempsey grumbled. "For now, at least. Depends on what our investigation turns up."

A concession, not that it appeared an apology would be forthcoming.

CHAPTER 13

Regardless of what Knox replied, which was that he didn't mind if Tinker stayed for the business, she opted to take Soldier and leave Knox to fight this battle on his own. She wasn't too sure she wanted to mix any further in his affairs. Added to which, the sheriff, and the way he looked at her, made her nervous. The dealings Maisie and O'Keefe'd had with the law in the past made her cautious and distrustful of those in authority.

She couldn't help thinking the result of her interference between Knox and Lowell hadn't been as favorable as she might like. Maybe for Knox, but not for her. Any time a good deed put someone like Anson Lowell on your trail, you had to question the decision that put him there.

Particularly, and here her thoughts turned sour if you were a woman. She wouldn't be safe until Dempsey either hanged Lowell or penned him up in prison for the rest of his life.

She and Soldier slipped past Mr. Adkins while his back was turned. Apparently, he didn't notice as he poured coffee from an ordinary blue enamel pot into something more impressive. She doubted the pretty china pot and matching cups were produced on Knox's behalf. More likely the clerk was trying to impress the sheriff.

It had been a little chilly in Eastman's office, and with Soldier restless and acting as if he needed to lift his leg, she hurried him out of the building. The sun shone, and though still early, warmth gathered in the canyon-like streets. The heat eased her sore knee.

With the attorney's office situated in the better part of town, the passersby proved more interesting to her than the motley bunch she'd observed in their hotel's dining room this morning. She eyed the women and their fashionable clothes. A deep blue walking suit, in particular, caught her eye, along with a matching hat the lady wore pinned to her high-piled hair. She felt a moment's envy. What would Knox do if he saw plain old Tinker O'Keefe so attired? Laugh at her?

Most of the men wore clothing like Thaddeus Eastman and she couldn't help contrasting their attire with Knox's denims and worn chambray work shirt. But Knox, he could hold his own with any man.

Reminded now of her own rough appearance and hoping to remain invisible, Tinker slunk farther into the shadows and settled in to wait for Knox. A little bewildered by all the activity, she leaned against the side of the brick building, wondering if she could find her way back to the railyard. Or if she should just retrieve her horse and hit the trail for home by herself. Fifty miles being a fair distance, she figured it would take her and Fancy a couple of days.

When she spotted the woman walking toward her, Tinker shot erect, her movement so tense and jerky

Soldier whined a question. Although she wouldn't call the woman's gait walking, exactly. More like mincing, a word one might read in an old-fashioned novel, denoting the short steps and swaying hips. What's more, the woman, though not the way she walked, was familiar, though changed. And beautiful. Still beautiful.

Lighter colored hair and only faint traces of paint and powder made her barely recognizable, even to Tinker. The woman's aim, no doubt. With her hand tucked under a prosperous looking fellow's arm, the woman wasn't paying attention to the way ahead of her. Too busy batting her darkened eyelashes and gazing adoringly up at the man as she hung on his every word.

But even she had to check in front once in a while, which she did just as the pair came abreast of Tinker.

Her half-caught gasp proved illuminating. So did the one aimed at Soldier, as the dog stepped into her path.

The dog, Tinker knew, expected a pet from this particular human. The woman, she clearly noted, would rather not. Just as she'd rather pretend not to see, let alone acknowledge, Tinker. Speechless, eyes fixed on the woman, Tinker tugged Soldier back, out of the way.

"Keep hold of your dog," the man said, sharp and short. "He's dirtying my wife's gown."

Tinker swallowed sharp words of her own. What did he think? That she was siccing Soldier onto them? "Sorry," she murmured.

Wife? His wife? She didn't know what else to say. *"Hello, Mother?"* came to mind. She put her hand over her mouth to stop an involuntary laugh. How about, *"Hello, Step-daddy?"*

The man was not the same one Maisie had left with three years ago. She'd risen a notch or two in the social sphere if Tinker were to judge by appearances. Could she?

Knowing Maisie, the pair were as likely, maybe more likely, to be partners in a scheme of some kind rather than a married couple. She didn't know which premise to favor.

But one thing Tinker did know. They, Maisie, hadn't anticipated meeting her.

A flush had spread over her mother's face, but she remained firmly in place as the character she was playing.

"Oh, Edward, I don't mind. You know I like dogs," she cooed, reaching out a hand gloved in kid leather. She patted Soldier on the head and tugged lightly at one of his ears.

He wriggled tail wagging, in appreciation.

As for Tinker, even as the aforementioned Edward railed against wearing dirty gloves to meet with *somebody*, Tinker didn't catch the name, she reflected that Maisie didn't lie. She *had* always liked dogs. Especially this one, as it had been she who rescued Soldier as an abused puppy and given him to Tinker.

The best gift she'd ever gotten. Maybe, Tinker reflected the only gift.

But Maisie's husband still complained. In the end, he reached into his pocket and extracted an eye-popping wad of bills, from which he extracted a few and handed them to Maisie.

"There's a store right there." He pointed. "A decent looking boutique. Buy a nice pair of gloves before I introduce you to George. I've told you how particular he is. I'll meet you in his office in say ten...no...fifteen minutes."

"Yes, dear. I'm so sorry. I forgot about George's aversion to dogs." Maisie smiled. "Thank you, darling."

The husband stalked off and turned into the doorway

of the building next to Eastman's. Waiting until he disappeared from view, Maisie giggled and reached down to give Soldier a hug.

Attention, Tinker couldn't help noticing, not accorded her daughter.

Maisie straightened. "Well, Tinker. I didn't expect to see you here. You don't look very prosperous. Business not good?"

It appeared Maisie expected her to have gone into selling herself, even though, to her credit, she'd protected Tinker from the trade as a youngster. Probably on the premise it would detract from her value. The really young ones didn't usually live long in the prostitution business.

Tinker's mouth twisted. "I'm not in the family business, mother." Her eyes narrowed. "Is that man really your husband?"

The question set Maisie to preening. "He really is. Colonel Edward Von Senkler. I met him in San Francisco a year ago."

"Are you running a scheme?" Tinker gawked at the bills Von Senkler had given her mother. "Looks like it must be going well."

Maisie laughed. "No scheme. Edward is for real. He's in the mercantile business and wants to add to his empire with a store here in Spokane." She gazed around. "There's a great deal of money in this town, you know, what with the mine owners and timber barons and wheat farmers. By the way, Maisie is a name lost in time. I'm Sarah now. Sarah Von Senkler." She shuffled the money, selected a bill, and thrust it at Tinker. "Here. Looks like you can use this. Buy yourself a pretty dress, Tinker. God knows you could use one. And for heaven's sake, do something with your hair. It looks like rats have been using it to nest in."

She whirled, then, and high heels tapping on the sidewalk, headed toward Mamzelle's Boutique without a backward look.

As if Tinker meant nothing more than a charity case to her.

No real surprise, Tinker admitted to herself. Nothing more than a truth first proven when Maisie left her daughter to fare for herself in an empty whorehouse. Once owned by Patrick O'Keefe, nobody questioned when Tinker simply continued living there. Not even when he disappeared. Blood drummed in her ears. First, she felt hot, then cold, then hot again.

She hadn't glanced at the money until then but now gasped in surprise. Not only a second-in-a-lifetime gift but a fifty-dollar bill. Tinker almost fainted. A pay-off to get out of sight, she assumed. Nothing more and nothing less. Crumbling the bill in a suddenly sweaty fist, she skittered back inside the office building lobby, pulling Soldier with her, and shrinking from sight as Sheriff Dempsey, who looked neither right nor left, trod down the stairs. He took no notice of her, huddled in a corner.

If Knox thought himself gobsmacked by what had happened in Thaddeus Eastman's law office just now, the look on Tinker's face matched his own when they met in the lobby. He wondered if she'd been listening at the door when Eastman broke the news. Further thought brought an answer. No. The clerk would never allow anyone but himself close enough to hear what had gone on inside. Besides, Tinker's expression was different from the astonishment his turn of fortune deserved.

What caused the stricken expression she tried to hide, but which left her cheekbones painted with bright red blotches? The color even overwhelmed the bruise Lowell had placed there. He'd gotten to know her a bit now and he could tell something had happened to upset her. Dempsey! Had the sheriff said harsh words as he left? A comment that had set her off? Hurt her?

Dempsey, after all, hadn't been pleased with Eastman's news. Distrusted it, most likely.

As for Knox, he didn't know if he was pleased or not. Not the proved innocent part. The other. Had the wind knocked out of him is all he knew right now and didn't know what to make of the whole shebang.

Soldier, who'd been lying at Tinker's feet, scrambled up as Knox approached. Tinker didn't even seem to see him, her gaze intent on the street outside. When Knox said her name, she acted as if she didn't hear.

"Tinker?" he said again, louder.

She jumped. When she turned her head to look at him, her blue eyes were watery. Not crying, exactly, he decided. Just...watery.

"What's happened?" he asked.

Tinker hesitated, her chin trembling. "See the woman who came out of Mamzelle's Boutique just now?" She pointed across the street, past the wagons, horses, people, and the odd horseless carriage stirring up dust, to where an elegant lady had stepped from a small store and paused to look around.

Sighting along Tinker's finger, he thought she meant the brown-haired woman who looked as though her duds cost more than Knox made in three whole months. High-toned and snooty, the lady was smoothing gloves the color of new grass over dainty hands. The gloves matched what he presumed must be stylish garb considering the attention she drew.

"Yeah?" The woman was a beauty but a little older than generally caught his notice.

Tinker swallowed. "That's Maisie. My mother. Only she's calling herself Sarah something or another now. Says she's married to an important man." Those flooded eyes came up to meet his. Slowly, her fingers unfolded, revealing the fifty-dollar bill they clutched. "She doesn't want to know me anymore. She gave me this. Payment to make me go away." She snorted. "As if I'd come looking for her. As if I ever came looking for her!"

He didn't know what to say, settling on, "You talked to her?"

"Not much. Enough to know she didn't approve of my attire or my looks."

Knox detected a quiver in her voice. He started to ask what made her think Maisie wanted her to disappear, then thought better of it. Not something he wanted to get into.

The woman, as though aware of their scrutiny, walked away without a backward look, passing from sight as she turned the corner.

"C'mon." He steered Tinker from Eastman's building, turning her in the opposite direction. "Let's get out of here."

Sunlight glaring into his eyes momentarily blinded him as they started off. He was more concerned with imparting Eastman's revelation to Tinker just then than watching for enemies. Taking a breath, he said, "I ain't sure I believe."

Her shove took him by surprise.

A shove that pushed him all the way into the

doorway recess of a men's shop. At that exact instant, the window beside him shattered into a million pieces. Shards of glass flew everywhere.

A woman inside the shop screamed.

A man shouted.

And Tinker kept pushing until she had him, her dog, and finally, herself, all the way inside the store. They joined several others already there, most of whom had sprawled flat on the floor. One clerk sheltered behind the mahogany counter. Another stood frozen in the middle of the room with his mouth gaping open.

"Everybody get down," Tinker yelled and followed her own advice by dropping below the level of the window and hugging a cowering Soldier close against her knees.

Knox, afraid his mouth copied the clerk's, snapped it closed as he crouched beside her. "What the?"

"Stay down, Knox. It must be Anson Lowell," Tinker replied crisply, though not loud enough for anyone else to hear. "Or one of his men. I glimpsed someone on the roof across the street."

A couple more shots followed the first. One blew a hat off a display head; another gouged a divot in the wood as it crossed the counter and carried on into the back room. Somebody bellowed, "Call the police!"

The upright clerk remained standing. He shouted, as if afraid they'd all gone deaf, "Is anyone hurt?"

A woman who'd been looking at some shirts asked querulously, "What is going on?"

Another said, "What are they shooting at?"

"One of us," the first woman said. "One of us is his target." She was holding a shirt close to her chest as though mere cloth would provide protection.

At this, everyone in the store turned to eye Knox and Tinker.

Cautiously, Tinker sat up. "A mad man must be on the loose," she said, eyes wide and innocent. "Who else could it be?"

Outside, whistles had begun blowing. Policemen converged on the street, waving guns, and shouting conflicting orders at each other. Knox dared to stand up, then venture outside. Several people who'd been on the street and out of the line of fire were pointing toward the river. Some of the men in uniform dashed in that direction.

"I think the shooter has cleared out." He ducked back into the shop with his report. "Police are giving chase."

The only question in his mind was whether they were after the right man. But when no further shots were fired, he deemed it safe enough to grab hold of Tinker and urge her along, moving between some of the others who scattered. Their way lay in the same direction as the shooter and the boys in blue. Not a comforting thought.

Knox, eyes open for a trap, walked fast, not speaking until they were well away from the store, its shattered glass, and terrified customers. They'd gotten within reach of the livery's odor before he stopped and let Tinker catch up.

Had him cussing at himself, too, when he noticed how she was limping again. "Here," he said, "stop and lean against this hitch rail. Catch your breath."

Her mouth firmed. "No need. I'm fine."

"Yeah, well..." He didn't move though. "I expect I owe you my life, Tinker. Again."

She may've said she was fine, but from the way she

sort of draped her body over the rail and lifted the sore leg to take the weight off, he knew it pained her.

"Pure luck," she said. "I just happened to catch sight of him when he moved. Maybe only his shadow. I don't really know, but I knew he had a rifle."

"Luck of the best kind." He grinned crookedly. "Wasn't 'nothing' to me. Seems I put some value on living another day." He figured she'd been trying to catch a last sight of her mother and spotted the shooter instead. He hoped she thought it a good trade-off.

When she'd rested long enough for the pain to ebb, they continued on to the livery. Soldier made a joyous reunion with the horses while Knox paid for their upkeep, and within minutes, they rode out.

"Maybe we could catch the train back?" The longing in Tinker's voice gripped Knox. "In the coach this time. I've got plenty of money."

He knew it would be best for her. He even turned Chick toward the rail yard, until he took a second thought. "The shooter. Lowell, his whole crew. If they got away from the sheriff, they're apt to be looking for us there. Or be on the train themselves."

"The sheriff?"

"Has hardly got started. Eastman had to do some persuasive talking to convince him of any kind of action. We don't know when or if the sheriff will ever catch Lowell. The only certain thing is Lowell will be out to get me. And you."

Tinker, her expression woebegone, could only agree.

They stopped at a little store on the edge of town for supplies. At least they didn't have to go hungry this trip. Although, come to think on it, that might not be the worst of their worries.

CHAPTER 14

Tinker had little to say after they left the haberdashery store. Her mind solidly stuck on the chance meeting with her mother, refused to budge. Seeing Maisie and watching her leave—again, had stirred up old feelings. Or maybe she meant to put them in a stew. The memory of waking up one morning and finding her mother gone without a word. Resentment? Anger? Hurt? Oh, yes, all of those and more. Here she'd thought these last few years had gotten her past those feelings. Apparently not.

She let Knox take care of things at the mercantile where he'd picked up the most basic of items without asking her advice. But then, she guessed, they weren't exactly going on a picnic. Which was fine. She wasn't in the mood for one anyway.

Knox, having taken note of her withdrawal, rode a horse's length ahead of her and kept his mouth shut. She saw him glance back at her every now and then as if wondering what to do with her now he'd done his duty by William Ault.

Well, she didn't know about him, but she had

nowhere to go but...home. And since she'd helped get Knox to Spokane, he could just escort her back to the Red Light Pleasure Palace.

Yeah, the good old den of iniquity. Where Maisie, now known as Sarah, had abandoned her fifteen-year-old daughter, left her penniless and bereft, to sink or swim on her own. At least Patrick O'Keefe, who'd disappeared about the same time, had paid the taxes on the place, so she'd had a place to stay. A big empty house, from which the working girls departed as quickly as they could pack. None of them had enjoyed living so far from a town, even though business had been good. Most slipped off in the night and neglected to tell her goodbye.

They hadn't been friends. In truth, she'd been glad to see them go. Or so she told herself.

A resourceful girl, Tinker soon acquired the post office business and managed to keep body and soul together by letting rooms to travelers. Nothing munificent. The fifty dollars Sarah had nonchalantly pressed upon her was more than she usually saw in two months.

At least Knox hadn't abandoned her. Yet.

"What are we going to do?" Her abrupt question broke the long silence. The first time she'd opened her mouth at all, come to think of it, whether to question or comment.

Knox shifted in his saddle and smiled at her. The smile faded as he eyed the expression that shifted over her face. "What's the matter?"

We going to do? What was she thinking?

"I said, what are you going to do now? Is it safe for you to go back to the Running T?" She hadn't forgotten the name of the outfit he worked for.

He paused, eyes narrowing a little as he studied her. Thrusting his hand through thick brown hair as if

143

missing a hat to tip, he cleared his throat. "Yeah. About that. I started to tell you something as we left Eastman's office, but then bullets started flying, and, well, the time hasn't seemed right since then."

Tinker whistled at Soldier who seemed to be thinking about chasing some wildlife, a chattering little chipmunk, into the brush. Not that it diverted her attention from what Knox had said. "Right time to tell me what?"

"You know those papers I handed over to Eastman?"

Impatient, she huffed. "Of course. I'm not likely to forget. We wouldn't be in this predicament, otherwise."

He quirked a half-grin. "Truth in that, seeing as how Lowell is willing to kill for them. I expect you have some curiosity about what those papers say?"

"Yes. But I didn't suppose it was any of my business." She paused. "You mean Mr. Eastman told you what they said?"

"He did. He called it an addendum." Knox pronounced the word carefully.

"And?" She drew the word out.

Knox's throat moved on a big swallow as if he might choke on what he was going to say next. "Ault left the XYZ to me."

She had a moment of silence. Her mouth formed a big, round O. Then, "Ault left you the XYZ? Knox Burdette! That's...that's..." Tinker wasn't quite sure how to finish her sentence. Wonderful seemed disrespectful considering the circumstances. Lucky struck her the same. "That sounds fair, what with Astrid passing and the way you tried to help him, there at the last. And you fulfilled his final wish, to keep Anson Lowell from profiting. A dangerous undertaking."

"Yeah." But Knox still looked unsure. "The sheriff

didn't want to take Eastman's word for it, at first. But Eastman said he had proof. That's what took us so long. Eastman had to show the sheriff the papers."

"My word," Tinker said faintly. "What a good thing I fished you out of the river. And that we recovered the papers."

"I'm of a mind to think so." But he still seemed pensive. "Don't reckon Lowell does. What's more, I haven't forgotten he's still on the loose. And Tinker, things aren't cut and dried. Eastman proved the will, and its addendum are real, but it doesn't prove I didn't kill Ault and Shorty. After forcing Ault to change his will, that is."

"What?" Tinker's squeal of outrage was shrill enough to make Fancy jump beneath her. Even Chick's ears twitched.

"So," Knox went on, "I'm not in jail yet, but I'm not free and clear, either."

She pondered a moment. "We need one of Lowell's men to confess. One or two of them."

"I agree. Meanwhile, the sheriff says to leave it to him."

Tinker hadn't liked the sheriff. She didn't trust him either. "Here's hoping he doesn't sit on his fat keister, then," she said darkly.

"Eastman told me he's up for reelection. A few words in the right places and he's sure to get moving."

Tinker quirked a tiny smile. "Is Eastman one of those in the right place?"

Knox shrugged. "I think so. He says so."

They made good time through the afternoon. The horses, after their overnight rest and a good feed at the livery, had perked up fine and frisky. Even Fancy's limp

145

had disappeared, and the small wound closed completely.

Knox said he thought maybe the pretty pinto was a good actor. Tinker cooed and made much of her brave girl. Soldier, tail drooping, stood by and growled at the horse for claiming so much attention.

Tinker laughed at the dog and when they got down to stretch their legs, fussed over him in a way that had his tail wagging again.

They met several travelers on the road during the day, exchanging pleasantries and asking for news. Word had gotten around about the shooting, but no names were mentioned, neither Knox's nor Lowell's. Most folks were more concerned with the flooding and destroyed bridges that extended their travels, the washed-out roads, fields with standing water, and the fact stock had been lost.

A few men with revolvers loose in tied-down holsters made Knox's eyebrows raise. "Did you recognize him?" he asked Tinker when out of earshot of a, particularly suspicious-looking pair.

She shook her head.

He still watched their back trail for a while.

At nightfall, they made camp in a small clearing a couple hundred yards off the road. A shallow, yard-wide stream ran nearby, providing water for them all while making a sweet sound as it trickled over rocks. Ferns grew at the edges, scenting the air.

"Can we build a fire for coffee and to cook something?" Tinker asked. They'd had nothing since morning except a somewhat shriveled apple each, and a lot had happened since then. The problem? Shadows under the overhanging trees indicated privacy, but firelight could carry a long way at night. If Lowell and his men were still on the loose, which she suspected, it meant she and Knox were still in danger.

"I say we give it a whirl." Knox smiled. "I bought some eggs and a chunk of cheese. Maybe you can whip us up a passel of eggs for supper."

"The eggs didn't break?"

"Nope. Hope not anyhow. The storekeeper put them in a box of sawdust and said they'd be fine as long as they didn't get bucked off."

Tinker may have had her doubts, but upon inspection, found the storekeeper had been right. "I don't suppose he put a frying pan in there, too."

At Knox's crestfallen expression, she relented. "I see you thought to buy a couple tin plates. I can make do with those."

She did, too, used a cedar stick to mix the eggs with some wild onions to impart a little flavor, then cooked them right on the plate. She stirred quickly to keep them from burning. They might not have been as tasty as those cooked in her own kitchen but were edible. Immediately after eating, Knox kicked dirt over the fire to extinguish the light, and they sat companionably in the dark for a spell before bedding down.

Along about midnight, Soldier growled.

A second later, he growled again, louder, with more authority. Tinker stirred and opened her eyes.

The dark outline of a man stood over her, his leg drawn back as he prepared to kick her in the head. She gasped, upon which, pandemonium ensued.

First, Soldier attacked, catching the would-be kicker at the back of his knee and gnawing fiercely. The man screamed, short and sharp as Soldier's teeth sank in.

Second, Tinker, with what she considered great presence of mind, without trying to rise rolled not away, but toward the man with all the force, she could summon. Cursing, both legs taken out from under him, he fell heavily. Tinker leaped atop him, grabbed his ears, and whapped his head hard where a good-sized rock happened to poke out of the ground. He went slack.

And third, Knox leaped to his feet swinging a stick of charred firewood and bashed the gun from a second attacker's hand. The man howled, cursed, and started to run off. Whereupon, Knox tackled him, then used his fists in an accomplished sort of way to subdue any resistance.

Except for Soldier's growls as he worried the unconscious man, the excitement died away.

"Well," Knox said. "Well." He was silent a moment watching Soldier before he nodded decisively at Tinker. "I'm thinking of getting myself a dog for a bodyguard. A big dog. Looks like they come in handy."

Tinker pressed her hand over the spot in her chest where her heart threatened to burst out of her body. "They do." She could barely speak. "What will you name your dog?"

"Warrior."

She nodded. "A good name."

Shackling the men with their own belts, Knox used neckerchiefs to bind their hands. Ever helpful, Soldier made a fearsome deterrent, especially when Knox threatened to stuff the men's own socks in their mouths to stop their swearing.

"Do you know who they are?" Tinker peered down at the man she and Soldier had bested. He had little to say, still woozy from having his head slammed into a rock. A pointed rock. A goodly amount of blood had run down the back of his shirt.

They were the same two Knox'd had questions about earlier when met on the road.

"Not right off. But they've been following us."

"Yes." Tinker's brow wrinkled. "But they weren't at Aults?"

"No. Were they at the...your house?"

"No. It's my guess Lowell hired them, though. Looks like he's adding men to his payroll."

"I agree."

Tinker pondered. "We need to turn them in at the sheriff's office. Maybe the deputy can get them to confess."

"Or they can lie and make everything worse."

"Then what shall we do?" She couldn't keep the worry out of her voice.

"Get some rest. We wait for daylight, find their horses, and decide then."

They turned to look at the two. Between them, they'd managed to drag the men over to a tree and secure them there with the lariat from Tinker's saddle. The one with the smashed and broken fingers, if not a whole broken hand, was trying to scootch around and rub himself loose. He quit when Knox threatened to break all the fingers that were still whole.

"Dang," Knox said. "I'll have to stay awake and watch these fellers. No rest for the wicked, they say, and I guess that's me."

"We'll take turns," Tinker said. "I'm not sleepy. I'll go first." She didn't think she'd ever be able to sleep again, something she wasn't about to admit to Knox. But the horrifying moment when she'd opened her eyes to see a large, boot-clad foot coming at her had a way of sticking in her mind's eye.

Besides, Knox still wasn't over nearly drowning and

being shot. He might deny it, but the way he'd slept on that lumpy hotel mattress the night before led her to believe otherwise.

Light was spreading across a sky graying with dawn before she gave Knox's cheek a tap. Or two, which proved her earlier point. He hadn't even heard her and Soldier's outlaw groaning when he awoke and complained loudly of a headache and having to pee.

Tinker hadn't been particularly sympathetic.

On her third attempt to rouse Knox, he caught her hand before it reached his face. "I'm awake."

"Could've fooled me."

Knox opened his eyes, blinking in the light. He sat up and stared around. "Why didn't you wake me earlier? Those yahoos?"

"Still here. Still secure." She yawned.

He got to his feet with an air of strong purpose. "I'll find their horses. We need to get off this road before we meet any more of Lowell's men."

Tinker couldn't disagree with that.

Finding the horses turned into an easy task. Soldier turned them up in about three minutes, helped perhaps, by one of them whinnying from over on the other side of the creek.

They were all mounted before it occurred to her to ask what Knox had thought to do with the prisoners. "I can do it," she said. "Turn them over to the sheriff. Nobody is gunning for me."

"Nobody but Lowell." Knox gave her a severe look and shook his head. "I've got a better idea. We'll head on over to the Running T. RT can hand them into the deputy and see where the land lies."

"This RT, he won't have turned on you?" Turns out

his idea struck her as fine as if it had been her suggestion in the first place.

Knox didn't hesitate. "Nope. Not RT."

This plan of action involved putting the outlaws' horses on a rein and leading them, then listening to moans and complaints throughout most of the day. Once, they rode into the timber when a group of four came loping down the road. Knox held Tinker's gun on the two to keep them quiet until the others passed by. Could be the grim look on Knox's face served a better deterrent than the cocked pistol.

Tinker felt ready to jump out of her skin when they finally crested the last hill and spotted a big white painted house looming out of the dusk.

Knox grunted.

"What?" she said.

"No lights. Where is everybody?"

"Maybe they've gone to bed."

"Not this early."

Still, it was full dark by the time they picked a cautious way into the yard. They stopped outside the two-story house, its wide front porch overlooking the valley spread before it. A pretty spot for a ranch, Tinker thought, with what must be a good spring nearby considering the greenery around the yard. Made the place smell fresh.

Happy to be home, Chick's ears pricked forward. He nickered, getting an answer from the half-dozen horses in the corral.

Knox didn't say anything, but something, she saw, had made his face turn grim.

A tall, though stooped figure stepped from the house. "Who's there?" the man bellowed, deep and forceful, though they weren't more than a dozen feet from him. "Stop now or I'll fill you full of lead."

Not the greeting Knox had been expecting, Tinker knew. Squinting, she saw no sign of a gun.

"It's Knox, RT," Knox called back. "Came looking for help, not to get shot."

"Knox? I was about to give up on you, boy, thinking you might be dead." The man's relief was clear. "I hear you're in a spot of trouble. Where have you been these last three days?"

"Among other places, to Spokane and back." Knox dismounted, leaving Chick ground-hitched. "News travels fast. You heard right about the trouble. Chances are, though, you haven't heard but half of it and probably none of the truth."

"Might've heard more than you know." Stepping forward, RT leaned in for a closer look. "Who is that with you? Friends of yours?"

Knox laughed, a rough laugh and not one of amusement. "A couple of gunmen hired to kill me, so I wouldn't call them my friends."

Tinker sure as the dickens wouldn't.

RT came to the edge of the porch and took a closer look, his gaze lingering on her an extra second before it moved on. "What you planning to do with these gunmen, Knox?"

"Turn them into the deputy in the morning. Thought maybe you and the boys might do that for me."

The older man nodded. "We will. Be glad to. I'll have a couple of the men lock 'em in the barn for now and keep an eye on them." His attention shifted to Tinker, then back to Knox. "You and me, we need to have a little talk."

"Thanks, RT. I appreciate it."

"What about the woman?"

Knox's smile flashed. "She's a friend."

"A friend, eh? Suppose your friend could stay here with these yahoos until the boys come to fetch them?"

Knox hesitated, so Tinker, embarrassed, said, "Go ahead. I'll wait here."

RT nodded. "Come on in. No use standing out here for the skeeters to chew on." Without waiting, the older man turned and started into the house, tripping over the runner on a rocking chair. It set him to cursing softly as he went inside.

The penny dropped. Tinker figured she knew why no lights showed inside. The precaution indicated the old man had run into some trouble here even without Knox being present. The realization must've struck Knox at the same time.

He stopped RT. "Wait. Why are you stumbling around in the dark, RT? What's going on? Are you all right? You and Geraldine? The hands?"

"We're good." RT let the door slam behind him.

Who, Tinker wondered, was Geraldine? She sat Fancy, guarding the outlaws, and feeling like the last biscuit on the plate. The one nobody wanted.

Knox turned to smile encouragement at her. "It'll be fine. Don't fret." Following RT, the door closed.

A moment later, she heard them talking as they stood just inside the house. Not loudly enough for Tinker to make out words. Just the rise and fall of their voices, which she found frustrating. It wasn't a long conversation, either, though it seemed that way to her.

CHAPTER 15

Timmons's men took the two outlaws and all the horses off to the barn, though not before eyeing Tinker with all the curiosity of cats at a mouse hole. They left her standing on the porch until Knox returned for her. He didn't quite know what to think about that.

"Did they scare you?" he asked.

"No. They were just curious," she said, but he was almost sure they had.

"Hurry up." RT, who'd stayed in the dark house while Knox fetched Tinker, urged them inside. "Get in here."

Taking Tinker's hand to lead her through the dark front room, they didn't stop in the parlor. That was for favored females on the rare occasion they came visiting. Distracted by the scent of fresh bread and roasting meat, they all fumbled their way down a pitch-black hall to the ranch office to where a lamp had been lit.

One of the first things Knox noticed was the shutter covering the window. A new shutter, but one with a deep gouge in the center of it. The gouge looked remarkably like a bullet hole.

"What the?" Knox started, just as a worried sounding

female voice called out from the kitchen. "RT, is that you? Who is with you?"

"It's Knox. He's made it home," the old man bellowed back. Being a tad hard of hearing himself, he apparently assumed everyone else was, too.

"Knox? Oh, praise be! For goodness sakes, you all come on into the kitchen. Supper'll be ready in a minute, and I'll bet he's hungry. I have a light burning in here."

RT picked up the lamp. "Got our orders."

"Yeah, but..."

"Don't worry. Zach and Andy will take care of them fellers you brought in. They know the score. I may be deaf but I ain't blind and neither are they. The way you have them tied up and on leading strings, they ain't going anyplace but where the boys say. For now, I figure you have a story to tell and I'm anxious to hear it. So is Geraldine. I'll call Warren over, too. He has a story of his own I want you two to hear."

He held the lamp higher and examined Tinker. "Think maybe you better tell me who this is first. She don't look dangerous, but you never know. You ain't gone and got married in the last two days, have you?"

Knox, glancing wild-eyed at Tinker, figured it was probably hard telling who turned the reddest, him or her. He decided his best move was to pretend he hadn't heard RT's last remark. "I won't say she'd not dangerous. She is, but only to somebody who's trying to kill us. Saved my life, in fact. Chick's too."

"She did?" RT grinned like a pussy cat. "Knox Burdette, you young hound dog, where'd you find a capable female in all this fusseration?"

Red-faced or not, Tinker, Knox was pleased to see, refused to let herself be intimidated by the likes of RT Timmons.

She spoke up. "I can talk for myself, you know if you ask like a gentleman."

Knox smothered a snort. How this would play out when RT and Geraldine discovered Tinker's connection to the Red Light Pleasure Palace, he couldn't say. And he was certain they would learn. They'd just better not cause Tinker any mortification, that's all.

"Hah! Well, let's not just stand here. Come on to the kitchen. Geraldine will want to hear how you happened to save Knox and his horse. I'll have her set another plate. You ain't fussy what you eat, are you, young miss?"

Looking like she might burst out with something outrageous, Tinker settled for a simple, "No, sir." Just like a proper young lady.

Knox smiled at her. "Geraldine is a fine cook, Tinker. You'll see." The day anybody dared complain about the way Geraldine Timmons set a table is the day he fainted dead away. The fact remained; he hadn't considered what introducing Tinker to his boss might entail. Not deeply enough.

He felt Tinker shaking as he led her into the kitchen, weak lamplight guiding the way. A light that illuminated a disheveled girl with a dirty face and hands, and a man who looked no better. Worse, probably, since the shirt he wore had come from Tinker's rag bag. And that was three, or was it only two days ago?

He leaned down to whisper in her ear. "Don't be scared. They won't bite." He hoped. Hoped Soldier, who had followed them inside as a matter of course, wouldn't either.

"I'm not scared," she whispered back. Clearly another fib.

Geraldine Timmons rushed forward to enfold him in a motherly embrace. Drawing back, she sniffed and broke into a scold. "Knox Burdette, you stink. What have you been doing; rolling in the dirt with pigs?"

He grinned. "Guess I just about have, Geraldine."

"Take yourself out onto the porch for a good wash. This minute, sir. I'll bring warm water out to you."

"Yes'm."

"And you." Geraldine spun to face Tinker. "You, too. I'll not have people sitting at my table looking like tramps and scarecrows. Come back with a clean face and Knox will make introductions."

Tinker's blue eyes widened. "Yes'm," she said, copying Knox's response.

"And this dog." Geraldine seemed bound to say more before sighing. "Well, he is a dog."

Soldier panted and wagged his bushy tail, intent on making a new friend.

"Still not scared?" Knox murmured once they were out of hearing.

She merely looked at him.

Giving Tinker first go at washing up, Knox went to greet Warren who walked suspiciously slow and kind of hunched across from the bunkhouse to meet him. Evidently, RT had rung the bell they had rigged up to summon him. Soldier trailed after Knox, causing a bit of stir at first because Warren didn't seem any too sanguine about the brown beast lumbering toward him. Enough so his first words were, "This the animal that savaged that outlaw?"

Knox's nod may not have reassured him. "Only because the outlaw was attacking his owner."

The two men shook hands. "I been feeling sorry for myself, but hell, you look worse than I do," Warren said.

A comment that puzzled Knox. "At least I'm not limping," he replied, then, "What happened to you?"

"I met up with the Anson Lowell gang, same as you," Warren said.

His story spilled out. "RT sent me over to lend a hand moving the XYZ cattle off the Running T. I seen where you'd chased them back, but I figured to catch up with you and we'd fix the fence together. But when I got closer to Ault's house, I heard shooting. A lot of shooting. Not being too smart, I snuck up on foot to see what was going on."

"Should've run like the devil," Knox said.

"Yeah. I found out. But turned out better than riding straight in."

Tinker, her face and hands scrubbed clean, moved to where she could listen.

"First thing, I seen Shorty's body layin' in the yard. I spotted Chick holding off in the woods, so I knew you must be in the house, and I saw you and Ault shooting at the men surrounding the place. Lowell yelled out something about you were gonna wind up as dead as Shorty Bonham if you didn't get out of his way."

Knox huffed. "I didn't hear him. Too busy dodging bullets and trying to help Ault."

"Yeah, I seen. Anyhow, after a while I seen you bust out of the house and take off for the woods. Guess I got careless, cuz I stood up and one of those yahoos saw me. They started taking potshots at me and I ran. Mounted up and didn't even know I'd been winged until I got out of rifle range."

Knox eyed him with alarm. "They winged you?"

"They did." Rather than hurt, Warren seemed proud of the fact.

"How bad?"

"Nothing much." Warren's "nothing much" came out sounding like it had been quite a lot.

The hand's eyes lit up when he heard the tale of how Knox and Tinker had got the best of Lowell's gang, not the easiest endeavor they'd ever taken on. "Anyway, Knox, we've got the pair you brought in locked uptight. You better get on in the house now, before Mrs. T goes on the warpath and comes to get you." The curiosity in the way he eyed Tinker spoke volumes.

"You coming in?"

"Nah, I et with the boys."

"Is everything all right?" Tinker asked Knox as Warren headed back to the bunkhouse. "With me being here, I mean?"

"Sure. It's fine." He hemmed and hawed a few seconds. "We'll have a good supper. I smell the pot roast Geraldine has cooking."

"Me too." Tinker sighed. "Onions and herbs. But I don't know, Knox. Maybe I should stay out here by myself. In case they recognize O'Keefe's name."

He shrugged. "It's your name. So be it."

"Well..." She drew the word out. "Not exactly."

"What's not exactly?"

"O'Keefe. It's not my real last name. It's just the one I go by."

If he'd had a hat, he would've had something to adjust. Instead, his hair got tousled yet again. "If that's what you go by, then that's what it is," he said, flat and final.

Even so, things became a little uncomfortable when introductions had been made and they all sat down to eat Geraldine's pot roast and mashed potatoes. RT kept looking at Tinker with a thoughtful expression.

"Knew a feller named O'Keefe a while back." He shot a look at his wife and added, "Heard he left town in a hurry due to some problem with his business dealings."

"What are you saying?" Geraldine seemed a little put out with him like maybe he wasn't using company manners.

RT pretended innocence. "Nothing at all. Just making conversation. Most likely there's a lot of people named O'Keefe around."

Nobody said anything. Tinker's mouth trembled, then firmed.

"He didn't look anything like you, young lady," RT continued, oblivious. "An ugly cuss, as I remember."

"Oh," she said.

"How did you and Knox come to meet?" Geraldine broke into her husband's line of questioning. "Last we knew about you, Knox is that you were involved in that shootout at William Ault's ranch. Warren, well, I suppose he told you about that, saw you riding into the woods with Anson Lowell hot on your heels trying to kill you. We've been terribly worried."

"And Warren got shot for his pains," Knox said.

"He did," RT said. "But not bad enough to prevent him getting back to the ranch and sending word to Deputy Caldwell."

"Which was a very good thing for you." Geraldine's face went an angry red. "It just makes me so mad. We all went into town the next day when Warren was better. There Anson Lowell was, big as life, trying to make Deputy Caldwell think you had killed Mr. Ault and his man. Thank God Warren knew differently."

Knox's fork clattered onto his plate, splashing gravy onto the oilcloth spread over the table.

"Tsk, tsk," Geraldine said.

"Caldwell already knew? That means I was on the run over nothing." Knox swallowed hard. "Except for the fact, Lowell's men are still trying to kill me. Me and

Tinker, both. If Caldwell and Sheriff Dempsy know Lowell murdered Ault and Shorty, what's his, Lowell's, point?"

"Why didn't the deputy arrest Lowell right then and there?" Tinker added. "And why didn't Sheriff Dempsey appear to know any of this?"

"That's a good question, one I can't answer. I guess because Lowell denied any part of it."

"My guess is Caldwell is scared," Knox growled.

"I don't doubt it. As for Lowell's vendetta well, that's something else." RT put a hand on Knox's arm as if to keep him seated. "We all know what Lowell is. You're a threat to him, which, being a witness to murder, you truly are. The only eyeball witness. I expect he figures if he gets rid of you, he can beat the charge. Plus, there's his reputation for anger, like a stick of dynamite going off. Just as unstable, too, happens he's crossed, no matter how small the matter. Lots of folks have been on the receiving end of his temper. And this is no small matter."

Knox had lost interest in his meal. Looking across the table, he saw Tinker had, as well. Eyes fixed on the plate, she stirred gravy into her spuds, making a gloppy mess.

RT chewed a bite of beef. "I noticed how you're curious about the shutters and lack of light here. See, Warren barely made it back from the XYZ ahead of Lowell's men and we had a spot of trouble convincing them to back off. As it happened, the boys had just come in for dinner, so we were all here and had that devil and his demons outnumbered. That's why it took us until the next day to get to town and talk to Caldwell."

"When Lowell and his men attacked us here at the ranch, he made it easier to convince the deputy of what truly happened with Mr. Ault," Geraldine said. "Whether it was his intention or not."

Which it wouldn't have been, Knox figured.

"And Warren having a bullet hole in him helped," RT added.

"Helped?" Tinker raised an eyebrow.

RT had the grace to look embarrassed. "Pardon my phrasing. Didn't help Warren any, but it helped convince Caldwell of the truth."

"Maybe," Geraldine said. "Hasn't stopped someone from spying on us though. The shutters stay closed until this business is finished."

They got through the meal without further embarrassment to either Knox or Tinker. Knox didn't want to leave Tinker alone for too long with either RT or Geraldine, but he likely wouldn't have much choice. Confirming his fears, Geraldine shooed the men off to the office while urging Tinker to help her clean up the kitchen and leave the men to their talk.

He had to hide a grin when Tinker glared at him in a panicked sort of way as if it were his fault. Nevertheless, he had a lot to tell RT, and he wanted to get it over with. It worried him a little, talking about the disposition Ault had made regarding his property. The fact it made Knox a man of means, just like RT himself.

The first thing he'd do with the place, he figured, was to set those fence posts in concrete to keep each ranch's cows on their own side. He made haste to tell RT exactly that, while RT was still struck silent with shock.

What he didn't expect was the way RT's eyes lit up. "By glory, Knox, if you ain't the luckiest son-of-a-gun I ever heard of then I don't know what."

Considering the fact he'd almost got shot to death, him and his horse drowned, then arrested for murder, Knox wasn't any too sure of that. What's more, he'd never be safe until Anson Lowell got put away. Or hanged. Hanged would be best.

"...you'll make a good neighbor," RT was saying.

"It's all right with you?" Knox asked.

"I ain't got anything to say about it, even if I wanted to. Which I don't. That was up to Ault, and I'm tickled with his decision. Wait until I tell Geraldine." Slapping Knox on the back, RT reached into the bottom drawer of his desk, producing two glasses and a half-full bottle of Old Crow. "This calls for a libation, I think."

Knox didn't disagree.

They drank. "I'm proud of you, son. Proud of the way you stepped up to help Ault. Proud of the way you've handled yourself." He fell silent, poured them each another finger of whiskey, and sat back.

"Now," he said, "about the girl. Tinker O'Keefe. Pretty name, pretty girl. But there's something you might not know about her."

CHAPTER 16

T inker knew she was in for a severe quizzing the moment Knox and RT left the kitchen. Far from allowing her to help with dishes, Geraldine cleared the table and set the plates and utensils in a vat of hot water to soak.

"Sit," she commanded, and not sure what else to do, Tinker complied. Satiated with scraps, Soldier groaned, lay with his head on her feet, and went to sleep. The older lady eased herself down opposite and toyed with a glass of water. She didn't offer one to Tinker.

"Now," Geraldine said, "you might've guessed RT treats me, after all the years we've been married as if I'm an innocent girl."

Tinker's eyebrows arched.

"Yes." Geraldine nodded. "You may not be aware of this, but a good husband will try his very best to protect his wife from the hard or sordid parts of life. Knox is a good boy and has the same kind of manners as RT, who is a good husband. Neither of those two tell me but half of what they ought, and nothing they deem unfit."

The coolness behind Geraldine's words served as a

warning. Heart thumping a little faster, Tinker swallowed hard and found her voice. She had a strong inkling where this conversation was headed. "How nice."

"Not always. They're keeping things from me right now. Things I should know about the people who invade my home."

"Invade? I didn't realize any of those men got inside. How awful for you."

The older woman sniffed as though at an odor. "No man did. But what would you call it when someone of ill-repute shows up unannounced and manages to wrangle a way in?"

"Ill-repute? Do you mean me?" Tinker swallowed. "You do." The food in her stomach turned to lead. "I didn't realize my presence is an invasion. Your husband opened the door to me."

"Don't be pert, Miss O'Keefe. I want to know about you." Holding up her forefinger, Geraldine said, "First, how did you and Knox really meet?"

"Knox told you." Hadn't the older woman been listening? "I fished him out of the river when he and his horse got swept up in the flood."

"That doesn't make sense. Aside from what happened to them, why on earth would you be out in a storm like we had? Watching the water? Don't make me laugh. Any thinking person stays holed up inside if at all possible."

If Geraldine sounded tart, Tinker was as much so. "In this case, it wasn't possible. I found his horse, first. It was caught on a tree in the river and couldn't get out."

Geraldine snorted in disbelief, but Tinker forged on. "So when I had him loose, I thought it logical to search for a rider. Or his body. When I found Knox, I got him to shore and took him...to shelter. That's all."

"But what were you doing there for a rescue to be so handy?"

"I wouldn't say it was handy." Tinker took a breath. "I live near the river. I heard Chick squealing and went to see what was wrong."

"You live below the bridge?"

"Yes."

Geraldine sat back and eyed her. "There are no houses along that stretch for a good five miles. Except one."

A sense of dread building, Tinker had nothing to say. She looked down at her hands twisting in her lap and forced them to stillness.

"O'Keefe," Geraldine said the name as if it were a brand of poison. "RT thinks I don't know, but I do. Women discuss such things where men don't hear, so I know all about that house, a low den of iniquity, where men go to..." She choked. "The Red Light something or another. Run by a man named O'Keefe. Although I heard he disappeared a few years ago. Probably murdered. All the women were supposed to have left at the time. It seems they did not. It appears you are a hold-over."

Tinker lifted her head, bowed during Geraldine's scathing exposure, and met her eyes. "What, or who I am is none of your business. But be assured, I am not a whore invading your home."

Plain speaking.

Geraldine was equally plain. "So you say."

"I don't have to prove anything to you." Tinker stood up, dipping a funny little move something between a bow and a curtsey. "Thank you for dinner. It was delicious." Until it had turned rotten in her stomach.

Geraldine stood up, too, clearly surprised. "You're going?"

"I don't stay where I'm not wanted. Come, Soldier," Tinker said, and as the dog rose, headed for the back door. Without another word, they slipped outside. Geraldine said nothing to stop her.

Halfway to the hulking barn, Tinker stopped to rid herself of the food in her stomach. Afterward, it took only minutes for her to find Fancy, saddle her, and mount. Silent, walking the horse to avoid making noise, she rode into the night.

A bitter thought arose. So much for respectability. A ball formed in her throat, making it hard to swallow. If she hadn't been made of stern stuff, she'd be crying. Attacked by Anson Lowell. Eyed askance by Sheriff Dempsey. Dismissed by her own mother. Attacked again by Anson Lowell. Any finally, reviled by Geraldine Timmons, who didn't even know her.

And Knox Burdette? What about him? What did he really think?

She clicked her tongue at Fancy, her horse plodding after a full day of travel. Soldier, also tired, lagged behind.

Thank goodness she was. Made of stern stuff, that is.

Sometime after midnight, she reached the bridge. The only real daunting part of getting home lay in crossing it. But not because of the river, flowing smoothly, starlight reflecting off the surface like sparkling diamonds. Because of what, or maybe she should say who, she found waiting there.

Soldier signaled a warning by stopping in the road with one foot up like a pointer dog sighting prey. When she peered ahead, she spotted a blob in the shape of a man almost hidden where he sat under a tree, his back leaning against the trunk. The remains of a small fire smoldered next to him, the scent of smoke lingering on the humid night air. A horse, either white or gray in color, was picketed between a couple of smaller trees. It had to be one of Lowell's men, one who hadn't been called off the hunt by his boss. Or pursued by the law, who evidently hadn't bothered to come this far.

Positioned where he'd have a good line of sight to the bridge, it did no good as his hat was tipped to cover his eyes. He snored with the enthusiasm of a steam-powered buzz saw ripping through a log. The noise drowned even the crickets' song.

Tinker, Fancy, and Soldier went past him like wraiths, and although the clop of Fancy's hooves on the bridge seemed to reverberate, nothing stirred the watcher. Soon they were out of his line of sight and a half-hour later, Fancy stood in her own stall in her own barn.

Knox's white cat came to greet them, meowing and wreathing around Tinker's ankles as, tired to the bone, she unsaddled and fed her horse. Longing for her own bed, and feeling exposed under the starlight, she hurried toward the house. Soldier trotted beside her, the cat keeping pace.

Until Soldier froze in place, a complete repeat of his behavior at the bridge. Tinker froze, too.

Only the cat kept going. Nonchalantly, he pushed open a door already ajar and went on inside.

Tinker, mouth open, watched him disappear. *What to do?* The cat hadn't been worried whether unwelcome visitors lay in wait or not. But Soldier, when she lay a hand on his back, she felt a vibration running under his skin. He sensed something worrisome and out of place. Something or someone?

Stepping off the path, she scooted right up against the house wall and inched around a corner that formed an ell. Bushes filled the area. Not wishing to provide evidence of her passing, she moved the limbs aside with care, remaining silent while ducking down and burrowing her way through the thicket. Soldier came with her until six feet in, they arrived at a door unused since before O'Keefe left. A key, slightly rusty, was hidden in a crack between the door jamb and lapped siding. Only a slight screech betrayed her as she inserted the key in the lock and twisted.

The door opened onto utter blackness.

Knox, when he'd spent time in the tiny closet she stepped into, hadn't realized the back wall was actually a door and egress to the outside. No one would, with the latch being cleverly disguised as a coat hook. Tinker, crowded by Soldier's big body, put her ear to the inner wall and listened.

Nothing.

Finding the hidden latch, she pressed open the door and peeked around. Finding the way clear, she stepped into the post office where Knox had stayed. Still silent. No one around, not even the cat. Which meant whoever had invited himself inside was somewhere in the main part of the house.

Tinker closed the closet door behind her but left the outer door open. A precaution only, she told herself, in case she had to make a run for it. She breathed in short gasps, working up her courage to investigate.

A weapon. She needed a weapon since she'd left her Merwin & Hulbert with Knox. Peeling off her boots, Tinker crept forward on stocking feet. The weapon she aimed for was a simple baseball bat. A memory of how it had gotten here floated to the surface. Two teams of seven players, each being short a full roster, had met at the Pleasure Place after a game in someone's empty

169

pasture. The men had proceeded to get very drunk and to...um...hobnob with the admiring doves. In a not too rare scene, a fight had broken out. Not between teams but between two players on the same team, or so Tinker recalled. Anyway, O'Keefe had confiscated the bat one of them wielded before too much damage occurred, and somehow, when the men staggered away in the early hours before dawn, it got left behind.

Tinker retrieved her weapon of choice from the corner by the couch. She'd thought of a different way to wield it.

Bat in position, she and Soldier moved forward, into the house proper. Passing the office, Soldier didn't even turn his head. Tinker put her trust in him and deemed the room clear.

Next came the kitchen. Weak light shining through the window illuminated dirty dishes littering the table. Her neat canisters and boxes were open. Foodstuff had been spilled everywhere. Her socks stuck to a floor sticky with residue from grease and what must be sugar. A little heat lingered on the stove, and she smelled burned food. Probably, she thought bitterly, from her spider pan. There she found the cat, his white form hunched on the workbench eating something and ignoring a mouse running across the floor.

Tinker shuddered. Geraldine had known nothing of an invaded home. Nothing! Her prissy, sanctimonious speech had been hot air, plain and simple.

She eased through the dining room, which she never used. It was mostly undisturbed, although she stumbled over a saddle flopped down on the pretty Persian rug. Where was the horse? She wouldn't have been surprised to find it inside her house since it hadn't been in the barn.

Tinker went on.

At the arched doorway into the front room, Soldier stopped, walking in front of her so she had to stop, too.

She'd loosened her grip on the baseball bat but tightened it now. Not too tight. She had to remain relaxed enough to properly employ the thing. Twiddling her fingers on the smooth wood, she said a little prayer. Did she wish for Anson Lowell to be her target? Someone else?

No answer occurred to her, unless... But no. Best not to think of that.

The front room, though empty, showed signs of occupation. The couch had been pushed beneath the window. For someone to sit in comfort and watch for her, she supposed. Her bottle of whiskey, empty now, was tipped over on a table beside it, the drips no doubt ruining the finish. A lamp, its glass chimney dull with soot from the poorly trimmed wick, had been left to smolder. The odor of coal oil permeated the room. Lucky for her she'd gotten home when she did, Tinker thought sourly, pinching out the wick. At least the house hadn't caught on fire.

Soldier, with Tinker following on silent stockinged feet, led the way toward a hall where the part of the house that had served the doves opened up. They didn't need to go that far. The dog stopped at the first room. The room Tinker, not wanting to live upstairs in the business part of the house, had claimed for her own when everyone left. The room had been Maisie's. *Or Sarah's.*

There was enough light for her to see a man occupy her bed. He wore a beard and lay on his side facing her, although his face was mostly in shadow. The short man who'd been here before wore a beard, she remembered.

So, one of Lowell's men, still on the job. He breathed deeply, not quite snoring. Problematic then, whether he was awake and waiting to surprise her, or if he was as deeply asleep as he seemed.

Only one way to find out.

Fury had lit a fire in her. Occupy her home, destroy her things, spread his filth, would he? She'd just see about that!

Tinker's grip on the bat tightened.

She glided forward just as the white cat trotted past her and pounced on the sleeping man's foot, conveniently sticking out from under the blanket. The cat dug in his claws, maybe even employed his teeth, because the man let out a shout and kicked violently. The cat went sailing, hissing, and roaring like a miniature lion.

Soldier, not that Tinker blamed him, set to barking, at the same time circling behind her for shelter. Not helpful, perhaps, but he left room for her to punch forward with the bat.

Straight out and with all her strength into the man's belly as he sat up and reared forward.

Air gushed from his lungs. He flopped back, his eyes wide with shock, his mouth in an agonized twist.

"How dare you?" she yelled at him, unmindful that he might not be alone here and, in the heat of the moment, not caring. Her bat poised; Tinker hoped he'd make a threatening move so she could justify hitting him again. The first time had felt good. No, it had felt *excellent*.

"Uh..." he said. "Uh...uh...uh...huh."

"Get your grimy carcass out of my bed." Tinker nudged him with the end of the bat. When flailing, he tried to grab it, she took the opportunity to punch him again, this time on the elbow. Bones may not have crunched, but his whole hand spasmed.

The fool lay looking up at her.

"I said, get out of my bed." It seemed clear they were alone. Tinker wasn't afraid to let loose, no matter that the cat's hair stood on end and Soldier slunk away toward the kitchen.

"Get." She prodded him again, in the shoulder this time, and when he proved too slow to suit her, gave him a whack that sent him rolling onto the floor with a thud.

He lay groaning and gasping for air.

"Shut up," she snapped. "That stray cat has more balls than you." So much for being a lady, but then she hadn't been raised by doves for nothing.

By the time his diaphragm began working and he had air again, Tinker had a lamp lit and had found some stout twine to bind his hands. It didn't take her long to have him trussed up like a roasting chicken.

He cursed her soundly. Big mistake.

"I said shut up." She slapped him across his face, one side and then the other, looked down, and shook her hand as if it was filled with bugs. "Who are you and why are you here?" she demanded, contradicting her first order.

His eyes rolled, whites showing all around. A trickle of blood formed on his lips. She'd slapped him good and proper.

"It was your dirty old toe the cat was chewing on, not your tongue. Tell me." She glared at him. "I could just shoot you; you know. Nobody would blame me, a woman alone and a strange man in her house destroying stuff. Stealing my things."

"I didn't..." he started.

"Shut up. Could be I wouldn't even have to tell anybody. I could just dig a hole and bury you some-where. Or throw your body in the river. That would be easier. Water is high. Your corpse might not show up for months."

He blanched. "You wouldn't dare."

Her laugh soared high and wild. "No? Try me."

"You ain't got a gun."

"No? Isn't that your six-gun I see hanging on the bedpost? I'm not particular where it comes from. Anyone will do." She fell silent and studied him while seconds ticked past.

He watched her, the whites of his eyes showing all around.

"I changed my mind," she snarled. "I'm not going to shoot you. I'm just going to beat you to a pulp. Then I'm going to toss you in the river. Even if you wash up in a day or two nobody will know but what the smushy parts are where you got thumped around over the rocks."

"Jones." He gulped. "My name is Kurt Jones. I work for Anson Lowell." He eyed her. "You knew that."

Tinker made her scorn clear. "Of course I did. You were one of his crew here the other night. Four of you, all trying to terrorize me. Didn't work out so well for you, did it?" She shrugged. "About the same as this time. What I can't understand is why Lowell is still loose and on the prod. The law knows he murdered William Ault and Shorty Bonham. And tried to murder Knox Burdette and me. So why doesn't he stop? Why isn't he in jail? Why are you doing his dirty work?"

Jones's beard waggled. "I ride for the brand."

Disgusted, with herself as well as him, Tinker left Jones hog-tied, a gag stuffed in his mouth, lying on the cold floor to deal with in the morning. She'd had all she could tolerate for one day.

CHAPTER 17

After his talk with RT and helped along by the whiskey RT had poured for him, Knox trudged off to bed in the bunkhouse and slept like he'd been poleaxed. Warren forcefully shook him awake in the morning, and they walked over to the main house together.

The screen door banging behind him, Knox was surprised not to see Soldier standing at the stove waiting for food. Tinker, he figured, must still be asleep in the Timmons' spare bedroom.

He found his place at the table and sat.

"Eat up." Geraldine Timmons set plates of beef gravy ladled over biscuits in front of the men, which included Warren as he was off duty due to his wound, and poured coffee all around. RT sat at the head of the table.

Knox picked up his fork. "Tinker not up yet?" If he hadn't been looking, he would've missed the strange look RT sent toward his wife. Didn't seem possible, but it struck him his boss looked like a guilty kid.

Nobody spoke. A queer sort of tension grabbed him.

"RT? Geraldine?" He pushed for an answer.

Warren ended up being the first to break the silence. "She rode out, Knox. Must've been real early. Maybe even during the night. Her horse was gone when I checked the barn this morning."

Knox half-rose out of his seat. "What? Why would she leave without telling me? She isn't safe at that house. Lowell has it in for her. If he hasn't been caught, he's sure to be after her. He's got a grudge."

"I'm sure she can take care of herself," Geraldine said. She turned back to the stove, still muttering. "Women like her always can."

Thinking he wasn't supposed to have heard the last part, or if he did, not to respond to it, Knox pushed back his chair, the legs screeching across the floor, and stood. "A woman like her? What do you mean by that?"

"Ignore her. She don't mean anything, Knox." RT's face had turned vivid red. He shifted in his seat. "Do you, Geraldine?"

She breathed hard for a moment or two, then spun around. "Yes, I do. Knox Burdette, you should know better than to bring a...a fancy woman into this God-fearing house. Into *my* home. And then, with her sitting at my table big as life, expect me to feed her. As far as letting her sleep under this roof? Shame on you."

"Now, Geraldine." RT began but fell silent under the force of the grim expression suffusing Knox's face.

He answered softly enough. "Tinker O'Keefe is not a fancy woman. Even if she was, there's still only one person," His glance swept over RT. "or maybe two, who needs to be ashamed. That one isn't Tinker. Isn't me, either."

There was more boiling up inside him that wanted out, but he figured he'd better stop. The Timmon's had always been good to him, and he owed RT a lot. In fact, he had a hard time trying to fathom Geraldine's attitude just now. Or last night. Somehow though, she'd managed to run Tinker off.

For fear of what his hot anger might let him say, Knox, damped it down until he got out of the house. The screen door slammed behind him as he stalked away, breakfast not only uneaten but forgotten in the heat of the moment. RT's plaintive, "Knox, wait up. Let's talk about this," followed him. Ignoring it, he kept on going to the barn where he threw Tinker's old saddle on Chick.

It was Warren, not RT or Geraldine who followed him to the barn. "What are you going to do?"

"Get over to Tinker's Post Office quick as I can. And hope to God Lowell hasn't caught up with her and she ain't already hurt or dead."

"Tinker's Post Office?" Warren's face screwed up, bumfuzzled by the shift.

"The old Red Light Pleasure Palace is the area post office." Knox reached under Chick's belly to pull up the cinch. "Has been for a few years, ever since O'Keefe and the women left. Tinker is not, and never has been, a whore."

Warren nodded. "I know it. Every man around would be panting after her if she was. I expect RT knows it, too. He just don't want to fight with his wife. Your Tinker is a pretty girl."

Maybe not put in the most diplomatic manner, but Knox nodded anyway, grateful for Warren's support. Until something, Warren said struck him. *Your Tinker?* Meaning *my* Tinker?

A denial died on his lips.

Mounting, he lifted Chick into a lope and rode away without looking back. He missed seeing RT standing on the porch waving at him to stop.

At the bridge, he crossed without seeing another soul, although a part of him noticed the remains of a small campfire and where the grass had been chewed down by a horse. Recent, too, new since he and Tinker had crossed the previous day.

He kept going, urging Chick to lengthen his stride. As they neared the Pleasure Palace, he slowed, then stopped before entering the open area around the buildings. A sense of wrongness heightened his senses as if a pall hung over the place even though he heard the river, its roar dimmed to a chuckle. Birds chirped, insects flew, squirrels skittered. But the barn door was closed. No pretty pinto mare graced the corral. Most telling, perhaps, no Soldier came to meet him. The place looked deserted, but somehow, it felt as if eyes were watching. Something wasn't right.

Slowly, still hidden from the house, he walked Chick through some woods to the back of the barn. A soft rustling noise sounded from within. A horse urinated. Feet stamped.

So. Not deserted at all. And, if he was any judge, which he figured he was having spent plenty of hours inside a barn, it took more than one horse to make all the noises he heard. Fancy was not alone in there.

Knox dismounted and took the rifle Warren had lent him from the saddle scabbard. Tying Chick to a tree, he went around the side of the barn. He elected not to pass beyond the corner. Stopping, he removed his hat, a spare he'd thought to collect at the ranch, and stuck his head out far enough to see the house.

A shut door, curtains drawn over windows, an ell where a triangular piece of ground was filled with bushes. Lilacs, maybe, he thought, not yet in bloom. They ran right up against the wooded area. It seemed the only spot he had a chance of getting close enough to see who was in the house. Besides Tinker. If she was.

Knox finagled his way through the trees and pushed on through into the bushes. Coming up against the house wall, much to his surprise, he found a door he hadn't suspected existed.

It hung open, no more than an inch or two. Tinker was not a careless girl, especially now. He didn't think this was an accidental oversight.

Knox slipped inside and came right up to an inner door, which he recognized.

"I'll be jiggered," he muttered, so softly the words were more thought than spoken. He recognized the cubbyhole as the one where Tinker had hidden him. This time, the outside gave light for him to see. And this time, what he saw was that the inner door, like the outer, hadn't quite shut properly. He had passage into the house.

———

TINKER COULDN'T HELP HERSELF. RESOLVING TO STAY awake another night and thinking her anger would serve to keep her alert for trouble, she ignored the beckoning couch and seated herself in a stiffly uncomfortable armchair in the parlor where the window had a view to the road.

Nevertheless, certain her captive was secure, before long she let her anger go and relaxed. Too much, as it happened. With the white cat curled on her lap and purring like a bumblebee, she slept on into the morning.

A sudden screech and claws digging into her legs brought her awake. But not fast enough. Toenails clawed into her thighs. A blow from a fist slammed into her cheek on the side opposite the one already bruised. She grabbed for the bat set beside the chair, but knocked askew, it fell beyond her reach. When she tried to rise, a rough shove knocked her backward. Tinker and the chair both overturned. She landed on the floor, her tailbone protesting.

Sunlight shone in through the window and revealed a menacing figure.

"Where's Jones?" A man stood in front of her, his scowl forewarning more of the same treatment. The man from the bridge, she guessed. Awake, and afraid he'd failed his job. Well, and so he had.

Tinker found her voice. "Who?"

"You know. Jones. The feller who is supposed to be sitting on this joint, waiting for you."

"Never heard of him. Haven't seen him."

Where was Soldier? Why hadn't he warned her?

"How did you get in?" Her fingers spread over her abused cheek. It hurt.

He sneered. "Busted a window. Surprised you didn't hear the glass fall."

She peered up at him through her lashes. "Me too." *Where is Soldier?* The question resounded in her head like a silent echoing scream.

For a moment, she thought she'd spoken out loud when he answered the question. "That dog of yours?" He made a noise one might call a chuckle, but to Tinker, he just sounded evil. "If you're wondering, I clonked him on the head with my pistol barrel when he came to the window. Down he went. Might be dead. Might not." He touched the gun riding his hip, and she saw a smear of blood.

Tinker choked on a sob and started to rise. Again.

Hand on her head, he thrust her back and snapped his fingers. "C'mon, slut, speak up. Where's Jones?"

"I don't know who you're talking about." As long as the man in question made no noise, she could hope this one would look somewhere else.

"No? So you're gonna insist I search the place? I find him, you'll be in deep trouble."

As if she weren't already. Heart beating hard, she met his eyes.

To her relief, he followed a different track. "Jones' horse. Where'd you hide it? It ain't in the barn."

She shook her head and shrugged.

His forefinger flicked out and snapped against her temple, and without meaning to, she gave a little cry. It hurt amazingly, more than she would've thought possible.

He must've known because he laughed. "Makes you want to cry, don't it. A taste of what's to come." He stared down at her as if willing her to talk. Or maybe he'd prefer not. An odd rustling whisper, or maybe a whimper came from down the hall. The man's head shot up. "What was that?"

Tinker flinched, scooting an inch nearer the bat. "I didn't hear anything."

"No? You deaf?"

"You hit me hard. My head is reeling." Truly, his blow had been enough to knock her silly. Her head spun in a dizzy sort of way. Or maybe the sensation came from pure rage. Hard to tell.

He hesitated until, just at the verge of returning his attention to her, the whimper came again. He took a step toward the room where she'd left Jones.

When he moved, she caught a glimpse of the cat circling around him, slinking toward the kitchen just beyond. "If you heard something, it's probably the cat," she said quickly.

"A cat." He snorted disdain. "A cat belongs in the barn."

"This one is an indoor cat. Cats, in my experience, go wherever they please." And right now, she was glad of it. She just hoped this one stayed far away from the brute and his cruelty.

But just maybe she protested too much. Maybe she spoke too loudly.

The back and forth speech and appearance of the cat sidetracked the man for only a few seconds, thwarting his intention of searching her house.

Until it didn't.

He bent down and punched her hard on the shoulder.

Unable to stop herself, she cried out.

Her reaction pleased him.

"Stay right here," he said. "I ain't through with you." Confident of her compliance, he glided into the hall to investigate.

Quick as a shot, she picked up the bat where it had rolled half-under the chair. Ignoring the pain flooding her abused shoulder, she got to her feet and followed him.

Unaware, or uncaring of her, he paused before entering the room. Looking for traps, she supposed. But when another of those muffled "uh, uh, uhs" sounded, he charged right in. He leaned across the bed and peered down at the bound and gagged man lying on the floor on the other side.

"What the Jones? Sonuva..." The imprecation broke off as he whipped around.

But not fast enough.

Tinker's bat, ready and cocked over her shoulder,

swung around with all the strength she had. Although she hadn't exactly planned it, the wood slammed into the man's face.

He screamed. Blood spurted. Three or four teeth washed from his mouth to the floor. His jaw made a sickening snapping sound and went askew.

Horrified, Tinker almost dropped her weapon. A good thing she didn't as somehow, he kept coming. She struck again, the bat driving as though to hit a home run. To his leg, this time.

He went down, clutching his knee and howling, his jaw sagging half-open.

Tinker felt as if she couldn't get enough air. The room, her room stunk of sweat, of blood, of filth. One of the men, probably Jones, had wet his pant while she slept.

Determined, she kept her momentum going.

As cautious as the white cat, she circled around the downed man and snatched his revolver from the holster. She backed away.

His knee, like his jaw, was already swelling. He probably wouldn't be moving far from this room without help.

But help wasn't going to come from her.

She kept backing. All the way out of the room, in fact, until stopped by an object barring her way. A body. A man's body, going by the "oof" he emitted. With a little scream, the outlaw's gun in one hand, her bat in the other, she whirled. Both objects flailed with wild abandon.

Until her brain caught up with her vision.

"Knox," she cried. With the pistol still dangling from a forefinger, she dropped the bat and made a move as though to hurl herself into his arms. Halfway there, she stopped.

His face, she thought, struck her as unnaturally pale as she stared at him. He looked funny, with both arms outstretched in defense of her attack. *Or had he, no.*

Like a fool, she wanted nothing more than to have a good cry. Figured she deserved a good cry. After what Geraldine Timmons had said, she'd believed she'd never see him again. Wasn't sure she wanted to if only to expect rebuff.

Her throat felt raw. "What are you doing here?"

Knox's arms dropped to his sides. "I didn't hear what Geraldine done until this morning. I'm sorry as I can be, Tinker. I sure didn't expect her to act this way. Nor RT, either, although I don't think.. anyways, I came to see if you're all right?"

"Kind of you." There may have been sarcasm implied.

"Your mouth is bleeding. You have a bruise on your cheek. That lousy peckerwood hit you!"

"He did. More than once. And I hit him back." She spoke with pride.

He stared down at the man who seemed to be trying to stifle sobs. "I see that. Did a fine job of it. Looks like Anderson ain't the he-man he tries to act."

"Anderson?"

"Him." He nodded toward the outlaw. "He's one of the men with Lowell when they killed Ault." He barked out a laugh. "Thought he was tough, but he ain't as tough as you."

"I am as you see," she said, sharp as lemonade. She wasn't any too sure his comment had been admiring.

"Yes. And I see you aren't all right."

"But I'm alive." She took a breath and shrugged. "You missed all the fun."

"Fun?" He snorted, eyed her a moment, then quick as could be, reached out and pulled her into his arms. "Are you gonna cry?"

"No."

"No? You sure? You can if you want to."

Generous of him.

Tinker, after a moment of thinking about it, decided she didn't feel like crying after all. She'd rather just be held, if only for a minute.

CHAPTER 18

"**S**oldier!" Tinker's pretty blue eyes went from watery with unshed tears, to snapping with fury. Happened about as fast as a man could blink, to Knox's surprise.

Knox released her, at a loss when she jerked away. She'd made a fine armful.

He looked around. "Where is he?"

"I don't know. Him.." A gesture indicated the man whose teeth she'd knocked out.

Knox winced and looked away as Tinker went on.

"He said he broke a window and slugged Soldier with his gun barrel when Soldier put up a fuss. He said he killed him. Or no. He said..." She stopped. "How did you get in?"

"The door at the rear of the cubbyhole." For Tinker's sake, he hoped to God the feller had been lying about killing Soldier.

Hand over her mouth, she gasped. "I forgot. I left the door open. In case I had to run for it."

"Smart thinking." He took her hand. "And he didn't find the door. Let's look for the broken window."

186

"I think I know." Her head jerked toward the hallway. "Down at the end, there's another entry. Back in the day, it was the customer entrance. A waiting room with a piano and some card tables and a bar." She led the way.

They found Soldier lying among the shattered remains of a window, showing how Anderson had gotten inside.

Tinker gasped. Sobbed once. They stood close enough Knox felt her trembling.

But as they approached, the dog stirred. He struggled to stand before falling back with a sigh.

"I'll get him." Knox stopped Tinker from walking through the glass. "You're barefoot. So is he. I'd better carry him."

She must've forgotten, because she stopped and said, "Oh. Thank you."

Grunting, Knox gathered the big dog into his arms and toted him toward the other room. He didn't know about Tinker, but he felt uncomfortable in this part of the house. This room, with its deep red and dark paneled walls, a bar where dust-covered bottles of booze still stood on glass shelves behind it. The couches and chairs upholstered in some gaudy; slick-looking fabric set randomly about clearly showed its former function as a bordello. Cards still littered one of the tables, the backs dusty enough the pattern was unrecognizable.

Velvet curtains, faded from years of sun damage, had at least kept the glass from scattering all across the room. It was obvious no one had been in here for a long time. Footprints Knox figured belonged to Anderson showed on the dusty floor. It seemed to Knox a gloomy place, despite being called a pleasure palace.

Tinker must not come here often, he thought, inwardly smiling. Not to check for damage or even to clean. It appeared she'd shut the door on the house's past. He decided not to ask.

He felt the dog's muscles gather, weak for now, but with a gathering strength.

"He's waking up." He glanced at Tinker, padding along beside him.

She gave a sigh when Soldier licked her hand. He growled as they passed the room where Anderson and Jones were stashed. Could be Tinker did, too.

"What shall we do with them?" Tinker pointed with her chin at the men.

"Dunno." Glad to have reached the kitchen with his burden, Knox lowered Soldier onto a rag rug Tinker kept for him next to the stove. Straightening, back popping, he took his first good look around. At the spills, spoiled food left in dirty dishes, and all the other depredations on Tinker's normally well-kept home. Things he hadn't noticed when he first found a way in. Now he thought about it, he figured the place had been ransacked, Lowell's man looking for money or whatever else he could steal.

Tinker knelt beside her dog, examining the gash on his head with a gentle touch while she checked for further damage. "Do you suppose he'd wear a bandage?" She looked up at Knox.

"Might if you tie it good and snug under his chin." His gaze lit the on the stovetop where the frying pan was full of leftover bits of something cooked to charcoal. They in turn bore a coating of flies. He shook his head. "I'll help you clean this up."

She got to her feet. "Don't bother. I'm thinking of burning the place down. I'll get rid of everything, every last stick of furniture. Every single thing from the old days. I'll leave no trace. Not of the Red Light Pleasure

Palace and not of me. I'll disappear once and for all. Maybe people will be happier, live better lives when I've gone. Lord knows they all seem to believe they will since I'm such a smut on the landscape."

Knox, startled at the bitterness and the drawn expression on her face didn't know what to say. One thing he was sure of. Geraldine's opinion had wounded her. Put the Timmons' rebuff together with the attacks by Lowell and his men, and Tinker had been badly hurt. Not just physically, but in her heart. As for her no-account mother, she had done something, too, when they'd met in Spokane. Tinker hadn't been real forthcoming, but he knew it hadn't been good.

She tightened her lips, and the tirade went on. "I don't know why you should be surprised, Knox Burdette. Your friends made it all very clear to me. And so did my own mother."

Just as he'd thought.

"What does it matter, anyway? I barely make enough money to buy food here. Wouldn't, if it weren't for the mail contract and the garden stuff I put up in season. I can't imagine how I'm supposed to pay the taxes this year. Worse, apparently, every outlaw in the country seems to think they can just break a window or jimmy a door lock and take up space any old time they want. These.." A gesture indicated the men in the room beyond the partition. "They're not even the first. Just the first with lethal intentions."

"Tinker.." he started, but she cut him off.

"No, my mind is made up."

So she said, but Knox saw her indecision. How she turned first one way and then the other. How her lips trembled. How she jumped like somebody poked her with a hot branding iron when the white cat appeared

189

without her noticing and wreathed around her ankles and bare feet.

He leaned against the table and folded his arms across his chest. "Where do you plan to go?"

"I don't know, right off. It doesn't matter as long as it's somewhere away from this place." She went over to the dresser and pulled out a drawer. Scraps of fabrics, maybe towels and such, were folded inside. She pulled some out and fashioned them into a long strip. "I'll take the train. Ride it until they kick me off. Me and Fancy and Soldier."

She wet a rag at the pump and dropped onto her knees beside the dog. Soldier whimpered, but his tail thumped, and he didn't move as she washed the gash, which had stopped bleeding. Knox got down beside her, holding the bandage in place as she wound it around the dog's head while he shook and flapped his ears. They finally got it snugged down and tied securely. The animal looked like one of those cartoons he'd seen in a magazine. The one featuring a boy after a trip to the dentist to have a tooth pulled.

Other times, he would've laughed at the sight. He believed Tinker would've too, but not today.

Knox helped her onto her feet. "I've got an idea," he said.

"About what?" She scrubbed her bloodstained hands on the trousers she'd been wearing since the day of the storm as if more muck didn't matter.

"About where you can go if you want to leave here. You don't need to burn the place. Give yourself time to think." The idea had entered his brain from out of nowhere, and truthfully, he wasn't sure it was the best idea. But there it was.

Tinker eyed him, a little suspicious. "Where? Not the Running T, that's for sure."

"No. Come to the XYZ with me."

Her eyes widened, lashes fluttering. Her mouth opened, though nothing came out.

"If you don't mind a house with bloodstains on the floor and bullet holes letting in dust. I got no doubt the house'll take some cleaning up but, Tinker, you and me, we need to stay together."

"Stay together? You're offering me a job?"

From the cautious way she said it, he figured she had her doubts.

So did he.

"Yes. No." He frowned.

Panic set in. Knox's heart raced worse than when he'd been about to drown in the river. Did she think the invitation was a lewd proposal? He didn't mean it as one. He meant it as a way to take care of her. Didn't she know she was in danger here by herself?

Sure she did.

"I mean, we should stay together until Dempsey and Caldwell have Lowell and his men corralled," he said. "You shouldn't be here by yourself. Look what almost happened. Them two you beat up are proof Lowell means to make you pay."

"But they didn't. I made them pay instead." She stood proud.

"I don't deny it. In the end. But seems to me you took some punishment yourself. I see you're hurting. Tinker, Lowell resents you even more than he does me. I figure he's in a rage because you ran him off."

She touched a hand to the new bruise forming on her cheek. "And shot him."

He grinned. "Yes." The grin faded. "So will you?"

Her gaze slid away from him, fixing on the mess Jones had made of her kitchen. "There," she said, her lip curling, "he just had to ruin my best cast iron frying pan, didn't he?"

It took less than a second for Knox to figure what the change of subject meant. It meant she wasn't ready to give him a straight answer. All it did was bring her back around to her earlier question. "What shall we do with them? With Anderson and Jones?"

This time he had the answer. "Dump 'em onto Caldwell. Let him worry about them." Hauling them into town would mean more time wasted before he got the chance to look over the XYZ. On the other hand, he didn't suppose it was going anywhere.

———

As it turned out, transporting their prisoners to town proved daunting. Jones spoke up and told where he'd staked his horse down by the river, meaning Knox had to mount Chick and go fetch him.

Tinker left Jones trussed and taking up floor space while Knox was gone. She didn't figure another half-hour would hurt the outlaw any and didn't care if it did.

As for Anderson, well, even Tinker could see he wasn't able to straddle a horse for the ride into town. They'd have to find a way to use an old buckboard that'd been stored in the barn since the doves fled the nest.

Tinker, viewing Anderson's battered condition, wasn't in the least regretful when his glare threatened to peel her skin off. His unintelligible mumbles left her in no doubt that he intended to pay her in kind, provided she allowed him the chance. Which she didn't intend to do. Considering the source, she supposed she'd been thoroughly cursed. Since she was dragging a heavy old mattress down the stairs and out to the buckboard at the time, she had no sympathy.

Straightening her back, and easing her sore tailbone, she glared right back. His misshapen face raised no guilt in her. "Shut up. You came after me. You tried to kill my dog. I should have killed you." She shrugged. "You reap what you sow."

Tinker lugged the mattress outside, ready to stuff in the buckboard when Knox returned. Meanwhile, she had to finish business in the post office. At some time while she'd been away, a mail recipient had picked up the last letter. A relief, which left a single final task. There were twelve locked mailboxes behind the counter. One of them had a false back. She pulled a small latch and removed the wad of dollar bills, a few silver and a couple of gold coins making up her stash. Together with the carefully folded fifty-dollar bill from Maisie, Sarah refilled the cavity in both of her boot's heels.

It was when she looked around for a sturdy box to put the cat in that she realized her decision. She'd go with Knox to the XYZ, even though doubts arose as to whether either of them would be any safer there than right here. And she wouldn't set the Pleasure Palace on fire. Not yet.

Minutes later, Knox, a dappled gray gelding in tow, got back from his horse hunt just as Tinker set a pillow-case stuffed with a few personal things on the porch. She hadn't had a real look at the river side of the house since she'd gotten here, and what she saw now made her sad and mad all over again. The rocking chairs she'd painted were overturned; the fresh paint chipped. A doormat she'd put out to catch dirt before it got inside had been wadded up and tossed over the rail like so much trash.

All she'd accomplished in the days before the storm lay in ruins. Just like her pride. And her peace.

Knox took in the stuffed pillowcase and the box containing a yowling cat and smiled a crooked smile. "Guess this means you decided to come along."

"Unless you changed your mind."

"No, ma'am."

Jones, his voice back after a bit of lubrication, took it upon himself to quarrel about his role in shifting the party into town. Partly because it was his horse Knox hitched to the buckboard.

The outlaw rubbed his wrists and stomped his feet. "No, sir. Why, this old horse'll be mortified, hitched up to a buggy like a good-for-nothing carriage horse."

Knox hid a grin as he worked the breast collar over the gray's head and down his neck. "Then I reckon you'll be full on occupied seeing he don't jump the traces on the way to town. Keep you too busy to talk."

"Me?" Jones looked around as if searching for someone else. "Driving?"

"You complaining?"

"No." He shot a wary glance at Tinker and repeated himself. "No."

Anderson lay on the mattress in the buckboard and moaned.

Tinker told him to shut up and to move over. "Make room for my dog. And don't try to touch him. I'll be keeping my eye on you. Lift a finger toward him and I'll pistol whip you. We'll see how you like it." She mounted Fancy, Knox mounted Chick, and they were off.

The gray handled the unaccustomed work of drawing a wagon quite well, helped by Jones's unexpectedly light hands on the lines. They spoke hardly at all, possibly because Tinker, in an overwhelming rush of caution, kept her eyes out for an ambush in every stand of trees all the way to town. Right up until they drove up to the sheriff's office and stopped. She was unaware of giving a large, relieved sigh.

Knox stepped down from his horse, pausing beside her before entering the jail. "Think you can handle this pair if I leave you with them?" He glanced around. "And them?"

They'd begun drawing a little crowd, a few women eyeing Tinker in obvious disapproval. Maybe at who she was, if they even knew; more likely because of the britches she wore. Men spilled from various doorways to watch and murmur about Knox.

"Looks like you're the biggest news around here," she said. "I wonder if they've heard Ault left the XYZ to you."

Knox turned a dull red. "I hope not. Eastman said I should keep the news under wraps until the murderer is proved guilty. Timmons is the only one I told. And you. Nobody else oughta know yet."

She twisted in the saddle, looking out over the street. "Then why do you suppose they're all gawking you?"

"Could be they're looking at you."

Tinker, appalled at the notion, shook her head.

Deputy Sheriff Caldwell emerged from the jail, strutting like a banty rooster lording it over his flock. Turns out he was a pouty appearing, smallish fellow who wore a revolver low on his hip like a gunslinger. Tinker had seen him once before, a few years ago when he'd visited Daring Dorothea at the Pleasure Palace. As she recalled, Dorothea had not been impressed with his performance and had become a little vocal in her description. O'Keefe had spoken sharply and sent Tinker out to do a chore in the barn, so she hadn't quite caught all of it.

"You folks settle down and move along." Caldwell's

loud voice rose over the gathering. He raised his arms like an evangelical preacher. "I got this under control."

"Got what?" someone yelled back.

"The situation," Caldwell said.

Knox grinned a little. "Me," he said, low so only Tinker heard. "I expect I'm the situation, but not because of the XYZ. More likely because when Lowell told him it was me who killed Ault, Caldwell couldn't wait to spread the word. Then he had to take it back. Doubt it settles well with him."

Tinker nodded. "Makes him look a fool, all right." She narrowed her eyes and muttered, "As if he didn't already."

Meeting with Caldwell was no picnic.

Tinker stayed atop Fancy, leaving Knox to deal with the deputy. Knox talked, keeping his voice quiet, while Caldwell made certain the bystanders heard his tough talk.

"Arrest them? What for? That place is open for business, ain't it? A man can't be arrested for going to a whorehouse to get him a woman, far as I know. A woman like that, she expects to get knocked around a little. Or knocked up." He laughed at his own wit.

Knox's fists clenched, his face flamed red. So, Tinker supposed, did hers, shame setting in. Still, no more than she'd expected.

To her surprise, and she supposed Caldwell's, too, a woman standing with her husband at the edge of the group spoke up.

"Miss O'Keefe is not a whore," she said. "We get our mail at the old..." she hesitated. "... house. There's never been a man there, nor even a sign of one, and she keeps the place neat and clean as a pin. Shame on you, Deputy

Caldwell, for trying to ruin a young woman's reputation."

Her husband nodded. "Yeah. And I want to know who beat her up. Somebody has, a little thing like her."

"Me too," a different woman said. "Who hit you, Miss O'Keefe? Your poor face."

"And that ain't all," another feller said, "I got to wonder about a lawman who takes the part of Anson Lowell and his gang of roughnecks over regular folks. I can't tell you how many times I've seen him, and his crowd start fights and push fellers around. And women, including his wife."

"In fact," someone else added, "I hear Lowell is up on murder charges. Talk is he murdered his wife and her father."

"That ain't proved," Caldwell denied.

"Sure, it is," Knox said. "There's a couple eyewitnesses to him killing William Ault."

"We all know Burdette, and it don't take a genius to figure out who to believe," the first woman's husband said. "But I'll tell you what." He turned to the proprietor of the general store who'd come out to see what the ballyhoo was about. "What do you think about contacting Sheriff Dempsey and having Caldwell fired. I'm sick of him sucking up to men like Lowell and ignoring law-abiding citizens."

A good many nods and mutters ensued. All of which caused the deputy, his face turned almost purple, to wave his arms again, this time to shoo people along. "Move on. There's nothing here for you. I've got to get these men into a cell."

Tinker, in a state of shock over the support from a woman, two women, who'd barely nodded a greeting to

---

her any time before, didn't know whether to laugh or cry. Maybe both at the same time?

In a cautious sort of way, she smiled her thanks at the women, and the women smiled back.

As for Knox, he shook a few hands and received a slap on the back.

He was also, Tinker noticed, careful not to mention anything about the XYZ.

CHAPTER 19

"**D**o you think Jones and Caldwell will concoct some sort of horse-stealing charge against us?" Tinker asked. They'd gotten all the way across the bridge without speaking, and she saw Knox give a start at the sound of her voice. He'd been deep in thought, while she had kept a sharp lookout in case any of Lowell's men made a try for them. She only hoped Lowell would run out of men before much longer.

Knox, leading Jones' horse as the wagon bore Soldier and the cat along laughed. "Don't think he'd dare after so many folks heard the talk. Tell you what, though. I'll be glad when Eastman and Dempsey break the story about the XYZ. Eastman told me to go ahead and take possession, but for now, if anyone asks, I'm to say I'm just taking care of the place until Ault's will is settled."

She clucked to Fancy, urging her even with Chick. "Do you know if anybody has...has taken charge of Mr. Ault and his hand's funerals? When and where they're to be buried?"

This got his complete attention. "I don't know. But I

expect when Dempsey got here, he had the undertaker come out and take charge of their bodies."

Tinker shuddered with so much force Fancy shook her head, rattling buckles, and bit. "Unless he sent Deputy Caldwell in his stead. I don't like the deputy. I don't trust him."

"I can't think of a soul who does like or trust him."

They rode a little farther, the road having become more of a simple track, as they got farther from the river. Up ahead, a smaller trail passed between a couple rolling hills. Knox halted Chick and the wagon horse. "We're almost there, beyond the gap. Ault's place is just out of sight. When I come upon the buildings from the Running T, I enter from the backside." He huffed. "And when I last quitted the place, I went through the trees. I want you to study the trail here for a minute, Tinker. What do you see?"

Tinker dutifully studied. "Nothing out of the ordinary."

"Yeah. Me either. Which I hope means there isn't anybody that beat us here and is laying in wait."

She made a sound like a hiss.

"But you'd best stay right here while I go see what I can see. I'll give a shout if it's clear." He grinned. "I guess if it isn't, you'll hear the row. In which case, you'd best get yourself back to town before you're seen."

She frowned but nodded and he set off.

Knox had barely passed through the gap when she tied Jones' horse to a sturdy ninebark bush just making leaves. Leaving Soldier and the cat, both of them thankfully asleep, she gigged Fancy and followed.

Knox didn't really think she was going to sit back with the buckboard and wait for his call, did he?

The ranch house and outbuildings were visible as soon as she cleared the gap. A cursory scan led her to believe the area was deserted. Even from this distance, Tinker could see the house bore a number of broken windows. Otherwise, it looked like a nice, well-kept home. The front door stood open, as if the latch had been forced, or perhaps the last person out never shut it. She doubted Knox had bothered as he departed. He'd said he ran through a hail of bullets, and from what she saw, she believed him.

Horses stood in a corral attached to the barn, also open. A watering trough, kept full by a constant trickle from a spring, kept them close. Chickens pecked in the soil around a henhouse. There were a couple open sheds, one with stacks of wood in place.

She watched Knox pull up at the front of the house and dismount. Tinker held her breath as he went inside. Halfway expecting to hear sound and fury, the silence was intense. After a bit, he emerged from around the back and went to the barn. A milk cow and its half-Hereford calf ambled out as he went inside. In a few seconds, he emerged. Even at this distance, his stance showed grim.

Satisfied, Tinker rode back to collect the wagon. She found Soldier sitting up, nosing the cat's closed crate, and appearing alert. Her relief brought tears, quickly dashed away.

They met Knox at the gap, Soldier walking beside the wagon on his own and in a straight line.

Knox didn't appear to notice the dog's recovery

"What's wrong?" Tinker reached her hand toward him.

"You called it. Looks like Caldwell was put in charge of the bodies. Only he's a slacker."

If she'd thought his face showed anger, it was nothing compared to his voice, like rocks being ground to sand.

"How do.." she started. A suspicion grew. "Are you saying Mr. Ault's body is still in the house?" If so, she wasn't going to stay. She'd go back to the Pleasure Palace and face down any of Lowell's men who showed up. Or she reminded herself, catch the first freight train to come through on the line.

But Knox shook his head. "Not in the house. In the barn. Him and Shorty Bonham both."

Tinker's first reaction was horror, although relief came next. Not in the house, at least. But it had been several days, and she didn't want to think about their condition. "Why would he just leave them there, unburied? Why didn't the undertaker do something?"

"Caldwell left a note on the kitchen table. Took me a while to make it out but I finally figured he's saying the Parsons Mortuary won't take the bodies until they know who's responsible for the cost. Makes me wonder if he contacted them at all. So, he, Caldwell, says he decided to leave them here until he got word." He snorted like a bull getting ready to charge. "Lying.." He cut his words with a glance at her.

Tinker gaped at him. "Why would anyone do such a thing? Everybody knows Mr. Ault was no pauper. If it came down to it, all anybody had to do was take a cow or two in trade."

"Yeah, and Ault had plenty of those. I'd say it's because Lowell wanted to get even with a dead man. And Caldwell is just the kind of man to help him do it." Knox spat on the ground.

Tinker gathered in Jones's horse's lead rein and started toward the buildings. Much as she dreaded it, she had an idea of what needed done.

Knox didn't move. "It's bad, Tinker. I shouldn't have asked you to come. This isn't going to be any safer than at the Pleasure Palace. Maybe worse. You should turn around and go back. Stay at the hotel in town until Lowell is caught."

She huffed and kept going. "If he ever is, which I'm beginning to doubt. As for the hotel? What makes you think they'd let me in?" Nor could she afford to pay for a room and eat in restaurants.

Knox, she figured, wasn't thinking straight.

———

As Tinker slipped inside Ault's house or did she mean Knox's house? She discovered it smelled sickeningly of old blood. Of rot. Maybe even of the gun smoke from the fight Knox and William Ault had waged against Anson Lowell and his men. The odor could have been her imagination, she supposed. The gun smoke part anyway. The blood was real, a great puddle dried and stuck to the floor where Knox said William Ault had lain. Flies were still busy in it. She shook her head, trying to rid her brain of an imagined scene all too easy to visualize. Hard on its heels came one of cleaning up, a job certain to take more than simple scrubbing.

Knox went past her into the kitchen. "Come on in here," he said. "Read this note Caldwell left. Tell me what you think."

Telling Soldier to stay outside, she tiptoed through broken glass into the kitchen. A spacious room, it looked as if Jones, or whoever had ruined her kitchen at the Pleasure Palace, had been at work here, as well. The blood staining the floor in here no doubt indicated where Knox had said the man he killed had fallen.

He pressed the note into her hands and waited for her to read it through.

"What do you think?" he repeated.

Frowning, she looked up. "I think this Caldwell is almost illiterate and unfit to be a lawman. It seems certain he's working for Anson Lowell. Who appointed him to office, anyway?"

"He applied for the job. Guess the sheriff before Dempsey didn't find anything against him at the time, so he got hired. I'm beginning to think he might've been one of Lowell's hangers-on and Lowell deliberately put him in place."

"It would explain how Lowell had gotten away with all the mean, dishonest things he's done the last few years."

Knox agreed, and as Tinker handed back the note, he started to crumple the paper into a wad.

"Don't," she said. "Put it someplace safe. You should show it to Sheriff Dempsey. I'm sure Caldwell's own words provide cause to fire him."

"Smart." He tucked the note into his shirt pocket, huffing out an indrawn breath. "Now comes about the most disagreeable part I know of."

She opened her mouth to ask what he meant but stopped the words. She knew. William Ault and Shorty Bonham. They needed respect and burying.

"Ah," she said. "So that's why you brought the buckboard. A makeshift hearse."

His mouth drew into a tight line. "No, I brought it to transport your dog. But it'll serve for people to see how Caldwell disrespected Ault and Shorty. Folks need to know how he treated these good people. How he neglected his duty." He hesitated. "I hate to ask it of you, but, Tinker, I'll need your help."

Tinker felt the blood drain from her face, sure to be turning pea green at the idea of touching those bodies. "Help you load them?"

"Yes." He eyed her sternly until she nodded.

They wore gloves, Knox saying he'd throw his away after he'd wrapped both men in blankets. He did this before he allowed Tinker to come outside to help lift the bodies into the buckboard. A job neither accomplished without turning aside and vomiting at least once. They wore masks made of some ragged towels Tinker found in a kitchen dresser drawer. Tied over their noses and mouths, they did little to smother the stench. And nothing could stop the clouds of flies from landing on them. Tinker brushed frantically at her hair in an ineffectual attempt to run them off.

"Sorry," Knox kept saying. "I'm sorry."

She knew the flies plagued him as badly as they did her. But when the time came, she downright refused to go back to town with him. Not riding in that buckboard with its awful load and not on Fancy. And she definitely refused to leave her dog in a strange place by himself, unless you counted the white cat who'd gone to prowl in the barn.

Knox insisted on returning the Merwin & Hulbert to her. "Keep your gun handy." A grin broke through. "You brought your ball-bat, didn't you? Best keep it close to hand."

Tinker barely mustered a return smile. A minute later, she watched Knox tie Chick to the rear of the buckboard and waved them off with a sense of relief.

He'd leave the buckboard in town at the livery, he said. "Don't want Jones accusing me of stealing his horse." She didn't care.

As soon as the buckboard disappeared from view, she

set out to explore. First the outbuildings and the surrounding area. A tidy barn where a breezy blew through, working to dispel the smell of death. Aboard Fancy, they made a wide circle around the place, seeing where Knox had said he blundered through the trees until he found Chick and rode for the river. Saw where he'd come down from the Running T, meaning to warn Ault about his runaway cows. Found evidence of where Lowell's men had taken cover during the shootout.

She marked those places, trying to make certain they were intact if Sheriff Dempsey, or one of his real deputies, she didn't count Caldwell, came to investigate.

When finished, she unsaddled Fancy and let her tired little mare into the corral.

Next came the house itself. This part she'd been dreading, especially without Knox there to give her credence. As she entered by the back, Soldier at her heels, she couldn't help feeling like an interloper, and if she did, Tinker could only imagine how Knox must feel. He knew Ault had intended the ranch he'd worked hard to build up as a legacy for his daughter. Knox as inheritor was a last-ditch effort to prevent a bad man from taking it.

All grim thoughts.

"We should get busy," she told Soldier. "Clean the place up. But first, I'll pump you some water."

Soldier huffed at her and padded over to sit by the cold stove.

The hint brought a small smile to her lips. "It's all right. I brought your rug. You don't think I'd leave your bed behind, do you?"

Knox had brought the small load of possessions she'd deemed necessary into the house and dumped them.

Going through them now, Tinker soon found Soldier's rag rug, which she spread beside the stove.

A couple open cupboards, one on each side of the pump, held dishes. Thankfully, most of them were intact, including a bowl with a crazed finish. She pumped water into it for the dog first, then filled a teakettle sitting atop the cold stove and got a fire going.

Sighing a little because she was not only tired but hurting from the beating Anderson have given her, she found a broom and began to sweep. Glass, spilled kitchen items, bullet casings. A whole lot of litter that had been dumped onto the floor and broken.

The blood bothered her, and she swept around it. But that wasn't all. The silence bothered her, too. The loneliness. The strangeness of an unknown house, in an unknown place with only partially known enemies seeming to lurk just outside.

It was getting dark, and hunger began to gnaw at Tinker's stomach. She was just thinking about making something to eat when Soldier sat up and barked. Not a loud bark. A low one.

His warning bark.

At first, Tinker's heart leaped with relief. "Knox is back."

But Soldier didn't agree. After more thought, she didn't either. He hadn't been gone long enough, traveling in a slow wagon. Or only if his turnaround time had been minutes only. Or if he rode Chick hard on the way back.

She'd lit a lamp. Reaching out, she pinched the flame, plunging them into a half-light.

"Fish guts," she muttered under her breath and grabbed Soldier by the scruff. If the visitor was anyone with good intentions, she expected a knock on the door.

If his intentions weren't good, he'd probably open fire the second he spotted a shadow of movement. Meanwhile, she didn't want Soldier getting himself in trouble again.

Tinker opted not to stay in the house, which felt a bit like a trap. She slipped out the back, dragging Soldier with her, and went around to where the front of the house became visible.

They waited there as the approaching rider came nearer. A man. A tall man, one who sat a big horse.

She heard him say, "Whoa," to the horse. He got down and, leaving the reins dangling, walked soft-footed up the porch steps. His hand, Tinker noted, stayed on his gun butt as he tried the door.

She'd set the latch.

The man grunted and raised his booted foot, prepared to kick it in.

"No, you don't," she muttered and called out, "Hold it. Stay where you are." She cocked her revolver. The soft click of the cylinder turning proved a more resounding warning than her words.

He revolved slowly toward her voice. "Who are you?"

"I'm the person holding this gun on you. Here's a better question. Who are *you*?"

Soldier, having napped while Tinker worked, was well-rested and feeling feisty. Despite her quick grab to stop him, he charged out to confront the visitor. His throaty grumble showed displeasure. His size signified formidable strength.

The man stood poised, standing rock still as the dog neared. Then Tinker saw his teeth flash in a grin, and he chuckled. "Look at you," he said.

CHAPTER 20

S tepping around the corner, Tinker stiffened. "Something strike you as funny?" she demanded of the visitor. Or hired killer. A bit hard to tell just yet. Her revolver held steady on his belly just in case it was the latter. The old pistol shot high, and if she had to pull the trigger, the bullet should hit somewhere in his chest. Better than a messy gut shot. She'd had enough of cleaning up blood for one day.

The man ignored the cool reception. "Kind of tough to take a dog wearing a scarf as a serious threat." The fellow's smile stayed in place. Still at ease.

"It's not a scarf." She said the word as if it were an unmentionable. "It is a bandage. A pistol-whipped dog is no laughing matter."

To his credit, the man stopped laughing. "No. No, it isn't."

Tinker ignored what some might have considered a pleasantry. "I still have my gun on you. You'd be wise to state your name and business."

He held up his hands, making sure she could see

them. "Yes, ma'am. Hope you'll excuse me. I wasn't figuring to find anybody here yet."

She waved her pistol in a "get on with it" sort of motion.

"If you can refrain from pulling that trigger," he said, "I'll fetch out my authorization and introduction. First, though, my name is Win...short for Winton...Collins. I work for Thaddeus Eastman and occasionally for Sheriff Dempsey when a special investigator is required. I'm here at their behest."

Tinker pondered a moment, thinking it sounded plausible. "You have a letter of introduction? Toss it to me."

He complied, cautious as could be, and didn't move when she bent down to pick it up. A problem presented itself. With night coming on, the writing was hard to see. She didn't know what to do.

Soldier took matters out of her hands. He'd been sitting close to the so-called Win Collins, and now his tail began wagging. Evidently, he'd made up his mind.

And then Collins helped make up hers. "Am I right to assume you're Miss Tinker O'Keefe? Eastman had a fine tale to tell about a young lady accompanying Burdette. Apparently, she's responsible for saving Burdette and his horse from drowning. And there was something about a cat, too. A white cat."

Tinker let out a breath she didn't know she'd been holding. This Collins must be telling the truth. Unless Knox had said something to RT about the cat, she didn't think anybody else had heard that part of the story. Not even the sheriff.

She lowered her gun. "You can put your hands down, Mr. Collins. I hope I'm not making a mistake, but I'll take your word for it. At least until I can look at your bona fides." Although she had to wonder how she'd know if they were the real thing or not. "Head on around the house. The front door is latched. We'll go in the back."

"Whatever you say," he said, and away he went, stumbling a bit in the dark with Soldier tagging along beside him.

Inside, Tinker got a lamp going and motioned for Collins to sit. She'd already noticed he was tall and well-built, by which she meant he was neither fat nor thin and had more muscle than flab. When he removed his hat, she saw he was older by several years than Knox and had sandy hair and light eyes. He appeared honest, as long as his open expression could be relied upon.

Her attention switched to the authorization from Eastman and a postscript by Dempsey. The missive was clearly addressed to Knox and carried Eastman's letterhead at the top. She didn't think Knox would mind her reading it.

Collins waited until she nodded and returned the document to him. He put it back in his pocket and said, "Is it all right if I ask where Burdette is? I expected to find him here. Or is he back at the Running T, waiting for this situation to be cleared? I'm surprised to find you here." He frowned. "Especially by yourself. It don't seem safe."

"Yes, and I'm just as surprised to be here. It wasn't my intention." A question occurred to her. "Which part are you here to clear? The part where Anson Lowell is on the loose with his gang of outlaws and trying to kill Knox and me, or the part where Knox is heir to the XYZ?"

Win shrugged. "Either. Both." He glanced at Soldier.

"Does this pistol-whipped dog have something to do with you being here?"

"It does." She didn't want to be the one to tell him. The whole situation with Lowell's men at the Pleasure Palace made her sound as if she belonged on the outlaw trail herself. Something better left to Knox, she thought. Or, by preference, no one ever.

What she didn't like was the way he stared at her, at her bruised face and black eye and the scratches on her arms. He'd better not ask, she decided. Just better not.

He didn't.

Collins rested both hands on the table as if to rise. Seeing her concern, he settled back. "Miss O'Keefe, I'm not here to do you harm." A thumb over his shoulder indicated the door Lowell's man had kicked through before Knox shot him dead during the fight. "I need to see where I'm told Ault died. And I need to see his office."

He gazed around. "It's too bad you cleared out the debris."

"It is? Why?"

"It's possible to tell a lot from the direction glass falls, for instance. I could verify which side shot out the windows, and that would give a clue as to who attacked who."

"You have Knox's word. And I think Warren somebody, who works for the Running T, saw the fight in action. I can tell you where the glass ended up. Mostly, right here, inside and under the window. It was the very devil to sweep up."

"Not good enough, Miss O'Keefe. You might be in cahoots with Burdette."

She jumped to her feet. "What? I never even met Mr.

Burdette when this was happening. I met him later when I fished him out of the river."

Collins raised a hand and smiled. An attempt to placate her. "Yes, ma'am. It's just I've got to be able to testify in court over my findings. Believe me, it's to Burdette's advantage."

Tinker sank back down. Her mouth firmed. "Oh. Well, I haven't been in the office. Only in these two rooms. That should tell you something. Apparently, it's a good thing I didn't get to the scrubbing. Only the sweeping in here." She frowned. "So much glass. Knox will need to hire a glazier before another big storm floods the place."

His sober expression confirmed the opinion. "I expect you're right. Now, what can you tell me about the fight?"

She blinked at him. "Not a thing. I repeat; I wasn't here. I only got here a few hours ago, to help Knox when he.." She stopped, unwilling to go into describing anything to do with Ault and Shorty Bonham's corpses.

This time he did rise. "Then I hope you'll excuse me while I get to work."

Tinker sighed. "And I should see if I can find anything to eat."

He turned a flickering smile on her. "Whatever it is, I hope I'll be invited to partake."

What could she do but nod?

She discovered three or four shriveled and sprouting potatoes, a smoked ham, and a tin of peaches that Lowell and his men had overlooked when they ransacked the house looking for Ault's papers.

Win Collins and Tinker had just sat down to eat when Knox burst into the house with the gun he'd

213

borrowed from Warren, drawn, and cocked. Soldier rose from his place by Tinker's chair to greet him.

Tinker popped up from the chair, clapping her hands and smiling. "Knox! I didn't hear you ride up. Thank goodness you're home. You must be starving. I'll get a plate." She pretended not to see the gun.

Knox didn't move. Or only his eyes, flicking from one to the other and on around the room. "Well," he said after a moment, clearly unhappy at what he saw, but holstering the pistol. "Ain't this cozy? I see you've been busy." His gaze settled on the stranger, "Who are you?"

While Win explained himself, Tinker got Knox settled at the table. Earlier, she'd had to fix it with a quick brace where a leg had been loosened, adding a shim to keep it level. Almost level, at any rate. Knox hardly seemed to notice.

Finally satisfied with Win's explanation and proffered bona fide document, Knox loosened up enough to talk. He narrowed in on Tinker as she bustled about. "Anybody else show up here while I was gone?" For some reason, he looked angry.

"Just Mr. Collins. At least, nobody else that I saw. Or Soldier, either. He didn't sound an alarm until Mr. Collins rode up and thought to kick the door in."

"But I didn't," Collins said.

Shaking his head, Knox scowled. "I don't think Soldier is as alert as usual. After I left the bodies at the undertaker and dropped off the wagon at the livery, I stopped at the general store on my way out of town. At the same time, a couple men rode in. I heard them talking to one of Lowell's men while I was tying a bag of supplies onto my saddle. They didn't see me."

Tinker, hearing bad news before it arrived, froze in the act of placing a slab of ham on his plate. The meat dangled precariously from her fork. "Shouldn't those men be locked up on sight?"

He shrugged. "Ask Caldwell."

"What did they say?" Collins leaned forward; eyes narrowed.

"They were making a report. Said they'd been here, at the XYZ, and seen a woman. Said she didn't see them." His look was accusatory. "You should've been keeping a better lookout, Tinker. It's a wonder they didn't come down on you right then and there. And don't think that baseball bat is gonna work again. You wouldn't be taking these two unawares."

Tinker gnawed at her lip.

Win stared at Knox. "Baseball bat? Unawares?"

"Tinker didn't tell you?"

Win shook his head. "She hasn't said much of anything."

To Tinker's disgust, Knox had plenty to say. The explanation made Collins scowl in parts and chuckle in others but in a serious sort of way. "I see why you're keeping her close," he told Knox.

Tinker was not so amused. Not at all, matter of fact. She interrupted Knox. "Did those men say anything else?"

"They did. One last thing."

"What?"

"Said to tell Lowell. So they know where he is, and he must be somewhere close by."

Figuring she'd had enough of Anson Lowell and his men, Tinker couldn't help the way she blanched at the news. "And by now he knows we're here."

"He does."

They both could guess what that meant, or so Tinker

thought. It was almost a relief when Collins had another question.

"You said, 'left off the bodies.'" He stared hard at Knox. "What bodies?"

Knox sighed. "William Ault and his wrangler, Shorty Bonham."

"What? They've been laying here for days? Unattended?"

Knox stared at his fried potatoes with a sick expression. "They had."

"What about the deputy? Caldwell? He knew what happened here. Why hadn't he taken charge?"

"Guess you'd better ask him. Add it to a list." Knox didn't sound any happier about it than he had earlier.

Tinker, who'd seated herself beside him during all this, without thinking reached out her hand. Knox took it.

———

KNOX HADN'T KNOWN WHAT TO THINK WHEN HE REACHED the ranch. A light shone from the window, or from where a window with glass ought to be providing enough illumination to allow him to see the horse standing there. Not Fancy. Though he couldn't think of a plausible reason why Tinker would have her little mare standing at the hitching post in the first place.

So, whose horse was it, and what was it doing there?

One thing sure, he intended to find out before anybody saw him coming. Except for Soldier. But then, when the dog didn't show up, he became even more worried and cautious.

Smelling food cooking, hearing voices, busting in,

and seeing Tinker sitting down with a strange man across the table from her.

He didn't know why, but it made him kind of itchy inside. Even when he saw she was perfectly all right after all the worrying he'd been doing on his way to the XYZ. He'd spent the entire ride afraid he'd be too late to save her from some unknown danger. At least Soldier wagged his tail, happy to see him.

The stranger's explanation mollified him, even if it didn't quite erase his reaction. He even knew what it was called. Jealousy.

Winton Collins's letter of introduction from Eastman cured that mostly.

"You work for Eastman a lot?" Knox slurped from the coffee Tinker had brewed from the supplies he'd brought.

Collins shrugged. "Him and others. Keeps me and my horse in food and lodging."

They talked more when Tinker fell asleep in her chair and Knox, grinning, carried her into a room Lowell's men had mostly let be and laid her on the bed. She didn't stir. He figured this had been Astrid's room when she lived at home, and maybe even a man like Lowell found it beyond him to destroy his dead wife's girlish ruffles.

In the kitchen, he poured more coffee while Collins took his horse to the barn, settling it in a stall between Chick and Fancy. When he got back, the two of them had more to discuss. Things Knox didn't want Tinker to hear and worry over. Truth is, he admitted to Collins, he had heard a little more while in town.

Collins held his cup between his hands and stared into it. "Tell me. I figured there might be more."

"Me, Lowell just wants to kill, but he put a bounty on Tinker. He wants her brought to him. His men were talking about it." Knox flushed. "Talking filth, about what they'd do after Lowell finished with her."

"After Lowell is finished with her?" Collins repeated. The tight clamp of his jaw showed what he thought of this. "This Lowell feller needs explained to me. I understand he's a killer who murdered his own wife and his father-in-law. Like a lot of men, he intended to get rich on other folks' efforts. And when you foiled his plot, I can even see why he's after you, but what's his beef with Miss Tinker? What did she do to him?"

"She saved my life, outwitted him, and ran him and some of his men off her place with a gun." Knox had to grin. "After nicking him with a bullet."

"She shot him?" Collins chuckled. "You know, I can believe it. She managed to get the drop on me when I showed up here. She's a pistol."

"She is."

They were quiet then, drinking their coffee and listening to the crickets outside, their racket loud through the glassless window. Knox liked their sound. If anything stirred out there, they'd stop. Advance warning, he called it.

A while later, he and Collins went out together to check the barn and around the ranch yard's perimeter. They found nothing amiss, although once know thought he spotted a man-shaped shadow. It turned out to be nothing more than a breeze driven tree branch projected onto the side of the barn.

Returning to the house, Collins found a bed the outlaws had left more or less whole, and Knox made do with a couch whose horsehair stuffing was making an escape through a rent in one of the cushions. Made by a knife, he suspected, but the fabric was tough and had resisted. He supposed that's why the damage wasn't worse.

Knox slept hard for a couple hours, then awoke. Sudden like, as if he'd been poked in the ear with a sharp stick. Fuzzy-headed with sleep, it took a moment to realize where he was and what had awakened him.

Then he knew.

The crickets had gone silent.

CHAPTER 21

They'd had a lot of coffee. Maybe Win Collins…
Knox's first thought, but he knew differently right
away. Win had left the bedroom door open, and Knox
heard the rise and fall of his snoring. Not loud, just regular, like a tired man is wont to do.

Silent, careful to keep the couch from squeaking, he
sat up and pulled on his boots. Buckling on his gun belt,
he went soft-footed down the hall to awaken Win.

"Win," he whispered. "Wake up. They're here."

He'd have liked to yell, but with the glass shot out of
the windows, the place was wide open, not much better
than a campsite in an open meadow.

"Win," he said again, only marginally louder. It
served. A break in Win's breathing answered.

"Wake up."

"…wake," Win muttered. "Give me a minute."

Hoping they had a minute, Knox left and hurried to
Tinker's room. He had his hand on the door when the
sound of a muffled cry reached him. Then a thud, a
curse, something like a chair scooting and Soldier
howling like an Irish banshee. Howling, barking, growl-

ing, all at the same time. A gunshot, loud as a howitzer, roared from behind the door.

Gun in hand, Knox ran his shoulder full force into the door. It flew wide and he stumbled inside. Something, a chair, he discovered as he fell over it, had been shoved under the knob. It hadn't held but did slow him. Long enough so when he picked himself up, only to fall again over the top of Soldier who wobbled toward the window, it was to see Tinker dragged through an opening where glass shards pointing upward shone under the starlight.

He didn't dare shoot, for fear of hitting her.

Or her dog.

Then she was gone.

Curses so obscene he didn't even know how he knew them spewed from his mouth.

Gunfire echoed from the front room. Knox ran through to where Win Collins stood in the doorway, taking aim at one or the other of two men racing away from the ranch. One crouched over the burden flopped across his lap in front of him.

He was the one closest to the house and Win, his rifle steadied against the door jamb, was drawing a bead on him. His finger tightened on the trigger just as Knox grabbed the barrel and shoved it skyward. The bullet flew in the general direction of the sky.

Collins roared his anger.

"What are you doing. I could've got him."

"Yeah, and put a bullet through both him *and* Tinker." Knox came close to busting the other man in the chops.

Win turned to him, his rifle lowering. "Tinker?"

"What did you think? That he stole a bundle of laundry?"

"How the hell was I supposed to know?" Win started

221

hotly, then stopped. "Yeah. Sorry. All I could see is him getting away."

"Get your horse," Knox said. "We're going after them."

No argument. They ran for the barn.

––––––––

TINKER, WHO'D BEEN SOUND ASLEEP, DIDN'T KNOW WHAT was happening when a man's rough hand smelling of urine and sulfur clamped over her mouth. Plain fact, it took her several heartbeats to figure out it was a hand. One sticking out the bottom of a ragged shirt cuff. Both gagged and without adequate air, she fought, wrestling out of his grip once and landing on the floor with a thud.

He hauled her up by her hair. Meanwhile, Soldier, confused and hurt when the man kicked him in the ribs with the toe of his boot, carried on in a disordered sort of way. A kind of cacophony of all the sounds dogs usually make when they're hurt, angry or scared. Or all three.

But Soldier was far from the only one scared and angry.

On the losing end of things from the outset, Tinker was wide awake when the man shoved her headfirst out the window and she felt her arms tear on spikes of glass. First came pain, sharp and sudden, then blood, hot and wet. More than simple scratches, she feared.

At that, she supposed luck came somewhere in the equation because the man on the outside of the house had her by then and lifted her head and shoulders through without further damage.

That one picked her up and, with her stomach jouncing on his shoulder, carried her away. He dragged her up with him onto a horse and gouged in with his spurs. They set off at a gallop, every stride a lesson in pain. The stinking one was already several yards ahead of them by that time and riding hard, leaving them farther behind by the second.

At least she could draw breath. Not, it occurred to her, that she should let the man who held her know it. Not yet. He squeezed an arm around her middle and, just to let him think she'd given up the struggle, she made herself sag over the arm. She hoped he'd relax quickly as her stomach churned under the pressure.

His horse, evidently not the best conditioned animal in the string, had slowed from a full-out run to a lope. Tinker sagged lower, trying to convince herself, and him, she weighed twenty more pounds than she did. Sooner than she'd feared, but longer than she'd hoped, his arm slackened, to the point she found it necessary to hang on to the saddle strings where his lariat hung. Her efforts would do no good if she fell off by accident.

No. She needed to choose her spot. Before her stomach gave up its contents, by preference.

The man who'd come into her room and captured her in the first place had disappeared from sight, although dust stirred by his horse's hooves hung in the air. Tinker wanted to cough, almost choking in the effort to stave it off.

But it seemed as though she smelled water. Greenery greener, air damper, and cooler. Although she didn't need to be any cooler. Too cool and her muscles were apt to freeze up.

The man holding her was muttering to himself. Cursing his partner in crime for not staying close and watching his back. Complaining about the blood, her blood, from a deep slash in her arm, dripping down the side of his saddle. The agitated way his horse moved, tossing his head and side-stepping. Tinker knew the way she hung to the side over the man's arm threw the horse off stride.

Tiring of it, the man gave her a shake.

Tinker moaned. Ever so slowly, she allowed her eyelids to open a slit.

"Hey, you, wake up." His gruff voice held impatience. "C'mon. Wakey, wakey." A string of cussing indicated his feeling for not only his partner but for Anson Lowell, who didn't know enough to get out of the country while he had the chance.

And for her. The victim.

"Stickin' around for some kind of vengeance. Damn fool." After this profound statement, he twisted in the saddle and looked behind him. "And you." He poked a forefinger into her sore ribs. "Another damn fool, a woman just out to cause trouble, if you ask me. Lowell will get his way in the end. Why're you fightin' it?"

Wincing, Tinker looked backward too, surprised to see dawn creeping over the horizon. But no sign of anyone following. No Knox. No Win Collins.

They were about to enter deep timber. An easy place to get lost. This, she figured, was the best chance she'd have.

With the man preoccupied with complaining, and blaming, she released the lariat and as they turned sharply toward what she figured must be Lowell's hideaway, she popped erect and slapped him, slapped him hard, with the coiled rope.

He flung up his hands to protect his eyes.

Quick as a rabbit sheltering from a hawk, she slid from the horse and, forgetting her lack of shoes, dashed for the woods.

He came after her. No surprise.

She dove between bushes. Panting hard, slipped between two narrowly spaced trees. Plunged over the top of a log, and fell into a deadfall that caught her like a coyote in a trap. Noise from dry branches breaking, the log creaking, birds taking flight from the trees. No way, nowhere for her to hide. He'd find her.

And he did. Reaching down, he yanked her up, not at all careful how he handled the rips in her arm. Drew back and slapped her with his free hand.

Tinker tasted blood. She hit him back only to think a second later it might not have been smart.

She was right. His next blow almost knocked her unconscious. Everything swayed and went black for a time. When she came to herself, she once again sat in front of him on the horse. This time, her hands were tied over the saddle horn. The rope, scratching and rough, looped around her neck. If she were to try to escape, she'd likely be strangled.

Another problem. Where were they?

She had no idea where they were or how far they'd come, but when she looked down at the ground, she saw fresh hoofprints marking a trail Knox could follow.

If he wanted. She had a hunch she might be more trouble to him than she was worth. Oh, Lord, she hoped not.

After a while, she said, "Where are you taking me?"

"You know where. Lowell says you're not as stupid as most women." He snorted. "He has to say that, even if it ain't true. Which it prolly ain't. But he thinks it makes him sound smarter."

The reply puzzled Tinker. This man, whoever he was, worked for Lowell, but his voiced opinion resounded with disgust. Not an admirer, at the least.

"You don't like him?" she asked.

"Hell, does anybody?"

"I'd be surprised. But then, why are you doing this? Kidnapping me? Going along with murder. A man who killed his own wife and his father-in-law?"

He grunted. "Didn't know about the killings when I hired on. I ain't sayin' I like it, but the money is good."

"What if he decides to kill you?"

The man laughed even as an odd shadow crossed his face. "He ain't goin' to do that."

Tinker begged leave to doubt his conviction.

On this note, their conversation ended, right up until they topped a rise and he said, "We're here."

Tinker had already figured that out for herself.

They started down a narrow trail toward what fifty years ago had been a trapper's cabin sitting close to a small lake. Tinker was willing to bet nobody knew the old place existed. Her heart beat faster, like keeping time with a runaway horse

———

KNOX AND WIN RACED TO SLAP SADDLES ON THEIR mounts. Knox got done first, setting spurs to Chick in an unaccustomed manner. Better sense took hold by the time he'd gone far, and he slowed, waiting for Win. It took longer than he liked but gave him time to think.

A few minutes later, when Win caught up with him, Knox had formed a plan of sorts. He didn't claim it was a good plan. Just better than nothing. For instance, both of them rushing off through the dawn with no idea where the trail might lead wasn't the most intelligent idea. It only set them up for an ambush. There were different jobs needing done.

One, somebody had to follow the trail.

Two, they needed to round up some help, and the Running T was the nearest source.

Win, his mouth turned down like he'd been eating a California lemon, agreed. "Sounds fine as long as you get cooperation. You sure you will? After what you said last night.."

During their talk the previous evening, Knox had revealed the reason Tinker had come to the XYZ with him when he'd meant for her to stay safe at the Running T. No wonder Win had some doubts. Knox had them himself.

"Don't let Mrs. Timmons overhear the request. For some reason, she took against Tinker and might not be too eager to help."

"Not even to save her life?" Win had a taken-aback look in his eyes.

"I just don't know."

Knox thought enough time had been spent on the question. His fear for Tinker overrode everything. "This operation'll go a lot faster if they'll help, but if they refuse, don't waste time trying to persuade them. Go on to town and round up a posse. I'll leave markers along the trail."

"Seems you should be the one going to the Running T," Win grumbled, but Knox shook his head.

"If the Missus was to see me, she might guess what I'm there for. Best if you, a stranger shows up. Show 'em your letter. RT won't refuse, I'm sure of it."

"Hope you're right." Win's doubts showed clearly but, following Knox's directions on how to find the ranch, he loped away.

As for Knox, setting his jaw, he kept on after the outlaws and Tinker.

After a while, he came upon the prints of small bare

feet in a dusty patch of trail. He whistled, although why he'd be surprised he didn't know. She'd been in bed asleep and taken unaware. But the lack of shoes hadn't stopped her from running first chance she got.

Dismounting, he followed the tracks, both Tinker's and those of a man wearing boots.

In only a few minutes, he found where she'd been frog-marched back to the horse. Knox consoled himself with the thought she'd been walking upright on her own two feet, bare or not. She was a fighter. She'd proved that over and over. Tinker must know he'd be coming for her. She had to hold on.

Setting an arrow-shaped stick in the trail to point the way, he mounted and rode on. He went slower now, sensing the end of the trail just ahead.

The sun was taking the chill off the morning when he spotted smoke rising from a stovepipe poked through the roof of a shack. Hardly even a shack, considering the south facing wall was crumbling as the mud mortar between logs fell away. Kind of a comedown for the high and mighty Anson Lowell, Knox thought.

"Whoa, Chick." He drew the horse to a halt before they broke into the open.

Knox recognized the place, having visited the lake on fishing expeditions a time or two. It lay at the outermost edge of the XYZ. Ault had never run cattle here. The timber was too thick for good grass and the ability to keep his cows in good condition. More predators, too, and ticks. Knox had heard Ault say he was going to lease the land out to a logging outfit and have them thin out the trees. He'd placed more value on grazing land than timber, but Knox sometimes wondered if he'd been right. Guess he might find out if he lived long enough.

Since the old shack wasn't even on Lowell's land, it

was a good place for him to hide out. Folks most likely expected him to stick to his own. Or at least something a bit higher class than this falling-down hut. Knox admitted he had.

He huffed out a breath loudly enough Chick pranced a little protest at the unexpected sound.

Since when did Lowell do anything like regular human beings?

Remaining within the trees, Knox guided Chick in a half-circle around the old cabin, the second half of which faced the lake. A corral made by stringing rope between the trunks of small trees had been fixed up at one side. He counted four horses in the corral, plus two standing outside, including a dun that looked as though it'd been ridden hard and left with the sweat drying on its hide. He figured those two belonged to Tinker's kidnappers.

As he watched, a tall man stepped outside and proceeded to unbutton his britches. It was Anson Lowell, out to take his morning piss.

Six horses. Six men?

Too many for him to take on by himself. Although tempted to gun down Lowell as he stood, it would put Tinker in too much danger. Dismounting, he settled in to keep watch until Win brought help.

CHAPTER 22

Tinker's abductor pushed her into the shabby excuse for a cabin, her bare toes curling against the garbage-strewn floor and unswept rodent feces. Shuddering at the filth and afraid the stench might cling to her forever, she figured even if she got out of this alive she'd never feel clean again. No matter how many times she scrubbed.

A couple men slept on bedrolls laid out close to the walls. At least she assumed they were sleeping. They might have been dead, or drunk. Her nostrils flared at the stale smell of alcohol among other pungent odors. None were pleasant.

Tinker swallowed hard. How could any living person bear to lie on a floor like this? Better by far, in her opinion, to camp out of doors on the clean earth.

She jumped when her captor, whom a man outside had greeted as "Lem," raised his voice and said, "Wake up, boss. I got her."

One of the men snorted and rolled over. The other didn't stir.

"Boss," Lem said again. Then louder, "Anson Lowell."

The body shifted this time. He coughed, broke wind, and sat up. A mouse ran from the folds of his blanket. It was Anson Lowell all right, looking as though he'd neither shaved nor cleaned himself in the days since the attack on William Ault's ranch. He bore a definite accumulation of dirt since Tinker had last seen him. Rather than the important man he professed to be, he looked more like the lowliest of bums riding the rails.

"What?" he demanded, blinking bloodshot eyes.

"I got her," Lem repeated. "Right here." Showing no signs of letting go, he still had a grip on Tinker's shoulder. The one she'd fallen on when Anderson tipped over her chair. It hurt.

Although Lem had removed the loop from around her neck, a rope still held her hands loosely together in front of her.

She stood passive. This wasn't the time to draw attention to herself.

Lowell made an attempt to focus. "Huh, so you do. So she is. Good."

From the overwhelming stench of spilled booze, Tinker surmised Lowell's condition stemmed from a massive hangover. Her heart sank, remembering he had the reputation of being a mean drunk. In her experience, he was just plain mean.

"Job's done," Lem said. "I figure to head out for less heated parts now. Pay me what I'm owed, and I'll be gone."

"Pay you off, you say? This job ain't done."

"For me, it is."

"Huh." Getting to his feet, Lowell held up one finger in a 'wait' signal. He buckled on his gun belt and stepped outside.

A sound of liquid streaming against the side of the shack made Tinker wince.

The man still lying on the floor spoke without turning, his voice lowered almost to a whisper. "I was you, Lem, I wouldn't wait for my pay. Anson has been in a foul mood for days. Ever since...you know. Don't think he's gonna appreciate you leaving before Burdette is dead and buried."

Lem stood his ground. "I don't like this. I didn't sign up to be an outlaw and kill folks."

"Then run," the other man said and sank back down feigning sleep as Lowell returned.

But if Lem could've been persuaded to run, the time had passed.

Lowell stepped inside. Stopping just within the shack walls, he paused to roll a quirley and light it. Taking a deep pull that used up half the smoke, he drew his pistol and shot Lem. A neat hole between the eyes before the back of Lem's head blew apart.

Lem hardly twitched as he fell over, although Tinker staggered as his grip on her let go. Blood and brains splashed onto her face and into her hair.

So shocked she couldn't have made a noise if her life depended on it, Tinker simply stood frozen in place, certain she'd be next.

"What in the.." The supposedly sleeping man rolled over. He scrambled to his feet clutching a rifle. Tinker had seen him before, the dark man at her house that first night. The one who'd stood back and kept quiet. He'd probably expected to see her body, as his jaw dropped open at the sight of Lem lying dead.

"I told him," he muttered. He might've thought he'd be next, Lowell covering his tracks, but the boss had already quit the room and walked into the clearing.

"Any more of you forty dollar a month men thinking about leaving?" he shouted to the group standing with their mouths sagged open. "I hired you to do the job, and by God, you're going to do it. That," he gestured backward at Lem's body, "is what happens when men say they're deserting me with a job half-done."

The three men staring into the cabin had nothing to say. Behind Tinker, the dark man said, "He's gone crazy. Crazy as a rabid coyote." Only he spoke so quietly it must've been aimed for Tinker's ears only. Or for no one. He inched past her, pointing deliberately at the gun belt buckled at Lem's waist as he went to the doorway.

Quick as his back was turned and while he was blocking the door from anyone looking in, Tinker bent down and snatched Lem's six-gun from his belt, shoved it into the waistband of her pants, and loosened her shirt over it.

The cold metal against her stomach made her guts curl and shake almost as badly as the dark man's knees as he went to stand beside Anson Lowell. Oh, not because the gun frightened her. Because of what she planned to do with it.

KNOX JERKED AS IF THE GUNSHOT ECHOING ALONG THE lakeshore had been meant for him. He thought his heart might've stopped for a minute there until the pounding in his chest told him differently. So maybe his heartbeat on, but what about Tinker's?

In need of support, he clutched at Chick's mane and ripped his rifle out of the saddle scabbard.

Although too far away to distinguish the words, he heard Lowell talking, loud and angry. Three men were lined up in front of him, and Knox didn't have to know what was said to tell they were taking a browbeating. Another bellow and a tall, dark yahoo exited the cabin. Lowell seemed to be yelling at him too and the yahoo nodded and retraced his steps inside.

Five men, six horses. Where was the sixth man? More importantly, where was Tinker?

A least the last question was answered when the dark man reappeared, shoving Tinker ahead of him. Knox's eyes narrowed as the outlaw made a show of it. More than seemed called for as Tinker wasn't protesting. Far from it.

One thing in her favor. She hadn't been shot, so when Knox practiced his arithmetic skills, he concluded it was the sixth man who'd been on the losing end of the gunshot. Why Lowell had taken to killing his own men he couldn't figure.

Lowell pointed at a low stump, from the looks of things telling Tinker to sit there. Without arguing, she did so. As she turned, Knox spotted the splashes of red running down one side of her. His breath caught. No wonder she seemed stunned, though he didn't think the blood was hers.

What Knox didn't like was Tinker sitting right in the middle of the clearing, an easy target if gunfire broke out. And Knox guaranteed gunfire in the near future. Maybe she'd have the good sense to get down when the time came. Maybe he'd be able to yell loud enough for her to hear.

A big lot of maybes.

Impatient with waiting for Win and the others, he inched a little closer to the camp. Lowell sent the fellow who'd been shoving Tinker back into the cabin. He came out with bedrolls, pulling at the door until it caught on a swollen doorsill as he exited, leaving a barely visible body inside.

Once Knox accidentally rustled some bushes, going still as the man stared toward him. After a bit, the outlaw shrugged, dumped the bedrolls, and went back to what he was doing, which appeared to be watching the fire burn.

As for Tinker, Lowell went over to her, standing close and saying something right into her face. Turning her head away, she held up her hands, still bound by a rope. Lowell pulled out a knife and hacked at the strong hemp until the strands parted. He backed away then and pointed toward the fire. Tinker got up, trudged over, and found a frying pan, which she sat over the coals. Breakfast?

Knox huffed out a lungful of air and lowered the rifle he hadn't been aware of raising.

What in Hades was taking Win so long?

As if in answer, a hand came down on his shoulder, almost startling him into pulling the rifle's trigger. But he didn't. Turning, he discovered the hand belonged to RT, who looked hangdog enough to almost make up for the way he'd acted yesterday morning. Not that Knox was in a forgiving mood.

"Was beginning to think you weren't coming," he grumbled. "Where's Collins?"

"Setting up the boys so they don't shoot each other." RT kept his voice as low as Knox's.

"How many?"

"There's four of us. Me, Collins, Warren, Russell."

Knox had hoped for more. Overwhelming odds to cut down on the resistance would've suited him better, but this would have to do.

"Let's get this started then," he said.

"Collins said to tell you we got to keep the action legal and above board. You can't just shoot them down. Gotta give 'em the chance to give up." RT's curled lip showed his disdain of the decision. "Said to tell you to holler at them. If they don't throw down their guns, then you can shoot 'em."

Knox shook his head. "A waste of time. A way to get good men killed, too, if you ask me."

RT nodded. "I don't disagree. Give me a minute to get into position before you start the fireworks. Just so you know, I'll take that feller sitting by the fire." He slipped from view, quieter than Knox had supposed him capable of even though the older man had sneaked up on him.

What should he say, when he yelled to Lowell and his men? Did deputies have a script dictated by a set of legal rules? His mind went blank. What did it matter? All he had to do was make some noise. He figured Lowell would be quick to act on it and his words wouldn't mean a thing. If anybody shot at him, he'd shoot back. That's all there was to it.

Seconds ticked by until he figured RT's minute was up. More than up.

He stuck his head around the tree. "Anson Lowell," he boomed out. "You and your men throw down..."

He'd been right. Without waiting for the meat of the announcement, Lowell snatched his six-shooter from the holster and fired it haphazardly toward the sound of Knox's voice. A shot to admire if it hadn't been aimed at him. The bullet tore a chunk out of the tree Knox stood behind.

"It's Burdette. Kill him," Lowell yelled and proceeded to empty his gun in Knox's direction.

Knox fired his rifle and slipped six feet to the side. He

fired again. Another miss as Lowell ducked behind a horse tied in front of the cabin and reloaded.

Across from him, Knox caught a glimpse of Collins almost casually shooting one of Lowell's men. The outlaw dropped to the ground clutching his side, then lay still. Collins must've suspected the man of playing possum because he fired into the dirt a few inches from the man's head.

Smart on Collins' part as the outlaw flinched and tossed his gun off to the side and out of reach.

Warren and Russell banged off shots with their carbines, hardly taking aim but keeping the remaining outlaws too busy ducking the wild spray of bullets to hit anything themselves. Taking advantage, Knox found a new position, bringing Lowell into clearer view as he hunkered next to the horse.

The dark man who'd been in the cabin sat near the fire with his hands up and staring into the woods. Following the direction of his gaze showed Knox what he was looking at, and he grinned. True to his word, RT had him covered, shaking his head with a ferocious scowl. Another one down and out.

A glance at Tinker showed Knox that, as he'd hoped she'd have the sense to do, she'd dropped flat on the ground. Not that it made any difference to Anson Lowell.

Burrowed in next to the horse like he was, Lowell, grinning like one of those powerfully ugly gargoyles Knox'd seen on Eastman's fancy office building, raised his gun and took aim at Tinker.

And Tinker knew it. She rolled, the bullet kicking up dust an inch from where she'd lain a half-second before.

Fury suffused Knox. He lunged into the open. "Lowell." The shout echoed across the lake, reverberating over the water. "Murdering..." He fired.

———

TINKER, WISHING SHE WERE INVISIBLE, WASN'T ANY TOO certain of Lowell's intentions when he walked over to her. Like the dark man had said, crazy as a rabid coyote. The wild look in his bloodshot eyes proved it, and the way he grinned as he leaned over her.

How she kept her spine straight and, refusing to look away, her eyes locked on his, she'd never know. God knows he was good at intimidation.

"I'm hungry," he said. "Fix breakfast." As if she were a hired hand and the man he'd murdered five minutes earlier meant less than nothing.

She swallowed. Breakfast? With a dead man's blood and gray matter stuck to her skin? It was all she could do to hold back a fit of retching. Turning from his stench, she held out her bound hands without saying a word.

Even then, when he whipped out a very large knife, though possibly not a very sharp one, she thought he might use it on her neck. But no. He sawed on the rope, rubbing her wrists raw while he was at it, and when she was free said, "Cook."

He pointed at some foodstuffs laying on the ground. In the dirt. A squirrel had been chewing on a bag of something. A haunch of uncovered venison had begun to turn green. Her stomach recoiled, even as she picked up a greasy frying pan and set it over a grate one of the men had placed over the coals.

Purely by accident, she happened to be looking at Lowell when Knox's shout started a frenzy of gunfire. She caught the way his nostrils flared, his eyes widened, his teeth gnashed. The only thing missing was the frothing of his mouth. *Crazy rabid coyote*. Or so the dark man had said. She would change the animal to something more lethal, like a badger. Or a wolverine.

Strange for Lowell's recognition of Knox's voice to be so instantaneous, as if he'd been expecting it all along. The draw of his gun matched in speed.

And he was glad.

The dark man, oddly enough, ignored Lowell's command to shoot and said something to her. With the gunfire pounding against her eardrums, she couldn't really hear, but thought he said, "Get down." Even if she imagined the words, they struck her as good advice. So she did. Right down onto her belly where Lem's gun gouged a painful furrow.

Easing the pistol from beneath her, she didn't bother to hide her actions but searched for a target of her own. She spotted RT Timmons, holding his rifle steady on the dark man. One out of the fight. She caught a glimpse of Win Collins, picking his shots as he wounded one of Lowell's men. Two of Timmons' ranch hands laid down a noisy if ineffectual covering fire. And there. There was Knox, his gaze fixed not on her, but on Anson Lowell.

Tinker followed Knox's gaze.

Lowell's gun pointed at her. He was grinning, rictus in a death-head. He meant for her to die.

Instinct ruled. She rolled. Events happened in jerks.

Lowell shooting.

Yelling, Knox jumping from cover.

Win Collins running forward, halting at the edge of the woods, firing from the hip. Flipping the bolt on his rifle, then ramming it home, ready to shoot again.

Lowell banging off a shot, then another and another.

She heard someone grunt, then Knox saying, "Lowell."

Knox shot. Missed. Levered another cartridge into the chamber of his carbine.

Time stopped.

Tinker rose onto her knees, Lem's pistol pointed toward Lowell, the barrel unwavering.

The horse Lowell had concealed himself behind reared, shifting its hindquarters and bumping the man to the side.

Tinker's pistol followed him.

With the horse out of the way, Knox had an open shot. He took aim.

Lowell, a grin on his face, went for the easy target. He banged off another shot. The combined thunder of Collins' rifle, Knox's echo, and the sharper report of Tinker's pistol was enough to rattle the treetops as they all came together as one.

And Lowell, like an awkward straw-filling dummy, fell.

So, in the throes of blinding pain, did Tinker.

CHAPTER 23

K nox and Win stood over Anson Lowell's body. Both, as soon as Lowell jerked two or three times like one of those string puppets doing a dance and then collapsing, had rushed forward to inspect the results of their handiwork.

Knox, though certain Lowell was dead, gave the.45 laying nearby a kick as Win Collins knelt beside the body. The.45 didn't go far. His leg seemed to have gone weak and numb.

"I'll be jiggered," Win said. "Look at that, Burdette. He's got three holes in him, every one within an inch of the other. Good shooting."

But then, at the same instant, their brows lowered, and their eyes met. Win shot to his feet.

"Three?" Knox said.

Win nodded.

Knox had the queer sensation of going cold all of the sudden. Worse than when he been in the river with icy water closing over his head. He spun around.

So, more slowly, did Win.

"Tinker!" Knox ran, clumsy and stumbling over his

241

own feet. Straight toward where Tinker lay on her side, one arm flung out beside her. She clutched a .38; fore-finger curled around the trigger guard. She wasn't moving.

RT, coming from the woods behind the dark man, had beat Knox to Tinker's side. The dark man had already knelt at her side. Their heads almost met as they leaned over her.

"Got to turn her over," the dark man said to RT, "slow and easy. Face up. Together on three."

Knox got there, pushing the man's hands away. "Don't you touch her!"

"We got to see where she's hurt," the man said, too logical and calm for Knox's taste. "If she ain't dead already."

Knox drew back his fist until Win caught it.

"He's right," Win said. "We've got to see if..." He broke off. "To see."

"I'm trying to help her," the dark man said. "How do you think she got the gun?"

Questions rose in Knox's mind. So, how had she? *Had* the gun helped her? Or had it gotten her killed?

Not the latter, because she wasn't dead, yet. Or so they discovered as they got her turned and found the site of the wound. A bullet had gone in through her side just below the ribs. She bled profusely while, and probably for the worse, the bullet remained lodged in her body.

The dark man pressed fingers into her neck and only RT's quick grab stopped Knox from hitting him. "Leave off," RT said. "He's checking for her pulse. Looks like the man knows what he's doing."

"Heartbeat don't feel right," the dark man said. "Fast and faint. It don't look good."

"We've got to get her to the doctor."

"She can't ride."

"Bring the doc here."

"Won't do no good. It'll take hours. She needs the doctor soonest."

Opinions, suggestions flowed. Knox couldn't seem to think at all until it struck him that the last thing said made the most sense.

"I'll take her," he said. "Let me get my horse."

"She can't stay on a horse, or get on in the first place," someone, Knox thought it was Warren, said.

"' Course not. I'm carrying her." It was all he knew to do.

But first came a thick pad to help stanch the blood. RT and the dark man got it rigged and in place. His last name, the dark man told them as they worked, was Lowell, first name of Jeff. A cousin to Anson. He didn't seem the least put out by the fact his relative was dead.

"Anson never did nothing but get me in trouble," he said. "Didn't even pay my wages most of the time."

Knox retrieved Chick from the woods and, with RT and Win carefully lifting her, got Tinker up and into his arms.

She didn't make a sound, a silence which worried Knox more than anything. He turned Chick onto the trail heading out.

That's when RT noticed what everyone, up until then, had missed. Including Knox, who was settling Tinker into what he hoped might be an easier position.

"Stop. You're wounded." RT put his hand on Knox's leg.

"Wounded? Me?"

"Yes, son. You." RT glared up at him. "Don't it hurt?"

"Hadn't noticed." Although now RT mentioned it, he realized the ache in his leg was something other than concern for Tinker and excitement and, well, he didn't know what else. "Don't matter anyhow. Tinker is the important one."

But RT was shaking his head. "You're losing plenty of blood yourself, Knox. What if you pass out? What if you come over weak and drop her?"

"I won't pass out. Won't drop her, either."

"You don't know if you will or not."

Cooler heads, regardless of his arguments, prevailed. Plans changed to Knox's disgust. A decision overruled him. He and RT would take Tinker to the Running T and load her into a wagon for the trip to town. RT would ride along with him, just in case. Win and Russell would stay with the captured outlaws while Warren rode for Sheriff Dempsey or his deputy.

That was that, except it wasn't.

Because true to RT's prediction, about halfway to the Running T, Knox did come over weak. He didn't drop Tinker though. He had time to entrust her to a very worried RT.

———

TINKER AWOKE, SHAKEN INTO CONSCIOUSNESS BY A JOLT AS the wagon transporting her...somewhere... thumped into a rut. Pain followed, overwhelming every other sense.

"Knox," she called out. Or thought she did. Maybe not. The cry might only have been in her mind, without enough force to sound aloud. At any rate, if he answered she didn't hear him because she went off in another swoon.

Minutes, or possibly hours, later, she awakened with a clear thought. *Shot. I've been shot.* She rested in the dark. Then a gleam of light again. *Am I dead?*

Agony, lightning-like in its intensity, bolted through her.

No. Not dead. The dead don't feel.

Or so she'd been told.

She tried the name again. The name of the only person she thought might care. "Knox?" And though she waited, he made no reply.

———

TINKER HAD NO IDEA HOW MANY DAYS WENT BY. TIME merged, night and day, day, and night. She remembered someone, a man, peering down at her through thick glasses and holding a bloody little knife in his hand. He said he was a doctor. She remembered waking from the ether and being violently sick. She remembered a kind-faced woman giving her water.

All that, but she still thought she was going to die. She begged someone to bring Soldier to her so she could tell him goodbye. They didn't; she cried.

She instructed Win, when once his face swam above her, to keep her boots for Knox. He opened his mouth as though to say something, then closed it again. "Your boots?" he repeated

"He'll know." Or so she believed. He wouldn't forget where she kept her money, would he? "For Soldier."

Knox would take care of Soldier when she was gone. The money might help.

But time passed and she didn't die. The day came when, though she was far from recovered, the doctor told her he'd done all he could. He released her to go home as he needed the room she'd been occupying in his surgery.

"I have other patients in want of the bed," he said, apologetic and gruff.

So it happened that RT Timmons brought his, or perhaps Geraldine's, well-sprung surrey to carry Tinker home to the Pleasure Palace. Most disconcerting, as Geraldine sat beside him. She eyed a thin, wan Tinker with a dispassionate eye and said, "You'll have the whole back seat to yourself. Lie back. Make yourself comfortable. Rest if you can."

"Thank you." Tinker hoped she wouldn't have to listen to a listing of her sins during the five-mile drive.

RT let down a step for her to climb into the surrey, whispering, "Don't you worry, Miss Tinker. We'll have you home in no time. Your Soldier dog is there, waiting for you. You'll be glad to see him, won't you?"

"Yes." At once, the day seemed brighter. "Yes, indeed."

They were halfway there before she spoke again although both RT and Geraldine made comments about this and that every so often. Tinker felt no need to add to them. She used the miles to question herself on whether the question she had in mind to ask was wise.

"Knox?" she said at last. His name formed a question. One barely loud enough to be heard over the clopping of the matched pair of chestnuts that were Geraldine's pride and joy.

She didn't miss the concerned look that passed between the older couple.

"Mr. Timmons, has something happened to Knox? Is he...is he dead?" Her voice trembled.

RT turned in the seat in front of her. "Dead. No. No. He's not dead."

"They why didn't he.." She couldn't go on.

To her surprise, Geraldine answered.

"Not dead, but he came close."

Tinker gasped. "He did? What happened?"

Turning, Geraldine studied her. "He was shot. Nobody thought it terribly serious. He lost some blood, but no one figured it would hold him back for long. But then he got an infection. No one knows why. Maybe he was still affected from almost drowning in the river. But it laid him low."

RT nodded. "Touch and go there for a while. He almost lost his leg. He was at home with us, Geraldine, and me. We got him over it."

Tinker let out a breath. "I...I wondered. I thought he would come see me. But he didn't. And no one would tell me anything. Win...Mr. Collins, he came to see me once, but he didn't say anything about Knox. He should have told me."

Geraldine eyed her. "Yes. I can see he should have. We should have. I'm sorry. But be assured. Knox is on the mend now."

As it turned out, even the daughter of a prostitute, albeit a high-class prostitute, is afforded a certain respect and concern when she is deemed a hero. And Tinker was. She'd saved Knox Burdette, another hero, from death in the river. She'd been instrumental in helping him keep the XYZ from falling into a murderer's hands. She had been kidnapped in retaliation and threatened with an obscene death. Her's had been one of the three shots that executed the outlaw at blame.

In what may have been an act of gratitude, but she liked to think was neighbor helping neighbor, the Pleasure Palace, make that the Middle Fork Post Office, had been restored to order. Broken windows were replaced, rooms thoroughly cleaned, the kitchen put back together. She couldn't help seeing even the parts belonging to the doves had been cleaned, which probably owed more to curiosity about what had gone on in there than concern about cleanliness. Tinker figured it had been easy enough to tell that whole section of the house had gone unused for several years.

Food was in the pantry; her bed made with fresh linens; a pretty nightgown once belonging to Maisie, and how had anyone found that? Had been laid out.

Geraldine spoke to her kindly. Almost as if they could be friends.

Best of all, there was Soldier, ecstatic with joy.

Tinker was grateful and glad to be alone when everyone left.

Three days later, as she sat on her porch listening to the river and resting after giving Fancy a good going-over with a brush, Knox rode up.

Soldier, who'd been lying beside her feigning sleep, apparently sensed a visitor on the way. The dog rose to his feet and, after stretching each of his legs in turn, leaped off the porch and trotted toward the road. A minute later, Tinker jumped to her feet when she recognized Chick in the distance. Her heart thumped hard as if trying to break through her ribcage.

"Knox." Her whisper was lost in a bumblebee's rumble as it burrowed into a honeysuckle blossom on the bush beside the steps.

She tensed, almost ready to run inside the house and hide.

But she didn't.

Chick stopped at the rail and Knox sat looking down at her, almost as if he were answering a question he'd asked himself. His expression struck Tinker as worried.

Her heart, though she wouldn't have thought it possible, beat even harder, faster. Her mouth clamped down, stilling her quivering chin. She didn't know what to say.

Didn't seem like he did, either. *Hello*, didn't strike her as adequate.

But then, her attention caught on an object hanging by a thong on what looked like a brand-new saddle. A good one. "Is that my boot?"

Knox huffed in a breath. "It is. I've got both of them here." He untied the one from the other side of the saddle and dismounting, handed it to her. "Win told me about you wanting me to have them. But you didn't die, and I figured you'd need them back."

She smiled a little. "Yes, well, I said that before they told me you were at death's door."

"Death's door? Me? Who told you I was?"

Tinker's legs wouldn't hold her, and she plumped down into the rocker. Her mouth trembled despite her best efforts. "Mr. Timmons. Mrs. Timmons."

"Oh." He seemed to think about it while fetching the other boot. "Guess I was a little under the weather for a while. Too long. But I'm well now."

In Tinker's opinion, he could use some fattening up. And the sun on his face to bring back his tan.

They were silent, Knox fondling Soldier's ears and scratching his back. The dog wriggled happily.

Knox cleared his throat. "So you didn't burn this place down after all."

A pointless observation, as at the same time, she said, "Have you moved over to the XYZ?"

"Ladies first." Knox, still holding her boot, pulled the other rocker closer to hers and sat. Easy, like he belonged there.

Lady? Did he think she was a lady? Or just a woman willing to shoot somebody. Whose shot had as much to do with a man's death as anybody's. Tinker couldn't meet his eyes. "I need a roof over my head.

With Anson Lowell dead, I guess this roof will have to do."

Knox winced and put her boot on the porch floor beside the other. "You've got a good view here. There's a nice view at the XYZ, too. Looks out over a meadow and some woods. I'm on my way to town to order new windows and paint and such for the house. You probably noticed it's a good house. I'm gonna fix it up and make it pretty again. And Ault's rose garden is coming into bloom just now. Makes a nice smell around the place instead of cow..."

She knew what he'd started to say. She glanced at him, a question in her eyes, but she said, "I remember. The roses were just leafing out when...when.."

On his way to town? The Pleasure Palace is miles in the wrong direction.

"Do you like roses?" he asked, maybe sounding a bit desperate.

Tinker nodded.

He cleared his throat again, which started Tinker wondering if he was coming down sick. Seemed to her he was kind of panting a little, too. As if he were running a race or fighting a battle.

Of a sudden, Knox jumped to his feet as if he'd been stung by the bumblebee and grasped her hands.

Alarmed, she stared at him. "What?"

"Tinker O'Keefe," he said, his voice rising with each word, "I'm a man of means, and all because you saved my worthless life. Will you share with me?"

She blinked.

She hadn't thought she said anything out loud, but his eyes clouded. "I mean to say, will you marry me?"

Oh.

Chick, for no reason, let out a neigh that sounded a

lot like laughter. Soldier got up, skipped around like a silly puppy, and barked.

Shock. Joy. Tinker's heart thumped. Didn't know what to answer.

But it turned out her mouth did. "Yes," it said.

Upon which, he kissed her. And doggone if she didn't kiss him right back.

TAKE A LOOK AT THE WOMAN WHO BUILT A BRIDGE: THE WOMAN WHO BOOK ONE

2019 SPUR AWARD WINNER

Shay Billings is pleasantly surprised at discovering a new bridge over the river, as it cuts several miles from his trip into town. Ambushed and left for dead, he has even more cause to be grateful when the bridge-builder saves his life. Shay's savior turns out to be a mysterious young woman with extraordinary skills. More importantly, she's a strong ally when he and a few other men are forced to defend themselves and their ranches against a power hungry rich man. Marvin Hammel seems determined to own everything in their small valley, his intention to gobble up not only their homes and their livelihoods, but the water that flows through the land.

January Schutt just wants to be left alone to hide her scars. She's rebuilt the bridge that crosses the river onto her property, and lives like a hermit in a rundown old barn. All that changes when she takes in a wounded Shay Billings. Now she's placed in the middle of a war over water rights. But has she picked the winning side?

AVAILABLE NOW

ABOUT THE AUTHOR

2019 Spur Award winner for *The Woman Who Built a Bridge*, and 2020 Spur Award winner for *The Yeggman's Apprentice*, C.K. Crigger lives in Spokane Valley, Washington, where she crafts stories set in the Inland Northwest. She is supervised by a feisty little dog with a Napoleon complex, and ignored—except when he wants to lay on the keyboard— by a reclusive cat. Not satisfied to write only of the historical west, she also writes contemporary mysteries and dabbles in the speculative genre. A member of Western Writers of America, she reviews books and writes occasional articles for Roundup magazine. Buried Under Books also features her book reviews.